KU-745-930

YOU SHOULD SEE ME IN A CROWN

LEAH JOHNSON

M SCHOLASTIC

Published in the UK by Scholastic Children's Books, 2020
Euston House, 24 Eversholt Street, London, NW1 1DB
A division of Scholastic Limited

London – New York – Toronto – Sydney – Auckland
Mexico City – New Delhi – Hong Kong

SCHOLASTIC and associated logos are trademarks and/or
registered trademarks of Scholastic Inc.

First published in the US by Scholastic Inc, 2020.

Text © Leah Johnson, 2020
The right of Leah Johnson to be identified as the author of this work has
been asserted by her under the Copyright, Designs and Patents Act 1988.

ISBN 978 0702 30432 3

Printed by CPI Group (UK) Ltd, Croydon, CR0 4YY
Papers used by Scholastic Children's Books are made
from wood grown in sustainable forests.

1 3 5 7 9 10 8 6 4 2

This is a work of fiction. Names, characters, places, incidents and dialogues
are products of the author's imagination or are used fictitiously. Any
resemblance to actual people, living or dead, events or locales is entirely
coincidental.

www.scholastic.co.uk

FOR MOM

All I am is because you are.

"THE PLACE IN WHICH I'LL FIT WILL NOT EXIST UNTIL I MAKE IT."

—James Baldwin

Campbell
Confidential

WEEK ZERO

They say good things
come to those who take.

Sign In

one

I'm clutching my tray with both hands, hoping that Beyoncé grants me the strength to make it to my usual lunch table without any incidents.

I shudder at the thought of a slip that douses me in ranch dressing or a trip that lands me in the lap of one of the guys from the wrestling team. Or, worse, a video of that fall blowing up on Campbell Confidential, the gossipy, Twitter-esque app some senior created a few years ago that has become my worst nightmare. I'm grateful that in a few months all this will be behind me. I'll be on my way to Pennington, the best private college in the state, living the life I've always dreamed about: one surrounded by people like me, in a place I fit, on track to becoming a doctor. It's so close I can taste it. All I need is the email confirming that I got the scholarship and—

"Lighty, watch it! I've got a *thing* to do." Derek Lawson leans into the word *thing* like what he's prepping for is some big mystery as he plants himself directly in front of me. I take a step back—tray still in my death grip—and brace myself. I know what happens next. We all do. This type of public spectacle is second nature in Campbell this time of year.

Before I have a chance to spare myself the very specific torture that accompanies watching a flash mob full of varsity athletes singing and dancing in unison like some sort of value-brand boy band, it's already happening.

Derek slides across the floor with the type of drama that would make the cast of *Hamilton* sit up and take notes. He climbs onto the long table where his crew normally sits and points down to his girlfriend and my not-so-secret rival, Rachel Collins. Someone presses play on a speaker somewhere, and that's when it starts: another freaking promposal.

Even though this has been happening at least twice a week since the semester started, I swear one of the freshman girls at the table next to me faints from excitement when Derek begins singing a remixed and prom-themed version of "Time of My Life." Her friends are too distracted to even help her up.

Prom in Campbell County, Indiana, is like football in Texas. The only difference is, we don't get our fanaticism out of our systems every Friday night for months on end. Nope, in Campbell we just hold it in, eleven months and twenty-nine days per year, until one day we explode. The whole town, covered in a heap of sequins and designer tuxes and enough hairspray to fuel the Hindenburg.

It might be impressive if it weren't so ridiculously, obnoxiously annoying.

"You're the one girl, I want to go to prom with!" Derek is belting at the top of his lungs and it is certifiably awful, but no one seems to care. The girls from the pom squad come in from the hallway, where they must have been lying in wait, fully decked out in their uniforms, and grab their partners from the basketball team. And suddenly, they're doing full *Dirty Dancing* choreo and not missing a beat.

The entire cafeteria is watching this show, and I sort of want to die. My stomach threatens to bring up the granola bar I ate for breakfast just at the sight.

Not only because it's Rachel at the center of the attention again, but because this public of a display of, well, *anything* really terrifies me—even when I'm the furthest thing from being involved in it. I mean, everyone is looking at you, watching you, waiting for you to do something worth posting to Campbell Confidential. The idea of people's eyes being on me for any longer than the time it takes for me to pass out their sheet music before concert band rehearsal makes me undeniably anxious. It's why I never ran for class president or auditioned for a school musical and can barely take solos in band without wanting to evaporate.

When you already feel like everything about you makes you stand out, it just makes more sense to find as many ways to blend in as you can.

But still, there's something about the way Derek is looking at Rachel that makes my heart sink. People like Rachel and Derek get the perfect high school sweetheart love story to tell their kids

5

about one day, but tall, black, broke Liz Lighty doesn't stand a chance. Not in a place like this, anyway.

I don't resent my classmates—I really don't. But sometimes (okay, *most* of the time) it's just that I don't feel like one of them.

"I've searched through every Campbell store, and I've finally found the corsage for you!" Derek extends his hand, and Rachel grabs it, fully sobbing now. How she manages to look like an Instagram model even as she sheds a bucketful of fake tears, I'll never understand.

Derek's grand finale—I kid you not—is The Lift.

With clearly practiced finesse, Rachel runs forward, leaps into his arms, and is lifted above the crowd in the cafeteria. She looks less like Baby and more like Simba looking over the Pride Lands if you ask me, but whatever. Everyone is on their feet by the time the song ends, and the entire fourth-period lunch booms with applause.

There is a look of begrudging respect on my best friend Gabi's face as she watches the poms and the basketball guys stand around clapping and looking up at the couple in admiration. Everyone in the room now has their phones out, no doubt recording for Campbell Confidential. And the freshman girls next to us are in literal tears—the one who fainted is even doing a CC Live recording from the floor.

I look past Derek and Rachel's table and the hordes of fans surrounding them, and my eyes lock onto the corner of the cafeteria that I've avoided like the plague since freshman year. I can't help myself. Some of the senior guys from the football team are cheering, standing on their chairs and shouting support to their fellow clichéman, Derek. All of them besides Jordan Jennings. I feel the

6

same anxious clench of my heart I always do when I see him, my ex-best friend. His smile is faint as he claps, half-hearted, and I can tell how artificial it is from this far away.

He's almost too cute to stare at for more than a few seconds at a time. And this isn't just me being thirsty; with his smooth brown skin, his waves where his curls used to be, he really looks like he belongs in a teen soap opera—all effortlessly flawless or whatever.

I remind myself of what he made sure I knew when we were freshmen: People like me and people like him exist in two different stratospheres, and it's best to keep it that way.

• 👑 •

"Ugh! Organizing a promposal on the day Emme vacates her spot as potential queen? It's Kris Jenner–level strategy. I'd be pissed if I weren't so jealous I didn't think of it myself." Gabi shoves a book into her locker and shakes her head. "The devil works hard, but Rachel Collins works harder."

"Jealousy is a disease, Marino. Get well soon." Britt smirks from where she leans against the wall, and Gabi narrows her eyes in her direction. "Seriously, who cares about Rachel Collins? I'd rather talk about who would win in a steel-cage match between Captain Marvel and Wonder Woman. Who are you putting your money on, Lizzo?"

Stone, sitting cross-legged in deep meditation, seems to be completely unconcerned with the fact that there's a furious between-class rush that threatens to flatten her. I haven't said much since the promposal at lunch—haven't been able to shake that weird

7

feeling of *otherness* that sometimes hits me in waves so strong they threaten to pull me under—but that doesn't stop Gabi and Britt from trying to get me to chime in anyway.

"G, that is so far from relevant," I start, linking my arm through hers as we all head toward our next classes. "It's not like any of us are next in line for the throne."

"I'd say we're a lot closer than some people," Gabi says, voice laced with faux sadness. "Closer than Freddy, at least."

I've been good, careful, not to ever have any cafeteria mishaps, but other people haven't been so lucky. Last week, Freddy Brinkley tripped over his own shoelaces (rookie mistake, you always double-knot before you start the trek into the battle zone) on his way to his seat and face-planted into a plate of spasagna, Campbell County's lasagna-spaghetti hybrid dish.

At least thirty people captured it on Campbell Confidential, and it's been remixed, remastered, and retooled so many times and in so many ways that I don't think poor Freddy is ever going to get past #SpasagnaGate.

Freddy got cocky, thought he could make The Walk without the proper precautions, and he paid the ultimate price: a public meme-ification. You hate to see it.

Britt and Stone leave us at the band room to head to their next class. Band passes quickly, too quickly for my taste. Between my anxiety about waiting for the scholarship email, which I know is supposed to come today, and the general buzzing energy of prom season kicking everything into overdrive, I'm not ready for class to be over when it is.

Gabi gathers her things quickly once the final bell rings, not

8

taking nearly the same care as I do to tuck her clarinet back into the soft velvet of the hard case. She's going to miss her favorite Campbell Confidential livestream—the Prom Projectioners, a group of girls who make predictions every Monday afternoon about who does and doesn't stand a chance at making prom court—if she doesn't leave right now.

The rest of our classmates are pouring out the side doors into the parking lot, but I'm staying behind like I do most afternoons. There's always something more to get done before going home.

"I still can't believe that Emme went ghost like that." She pulls her sleek black sunglasses from her bag and adjusts them over her eyes. She pauses for a second. "You think Jordan is okay?"

Emme Chandler: Jordan's girlfriend of three years, the sweetest person alive, and mysteriously disappeared shoo-in for prom queen. We weren't friends with her—we were barely in the same area code, socially—but since she's practically Campbell County royalty, it's hard not to wonder where she went.

But the question still catches me off guard. Back when the three of us were friends, G and Jordan fought constantly. I wonder if a part of her cares about him still, even if she doesn't want to, the same way that I do.

Jordan, G, and I were closer than close in middle school. For years, the three of us did everything together. We all met in band in sixth grade, when me and Jordan were battling (auditioning, technically) for first-chair clarinet. And whenever he landed first chair, his smile smug and shining with his braces, he'd say, "Don't be embarrassed, Lighty. A first is nothing without a good second!"

During the school year, we would watch Jordan hang up his nerd hat on Friday nights to play football for our surprisingly good middle school team, and then we'd practically camp out at Gabi's house for the rest of the weekend—me and Jordan putting Gabi on to black cult classics from the '90s like *House Party* and *Friday*. We were so goofy back then, so unconcerned with what other people thought of us as long as we had each other, we even performed in our school's talent show together. Or at least me and Jordan did. Even then, Gabi had a pretty refined aesthetic.

Jordan and I dressed up in these awful, thrifted, super-baggy '90s outfits and did the Kid 'n Play dance sequence from the first *House Party*. We got second place, but honestly, we were robbed by Mikayla Murphy and her stupid Hula-Hoops.

But things change, people change, and Jordan is no different.

At some point, he made sure I knew that our friendship was just a phase. And there wasn't much I could do about it by then.

Gabi is still looking at me, and I realize I don't know how he's doing. I don't know anything about him anymore.

"I'm not sure, G," I say.

And despite how I feel about him now, I can't help but think, *But I hope so.*

two

"Is it just me, or was your section particularly out of tune today?" Mr. K asks as I stop by his desk to hand him the sight-reading quizzes we took. His eyebrows are raised in a way that tells me he knows that I know my section was all out of whack today. And as first chair, he expects me to straighten them out. Mr. K is a good guy. He's young, younger than most of our other teachers, and it shows in the way he's still all excited every time he walks into the band room. He's what my granny would call "wet behind the ears."

Plus, he really cares about us. He spent a lot of his own time helping me prepare for my Pennington music scholarship and orchestra audition, rehearsing the perfect piece—classic, not too contemporary, just what they prefer. And when my granny couldn't get off work and G had some family thing at the resort in French

Lick, he even drove me up there. We'd worked hard—*I'd* worked hard—and the audition was in the books. My future felt as good as set. I'd gotten accepted to the school itself. Now I just needed to be accepted into the orchestra and awarded a scholarship for outstanding musicianship, and my future would be set, too.

Music is something I understand—the notes are a thing that I can always bend to my will.

Between the promposal at lunch and stories about where Emme has disappeared to since last Friday though, the entire school hasn't been able to focus on much of anything today, let alone the new arrangement of "Once We Leave This Place" by my favorite band, Kittredge, that Mr. K handed out today.

"You know what? Don't answer that. I'm hoping it was just me and not the mark of prom-mania descending on my precious concert band again." He laughs with a shake of his head. He takes the sight-reading quizzes from me and cocks his head to the side.

I look down at my phone, clutched tightly in my hand, and will an email from the Pennington College School of Music to appear. All it takes is one email, one confirmation, and I'll be on the fast track to the rest of my life.

"You feeling okay today? You're not looking like the cautiously optimistic, 'you can catch me smiling at my sheet music only when I think no one is paying attention' Liz Lighty I've come to know. I thought you'd be more excited to play your own arrangement for the first time."

The classroom has mostly emptied out, the few people left behind far enough out of earshot that they can't hear us. Mr. K knows I don't really want anyone to know that the music we'll

12

be ending our spring concert with is a piece that I arranged myself.

My cheeks heat. I'm not sure why it makes me feel weird to know that people are playing something I had a hand in creating, but it does. It feels too public somehow. Like this thing that I do on my own to stay sane doesn't belong completely to me anymore or something.

"I am excited, I just—"

My phone buzzes in my pocket, and I pull it out faster than should be humanly possible.

And it takes less than a minute for everything around me to completely fall apart.

I read through the email quickly.

We regret to inform you that despite your admirable academic and musical achievements, competition was incredibly tough this year, and you were not selected for the Alfred and Lisa D. Sloan School of Music partial-tuition scholarship, nor will you be offered an advanced seat in the orchestra, which means you're out of luck to the tune of $10K. And while, yeah, it definitely sucks that you didn't get into the orchestra you've wanted to be a part of your entire life, feel free to audition again once you're on campus—not that you can pay to go!

That scholarship was my ticket to Pennington and all that comes with it. It was the last piece of the puzzle I've been putting together for the past four years. Excellent grades? Check. Solid, albeit modest, extracurriculars? Check. Outstanding enough musicianship to earn me a spot in the world-class Pennington College Orchestra and bridge that final gap between the money I've saved, the scholarships I've managed to get, the loans I qualify for, and the cost of tuition at the most elite private college in Indiana? Not so much.

My mouth goes dry. I open and close it, trying to gather words to explain what's happened, but nothing comes. All I can feel is dread. All I can think about is what Mr. K said to me as we waited for my audition to begin:

"You'll fit in so well on Pennington's campus next year. I know that Campbell isn't always the easiest place to be, but Pennington was a dream for me," he'd said as we pulled into the visitor's parking lot of the music school. As the gorgeous limestone building had come into view, my stomach did what it always does when I get nervous or scared or excited—tightened up, and not in the cute butterflies-in-my-stomach way. Tightened like it was threatening to force out everything I'd consumed that day. I thought I might puke then and there, might just call it quits before I even went inside, but Mr. K cut the engine and pressed on. "This isn't the only place where you can be yourself, but it was the place where I figured out what it means to be who I am. And that's worth how you might feel right now."

And now, two months after that audition, I learn it was all for nothing. All that time, that work, and I failed. And I don't know where to go from here.

"Liz. Liz?" Mr. K waves his hand in front of my face with a smile. "Are you okay?"

My chest feels like it's starting to constrict, and the feeling is familiar. I'm on the verge of a panic attack, and I know I have to get out of there fast before I completely fall apart in front of Mr. K. Before I have to tell him that all his help, all the time he spent working with me, has been for nothing. That I failed him and all the other people who were counting on me to make this work.

I open and close my mouth again, trying to find the words. But nothing comes out. I shrug my back up on my shoulder and head for the door.

"Hey, you don't look so great." His eyebrows knit together in concern. "Do you need to sit down? Get some water maybe?"

I shake my head.

I don't need any of that, I can't tell him. What I needed was Pennington.

And it's gone forever.

three

It's been three days since I got the email, and the only solution I've come up with is to sell one of my nonessential organs to pay for school in the fall. That, or take a gap year and work with my granny at the nursing home where she's a CNA. I can earn some money to help cover expenses around the house, reaudition for the spot and the scholarship that comes with it, and maybe next fall will be my time. I'll be a year behind all my friends, a year delayed on all my dreams, but it's the best—the *only*—option I have.

My brother, Robbie, throwing a sock still warm from the dryer at me is the only thing that keeps me from full-on anxiety spiraling like I've done every other day this week when I've thought too hard about next year.

"What?" I shake my head, trying to clear it. "Did you say something?"

He bumps his hip into mine gently. We're folding laundry while Granny's at work and Grandad dozes in his rocker on the front porch, and the monotony of the chore is almost soothing to me. Or at least it was soothing, you know, before I started thinking about how my life has been completely derailed.

"I *said* you're being mad spacy." He folds a pair of dress pants he wears when he has a debate meet and drops it into the basket. "You gonna tell me about the scholarship, or do I have to keep pretending like I didn't see you reading the rejection email over breakfast two days ago?"

"Ro." I flop down on the couch and put my face in my hands. Of course Robbie knows. "I was going to tell you. I just needed . . . time."

"Liz. Lizzie." His bare foot nudges at my bunny slippers until I look at him. I wrap my arms around my stomach, the sleeves of my mom's old Pennington Penguins crewneck warm and extra soft from years of wear. "Look, we can fix this. Money has never stopped us before. You know Granny and Grandad will—"

Sell the house, is what I don't let him say. I know what this looks like if I tell Granny and Grandad the truth. They'll sell the house, move into an even smaller space, and use all the money to make sure I get to go to my dream school for four years. I won't let that happen.

We've lived in the same boxy brick house on the edge of town for as long as I can remember. And it used to be pretty tight, three bedrooms for five people. The five of us have always been the "small and mighty Lightys," my granny used to say. My mom busted her butt to raise us practically on her own after my dad

18

left, and my grandparents did the same to raise us after she got really sick. We work hard, harder than the people around us, and we make it work. We succeed in spite of, or maybe even because of, the odds against us. That's just the Lighty Way.

So whether or not I was going to attend college has never really been a question for me. Neither was where I was going to go and what I was going to study. I was going to attend my mom's alma mater, Pennington College, and take the premed track while playing for the Penguins orchestra. I was going to become a hematologist and work with sickle-cell patients like my mom and my little brother, and it was all going to be possible because I grinded hard, kept my head down, and survived growing up poor and black in Campbell County—a place that's anything but. Because that's the Lighty Way too.

But I didn't account for my mom not being around to see me graduate high school. I didn't factor in not getting the scholarship it would take to go to college. I didn't consider that, despite everything, my hard work might not ever be enough.

"They can't know." I shake my head. "Granny and Grandad can't know about this. I'll come up with something; there's gotta be another way."

Robbie moves the clean-clothes basket to the floor and plops down next to me. Our old couch dips as he sits.

This house is the last place we ever heard our mom's voice, the last place she was ever loud and vibrant and irrepressibly alive. Her touch still lingers on the couch in the living room, even though it's bursting at the seams, because my grandparents can't stand to get rid of it. Even the smell of her perfume still clings to the living room wallpaper if you try hard enough to smell it.

If they sell the house, we forfeit the only thing that's left of our mother. And the thought terrifies me. It's either take the money and lose Mom again, or skip college and abandon one of the last wishes she ever had for me: that I attend her alma mater. Either way, I lose.

"It's funny you should mention it." He grins and jumps to his feet. "One moment, please."

He dashes into his room and comes back with nothing but a sheet of paper. He holds it out to me expectantly. Even though he's technically my little brother, I have to crane my neck to meet his eyes as he stands in front of me.

"Ro, what—"

"Just read it." He rolls his eyes and shakes the paper until I take it.

DECLARATION OF INTENT AND PETITION TO FILE is printed boldly across the top. I almost laugh.

"I'm not running for prom queen." I fold the paper and shove it back into his hand. Now I am laughing. I seriously can't help it. "Are you kidding me?"

"I'm serious as an inherited blood disease, big sis." He smirks. He knows I hate it when he jokes about sickle cell like that, but because it's law that little brothers have to be annoying, he does it anyway. "You need the money, and they're giving money away. It seems like the perfect solution to me."

Other schools have huge endowments for athletics or the arts, but Campbell County High School has one for prom. It's such a big deal, our rich alums give back faithfully to ensure that we have the biggest, most elaborate spectacle of a prom season in Indiana every year. And part of that spectacle happens to be the massive scholarships they give to the prom king and queen, for what they like to call the "outstanding service and community engagement" the winners must display.

But mostly, the alums are just writing checks to one anothers' stuck-up kids—checks in the neighborhood of ten grand. Robbie is right: It's almost exactly what I need to make Pennington work.

"Look, this money could be enough to at least get you to Pennington, you know? You win, and Granny and Grandad keep the house."

My stomach churns at the thought of one of my classmates getting that scholarship. All that money just for playing dress-up and picking up trash on the playground. All that money going to another Campbell County rich kid with too much time on their hands and no fear of the spotlight. It isn't fair. None of it is fair.

I think about the speeches and the public events and how visible the prom court candidates are every year. My hands get sweaty just thinking about the posts about the hopefuls that appear on Campbell Confidential—the rumors and the polls and the drama— or posters with my face on them plastered around the hallways and the events with eyes of the entire town trained on me. There's no way to hide when you run for prom queen; there's no way to fly under the radar when you want that title. And I've never been one to break from the ensemble to go solo.

Everything about the idea is ridiculous, but I can't stop thinking about it. I mean, I don't come from a legacy family—one of those families where everyone has run for or won king or queen—even though we do still have my mom's prom dress hanging up in my grandparents' closet. It's bad luck in Campbell to get rid of your dress.

The hallway near the front office at school has photos of every king and queen dating back to when they started this whole tradition. I think for a second about what it would be like to have my likeness plastered next to Eden Chandler's, Emme's older sister, the crown nestled into my tight black curls, my hair all defiance where hers is tradition. I chase away the idea as quickly as it came.

"Ro, be realistic." I shake my head and slip down to the floor. "I'm nobody's prom queen."

"Pennington is important to you, right?" He sits down next to me and bumps my shoulder with his.

I nod, even though he already knows the answer to that. Pennington has always been my North Star, the place where all my missing pieces would suddenly fit. Where I could play the music that's kept me grounded all these years, with people who take it just as seriously as I do. It's the only school in Indiana where I can start a specialty bachelor's degree enrichment program that feeds directly into a med school. The fast track to the rest of my career. The rest of my life.

"And it's three hours away." He scratches at his eyebrow, understanding. "Far enough to feel like you're really gone but not too far to come home if things get really bad with my SCD or something." His smile is a little sad as he adds, "Right?"

I won't lie to him, because me and Robbie don't lie to each other. I nod.

I know I could go to Indiana University, my backup, and things might be fine. I might be okay. But I'd be slipping further and

22

further away from the vision I've always had, the vision my mom always had, for my future. And that feels like a betrayal I can't begin to fathom.

"Look. The odds have never been stacked in our favor, but that's never stopped us before."

He doesn't even have to mention all the odds. There isn't a day that goes by that doesn't remind me just how bad my odds are in this place. Robbie reaches for the pen that's constantly tucked behind his ear and flips open the Declaration of Intent again. And right there, on the first signature line, written in his all-caps handwriting, is the name of my official endorser.

"You got three days to get thirty signatures and declare yourself a candidate. You've got my vote, big sis. Don't count yourself out."

four

Spring in Indiana is an unpredictable thing. You're just as likely to get caught in an aggressive snowstorm as you are to need to strip down to a tank top and booty shorts because it's too hot to wear anything else. And then sometimes, on days like today, you'll start the day with a cloudless sky, and by the time you hop off your bike outside your part-time job, you're drenched to the bone from a surprise thunderstorm.

Robbie's signed Declaration of Intent form is in my backpack, no doubt dripping wet by now, but I swear it feels like it's burning a hole straight through to my hoodie. I haven't left home without it since he handed it to me two days ago, but I can't seem to bring myself to do anything with it. It's like I'm wagering a potential future at my dream school against a very real, very present danger of making a fool of myself in front of not only our student body but the entire town.

"Jeez, Liz. I could have picked you up, you know," Britt says after I lock my bike to the rack under the awning in front of Melody Music—the music store where I work—and step inside. "You're such a masochist—and that's coming from me."

She gestures at her face full of piercings, and I laugh a tight, strained laugh.

Britt thinks I ride my bike everywhere because I like the exercise, and I've never gone out of my way to correct her. She's partially right, but mostly I ride my bike because I don't want anyone coming out to my house to get me. I don't want anyone but Gabi seeing where I live. It's just easier that way.

"Lizzie! You're finally here!" Gabi turns away from the counter where she'd been taking Stone's measurements before I came in, and Kurt, my boss, mouths a very distinct *SAVE ME* in my direction. G may be his niece, but he's never quite figured out how to manage her, um, exuberance. "Please tell him how critical it is that I make Stone a prom dress where the shade compliments her tawny undertones."

Kurt rounds the counter, rubbing his temples. He doesn't have the heart to tell us that we can't use his store as our number one hangout spot, since Gabi is his blood relative and because I've worked here on most afternoons and every weekend since I was a freshman.

"You're right. How could I ever have misunderstood the importance of . . . What were we talking about again?" He smirks and winks in my and Britt's direction.

He leans in and lowers his voice as I take over for him behind the register. "I'm going to miss you when you graduate, kid, but you have got to take my niece far, *far* from here." Kurt hums the melody to some Ariana Grande song about leaving as he disappears into the back room.

I cross and uncross my arms. I'm nervous even though I probably shouldn't be. I love my friends. I trust my friends. I need my friends' help if I want to make it to Pennington.

"Yeah, so look. I, um . . ." I look at their faces and am reminded why they're my people. All three of them look ready to leap into action, and they don't even know what I'm asking of them yet. "I didn't get that scholarship from Pennington."

Their reactions are immediate.

Britt cracks her knuckles. "That's such garbage! Nobody deserves that scholarship more—"

Gabi shakes her head. "I'm going to take care of this. I'll have my parents' lawyer call—"

Stone grabs the crystal pendant hanging from her necklace. "I have palo santo in my purse. We can cleanse your clarinet and—"

I wave my hands in front of me with a quiet laugh. These weirdos are the best sometimes. "Guys, it's cool. It's fine. Well, not fine. It's pretty awful actually. But it'll be okay. I have a plan."

Like a lightbulb, Gabi's face instantly shifts from rage to recognition.

"We're going to make you prom queen," she says simply, reading my mind.

"We're gonna *what*?" Britt narrows her eyes.

"My sentiment exactly," I mumble. I add so that Gabi can hear me, "Robbie said the same thing, and I'm starting to believe that

I'm in some alternate universe in which I am a viable option for prom court."

In a concert band, you're arranged into sections so that the instruments and sounds in your ear are the most similar to your own—so that what surrounds you *is* you, to a degree. It's easier to know your clarinet part when you're not fighting against a cello on one side and a tuba on the other.

High school friend groups are something like an ensemble in that way. My friends are certified oddballs, the inkblots on an otherwise pure white page, and it's why we work together so well. Because as long as they're my people, as long as they're the ones on my left and my right, sometimes I can forget that I don't fit in anywhere else in this town.

Stone adds, "My horoscope predicted something untoward might present itself today, but I wasn't anticipating anything of this nature."

"It's not *untoward*. Ugh, you're all so dramatic. Lizzie, I was born to be a fairy godmother; it's my destiny." Gabi plops her highlighter-yellow Chloé bag next to the register and pulls her phone out of it. Her fingers fly across the screen so quickly, I almost don't notice she's speaking. "A couple slight changes, and you'll be as good as new. Certifiably prom queen ready."

Her tongue darts out to the corner of her mouth quickly like it always does when she thinks. I brace myself for what that face means for my life, even though she hasn't said quite what she has in mind yet. Gabi is sort of magical in that way—she doesn't really have to say what she wants from you in order for you to just know.

"With Stone running the data from mentions on Campbell

Confidential and the point-collection system, and my powers of strategy or—shall we say—*shrewd deduction*, we'll know where you stand in the polls at all times," she says. "Nothing a quick algorithm can't do, right Stony?"

Stone looks to the ceiling, and I think for a moment she might be asleep with her eyes open. Until she speaks.

"I've consulted my star chart, and yes, Liz, I can do this for you."

I shake my head. I don't know how this runaway train started chugging along so quickly, but I have to stop it before I get knocked completely off track.

"Thank you, Stone, seriously but—"

"Perfect! It's settled, then. Stone, come with me. I'll explain—we have some work to do." She doesn't look up from her phone, but she doesn't have to. Stone is already grabbing for her own phone to get to work. "And Liz"—she looks me up and down—"we'll need to revamp your look soon. The grunge aesthetic does not a prom queen make."

I glance down at my outfit, and frown. Melody doesn't have a dress code—pretty much all we do is sell sheet music to middle-aged men looking to learn how to play Beatles songs on their acoustic guitars, and that doesn't require a ball gown—so I'm wearing a variation of what I always wear: a white V-neck T-shirt, black skinny jeans with holes in the kneecaps, and high-top black Chucks. Sometimes I switch the game up and opt for a cool thrifted logo tee from the '80s or '90s, but for the most part, this is it. Simple and to the point.

But Gabi has been like this since we discovered her mom's massive stack of old issues of *Vogue* in the basement when we were eight—and she's had one foot out of Indiana since then. Fashion is her everything. It's why she's already such a talented designer that she got accepted early into the Fashion Institute of Technology in New York for the fall. When G knows what she wants, nothing keeps her from getting it.

I look over at Britt and raise my eyebrows in question. She holds up both her hands in surrender. "Don't look at me, dude. I missed the memo where we decided to go all debutante ball on steroids."

Britt's right. We've had a plan, practically since the day we met, that we'd all go to prom as a unit. Just the four of us, together, wearing Gabi Marino original dresses. It was simple, ideal. This was never part of that plan. Prom court is anything but simple.

"Britt, why must you be so negative? This is going to be amazing!" Gabi offers me her warmest smile. "What you need to focus on now is the fact that you are officially in the running for Campbell County High School prom queen, and these are the logistics that are going to help you win. We're going to need some major work if we want even the slightest chance of moving you from here"—she holds her hand down near the floor and then moves it up near her face—"to here."

Britt winces. "Are you going to get any more superficial, Marino? I just want to prepare myself now if you're going to be firing shots like this for the next five weeks."

Gabi ignores her and smiles at me instead. It's bright and reassuring, the one she uses when she feels confident and needs me to feel it too.

"Don't you worry about a thing, Lizzie," she says. She holds out her hand and wiggles her fingers expectantly. "If you would hand over your Declaration of Intent, please. I'll take care of those signatures."

I reach into my backpack and give it to her hesitantly. This is really happening.

"You've made the right decision, Lizzie." She slips the paper into her purse and places both her hands on my shoulders, and although she's so much shorter than me, it somehow makes me feel like we're on completely even footing. "Call me tonight, okay? If you go into the prom court kickoff meeting tomorrow without me prepping you on what to expect, it'll be like seasoning yourself and stepping directly into a lion's mouth."

She shakes her head sadly as she slips her black, cat-eye sunglasses down from her hair and adjusts them over her eyes. She grabs her purse from the counter and slides it up onto her shoulder. Like always, her movements are elegant, graceful, and completely sure.

"My God, imagine the carnage."

And just like that, I'm Campbell County High School's newest prom queen contender.

WEEK ONE

All's fair in love and prom.

five

I'm running late for the prom campaign orientation meeting Sunday afternoon, speed-walking through the empty hallways of the school. I'm mentally running through the checklist of instructions from Gabi on how to handle this meeting and thinking about the candidates that she has projected will be in attendance, people I need to consider making an alliance with early in the game, how I'm going to look Jordan in the eye after so many years of avoiding being in the same room with him, and—

My phone buzzes in my pocket, and the message couldn't have come at a better time. G's best-friend telepathy strikes again.

Gabi Marino: **Don't forget to show teeth when you smile, but show no fear.**

I head inside the auditorium and find a seat in the back. From where I'm sitting, behind everyone else, it looks like there are about fifty people present, an almost even split of guys and girls. All the people I expected to see are here.

There's Lucy Ivanov and Claire Adams, two members of the pom squad (which is *remarkably* different from and *definitely* superior to the cheerleading team, and don't you forget it) seated near the front, red-and-white sparkly bows in their high ponytails to match their perfectly pressed pom uniforms. I can also see our local catalog model and eternally peppy ray of sunshine, Quinn Bukowski's bright blond head sitting near Jaxon Price, one of the football guys, giggling as he whispers something into her ear. I don't even bother trying to ID everyone, because it's pretty clear: All of Campbell's elite, Jordan Jennings among them, are scattered throughout the first few rows. And there's Rachel Collins, our class president and the PomBots' fearless leader next to her boyfriend and varsity basketball captain, Derek Lawson, seated directly behind them.

Thanks to my briefing session with G and an all-night cramming session with Ro, I know exactly who I need to be paying the most attention to in the race.

My sights are set directly on Rachel. Her mom is one of only two people in the history of Campbell County to win queen both her junior and senior year. This prom stuff is in her blood.

The thought makes me feel like I'm in an airplane getting ready to take off, all anxious and more than a little lightheaded.

But there are plenty of wild cards too. A couple of guys who I know are running as either a joke or a dare (if the way they haven't stopped laughing or talking since we arrived is any indication of their interest in making court), and girls like me who don't exactly scream prom court at first look for one reason or another.

The lights shut off in the room, and I swear to you, the Olympics theme music starts playing.

I practically jump out of my skin when the first horns start blaring, but the spotlight hits Madame Simoné where she stands onstage, her long black kimono dragging on the floor as she gestures at the screen behind her.

"Ladies and gentlemen, you have entered into a time-honored Campbell tradition that will soon change the course of your life forever!" The room erupts in applause. She speaks with an incredibly convincing French accent, like she wasn't born and raised in Campbell County and like we haven't all seen her photo in the Gallery with her very own placard underneath: *Roberta Simon, 1987.*

Madame Simoné is talking about all the powerful men and women who have left this race and gone on to great things, when the doors in the back bang open, and she shuts her mouth with a snap.

"Sorry I'm late!" a blur of a girl whisper-shouts as she bursts through the doors. She has a skateboard tucked underneath her arm, and a messenger bag that keeps slipping down her shoulder as she makes her way up the center aisle. "This school is surprisingly labyrinth-like. They don't mention that on the website."

Everyone stares at the intrusion, but the girl doesn't seem to notice. She just keeps going. She reaches my row, the last row where people are seated, and climbs over the two people closest to the aisle to work her way inside. She's speaking to everyone and no one in the room, her eyes never fixing on any one person for long.

"I didn't realize that the auditorium and the performing-arts space were two different things, you know? Most schools only have one. But this place is *massive*. I was just telling my dad that—"

Madame Simoné coughs dramatically and the girl finally stops talking. Rachel and her crew don't even bother to conceal their giggles as they turn back to face the front.

"Now that everyone has finally decided to arrive, may I continue?" She shoots a pointed look at the girl, who is slumped down in the seat next to me, before continuing her speech.

"I have her for second-period French," the late girl whispers in my ear, and I can feel her breath on my neck. "I like her energy. She seems pretty no-nonsense."

I don't want to look away from the stage, to miss even a moment of what Madame Simoné is saying, but I can't help myself. This girl is bold enough to come in late and talk during her lecture? I gotta know who I'm dealing with here. I'm sure Gabi would be proud of me for being vigilant about the competition.

I turn to face her, and seriously, her eyes are the kind of green that I thought only existed in books and on models post-Photoshop. Just a little bit south of olive, with brown flecks in them and everything, like someone painted them by hand. It trips me up for just a second.

"Wait, what?"

"She's cool, right? I'm getting a cool energy from her." She bites her thumbnail. "I'm not super good at French, but I feel like she takes no prisoners."

I just nod, because I'm not sure what to say. I mean, I've taken honors and then AP French with Madame Simoné for the past three years, but I don't know that it's even all that relevant to this girl. She seems to just like to talk for the sake of talking. And I'm not into that, noise for the sake of noise.

"You all know how this works, *les élèves*. But if you want to have your chance at making prom court, you'll listen very closely to the *nuance*."

Some of the rules Madame Simoné goes into next make sense, are obvious even, but some are completely antiquated. She covers all the bases for the campaign as well as prom night itself: no drinking, no vaping, the usual. But the hardest ones to hear are the ones she says with the most authority: Girls will run for queen, and boys will run for king—there's definitely no accounting for people who might not identify as either. And the hardest for me to ignore, same-sex couples aren't allowed to attend together. They can dance with each other once they get there, maybe, if no chaperones care enough to stop them, but they can't officially go as dates. And just in case they hadn't made their prejudice clear enough, if your gender identity doesn't explicitly align with the one you were assigned at birth, you can't come dressed the way you might want. Girls wear dresses, and boys wear tuxes. And that's the end of it.

The whole thing royally sucks in my opinion.

"Prom court is decided by a point system, determined by your attendance at a combination of both mandatory and volunteer community service events and public appearances, and your class rank." A chorus of groans erupts again, and I feel a little giddy inside. Finally, some payoff for being the nerdiest nerd this school has ever seen! "This is about more than where you sit in the cafeteria, *les élèves*; this is about your overall ability to represent the best of what Campbell County High School has to offer! Each event is worth twenty points, and the eight of you with the highest scores— four boys and four girls—will be selected as this year's prestigious prom court. And in the event of a tie, the administration will weigh in to make the final call on who gets to represent the best and brightest of what Campbell County High School has to offer!"

Five weeks of campaigning for prom court, and if you get selected, one more week to campaign for king and queen specifically. Five weeks to take myself from "Liz Lighty: Unapologetic Wallflower" to "Liz Lighty: Slightly More Apologetic Prom Queen Contender."

Everyone begins clapping, and I chance another look at Jordan and his teammates. This time, my eyes meet his. I'm so mortified to have been caught staring like a creep, I snap my head forward so quick I swear I hear the girl next to me giggle. If my skin weren't so brown, I'm sure I'd be beet red. But because I'm a glutton for punishment, I cheat my eyes in his direction again.

"Excuse me, Madame Simoné?" Rachel Collins's hand shoots straight up, her pastel-pink manicured nails wiggling in the air. "I just have a question about the scoring process."

Madame Simoné, clearly annoyed with having been interrupted before asking for questions, tells her to continue before she "cashes out her pension." Or at least I think that's what she's saying.

"Okay, well, I just wanted to make sure there isn't going to be any funny business going on with the scoring process. Like we're not going to have to deal with an"—she turns around to look pointedly at me—"affirmative action aspect, perhaps?"

Here's the thing: Rachel and I have never liked each other. We've been battling back and forth for everything since the second grade: spelling bee champion (I won), field day distance winner (I'm not an athlete, but my legs are incredibly long—I beat her by half a second), and now valedictorian (all mine, baby). And this victory, having the highest rank in our class, has made this a rivalry with the likes of Burr versus Hamilton. I'm half convinced that she's going to challenge me to a duel at graduation.

But she's never said anything like this to me before. Anything this obviously racist. I cycle through like eight different emotions before I settle on a combination of rage and embarrassment.

The voice beside me pipes up immediately.

"Actually, Rebecca, before you start concerning yourself with *skewed scoring*, you should probably know that the biggest beneficiaries of affirmative action are white women."

The girl's smile is cloyingly sweet as she stares Rachel down. A couple of people laugh and "Ooh, she got you!" after she speaks. When I look around, Rachel is narrowing her eyes and mumbling, "It's *Rachel*," under her breath loud enough so that we can still hear it from where we are.

"Ah yes, now, if that's all, I think I'll continue." Madame Simoné nods at the girl and finishes her speech. "While court is decided by your civic engagement, your king and queen are decided by popular vote. By the sheer will of the people."

"You didn't have to do that, you know—respond to Rachel," I whisper to the girl without taking my eyes off the stage. "She's been like this since we were in elementary school."

"Of course I did." I can feel her looking at me, but I can't bring myself to make eye contact. My heart is beating faster than I know what to do with, and I'm not sure why. I'm used to Rachel saying shady stuff, but I'm not used to people outside of my friends jumping in to defend me. Especially not beautiful girls I barely know. "I have rules."

I look at her then—I can't help myself.

"What kind of rules?"

"Well, for one"—she smiles at me with a flash of something that looks like trouble in her eyes—"I never let terrible people get away with doing terrible things. And two, if something is wrong, I say something about it. Always."

"Aren't those pretty much the same thing?" I'm smiling too, because there's just something about how sure she is, how secure in those ideals, that makes me happy.

"Maybe. But terrible people aren't always the ones doing something wrong. Good people mess up too, but that doesn't mean we should let it slide."

I swallow and nod.

"Now, if everyone will just bring up their Declaration of Intent and Petition to File, I will give you your *calendrier officiel* of both the mandatory and optional events for this week." Madame Simoné pushes her wire-rimmed glasses up the bridge of her nose and puts her hands on her hips. "And I will leave you with this advice: Do not think *pour un moment* that the next month will be a walk in the park. I expect all of you to take this seriously."

When everyone gathers their stuff, I stand quickly. I look at the new girl, who smiles at me brightly.

"This should be a lot of fun," she says, tucking her board under her arm. "I'll see you soon?"

I simply nod, even though a part of me wants to keep talking to her. As she waves and heads toward the stage, I realize I'm more than ready to get out of the auditorium, back home, and to my music. I can't wait to close the door, put in my headphones, and turn up Kittredge's new album so loud I can't focus on anything else. Some sort of escape from thinking about how in the world I'm supposed to do any of this, with these people, for the next month of my life.

six

I'm practically a zombie in school on Monday morning. The prom meeting ran long. Way longer than I thought it would. Even after Madame Simoné finished her speech and we handed in our forms, there was at least another half hour of waiver and photo release form-signing to be done.

With all the papers and signatures and talk of photoshoots and public appearances, I felt like Beyoncé's personal assistant (because I'm sure Queen Bey doesn't have to actually use her holy and precious time for that sort of thing anymore).

I went home to finish my homework and practice my solo for the spring concert but ended up helping Granny cook dinner and then debriefing on the phone with Gabi about who was at the meeting and what was said for two hours afterward instead. By the time I finished my lab report for AP Chem and the rough draft of my paper for AP Lit, I was almost too tired to run through my music, but I forced myself through it anyway. I barely got any sleep.

So believe me when I say I'm definitely too tired for the fifth-degree interrogation I'm currently getting from Gabi.

"I told you that I never actually got her name." I grab my case from my locker in the back of the band room as Gabi grabs hers. "I just know that she's new and she seems to be . . . different. But, like, in a good way?"

"Well, I don't like it one bit." Gabi tsks as she sits down and adjusts her music stand. "Do you think she's an agent of Rachel's sent to scope you out? I wouldn't put it past her. You know she's wanted to find a weakness in you since the day you beat her out for line leader in the second grade."

I pause. "Let me just get this straight. You think the new girl's . . . a spy?"

Gabi looks at me with her carefully plucked eyebrows raised to her hairline. "You kid! But I'm telling you, watch out. Remember: There are no real allies in war, only people who are valuable enough at the moment to delay the inevitable destruction they will eventually face at your own hands."

"I can't tell if you've been reading *The Art of War* again or *The Hunger Games*."

"Both. Obviously."

The bell rings, and something inside me settles. The world may be spinning at a thousand miles per hour, and I'm not sure where I'm headed or how to get there, but here, in front of my music, I'm grounded. I'm centered.

Mr. K stands in front of us to make his announcements before we start playing, and—

"Sorry I'm late!" The girl from the meeting—the double agent with the gorgeous eyes—rushes in, late again. She doesn't have a skateboard this time, but she's just as frazzled as she was at the meeting yesterday evening.

Gabi elbows me and mouths, *Is that her?*

I nod back and try to keep my face impassive as Mr. K brightens. Even if I hadn't already met her, she would have been hard not to clock as a new student.

Everything about her screams "I'm not from around here!" and has an edge of "But don't even think about messing with me." Her red hair is cut into an asymmetrical bob that reveals a dandelion tattoo behind her right ear, and her outfit looks like she walked straight off a *Thrasher Magazine* cover—rolled black mom jeans, dirty bright-orange-and-white Vans, and a camo jacket over her FEMME THE FUTURE hoodie that she clearly has carefully bleached and distressed herself.

Her nose is pierced with one simple emerald stud in the right nostril and two silver hoops in the other. I think for a second she might be ready to give Britt a run for her money as the most idgaf-I-wear-whatever-I-want student at Campbell.

"Class, this is our new drummer." He turns to her. "What would you like to be called?"

She waves a little and smiles. "My name's Amanda, um, McCarthy, but everyone calls me Mack."

"This is our new drummer, Mack. Mack is stepping in for Kevin for the rest of the semester, due to his . . . unfortunate

47

prom-related injury." He shakes his head.

Three weeks ago, we lost our drummer, Kevin Kilborn, to a promposal gone wrong. He attempted a backflip off the roof of his garage, holding a sign that said: LAURIE FERRIS, I'VE ABSOLUTELY FLIPPED FOR YOU. PROM? and, well, he didn't quite land on his feet. Literally or figuratively. Not only did Laurie turn him down (citing "commitment issues" on her Campbell Confidential feed later that night, according to Gabi), but he broke his left wrist and both index fingers in the process. The whole thing was live-streamed on CC, and Kevin hasn't come back to school since.

Mr. K gestures in my direction. "Liz can help you get all set up after class at some point this week, but for now, you can grab a seat at the kit in the back and maybe just try to get a feel for the music today?"

She meets my eyes and offers me a little wave as she goes to her seat, and my mouth gets all weird and dry. All the feelings of being at peace and at one with the music are out the window as she breezes by me. I don't believe in fairy tales and love at first sight and all that, but for just a second, I think this girl and those eyes and the way her freckles dot the entire expanse of her face are cute enough to make a believer out of me.

When Gabi elbows me again though, I snap out of it. She mouths, *Definitely a secret agent.*

And yeah, my best friend might be a little unhinged, but I have to get real. Fast.

After all, Lightys don't get fairy tales.

seven

My phone is buzzing with another text from Granny, and I know I should be getting home soon for dinner. But Gabi is talking a mile a minute, and I'm taking notes like everything she's saying is going to be on an exam later. I don't want to miss a single thing.

We're in her massive basement—which I have a feeling is going to become our prom war room—pretending not to hear Gabi's parents arguing upstairs, and listening to her lay out an impressively detailed plan for how she's going to *Pretty Woman* the hell outta me.

"Okay, so I had my mother's personal shopper send some options over to your house today." She holds her hands out in front of her. "No pressure! I just thought it might be a nice solution to the wardrobe concern."

Me and Gabi have always seen things very differently. For her, there is always a way if her will is formidable enough. Though she be little, she is fierce. Or whatever it is they say about short girls with big personalities. So if she thinks a wardrobe change is the fast track to winning prom queen, no amount of arguing is going to change her mind.

It's annoying, but I've learned to deal. Me and G aren't just friends, we're family.

I think about telling her that there's no way I'm accepting an order courtesy of her parents' AmEx like some sort of charity case, but then I remember her being there for me every day after my mom died without complaint. Bringing me homework for the weeks I missed school, sleeping on the floor of my bedroom every night in the weeks after the funeral to keep me company. Holding my hand when I couldn't stop having nightmares where my grandparents and Robbie were all lined up in identical hospital beds, the low, steady beep of a flatline multiplied by three. So I keep my mouth shut and swallow down all my protests, because even if I don't want to accept the gift, she wants to give it, and I know her heart has always been in the right place.

Even if her execution is . . . a bit shoddy.

"You were the only one with a *wardrobe concern*!" Britt huffs from where she sits. She crosses her arms over her Campbell County HS Varsity Girls Rugby hoodie. "Despite her impressive height and ridiculously perfect cheekbones—they really are crazy high, Lizzo, it's almost obnoxious—Liz isn't some Barbie for you to play dress-up with."

"Well, I'm just trying to be helpful. Someone has to take initiative here and—"

"Um. I'm right here, guys. Me? Liz? Your friend and the one whose life you're talking about?"

"You're so right. We should table that discussion for later," Gabi sort of concedes. She pauses briefly as her parents' muffled shouting from upstairs gets slightly louder, but she straightens quickly like we heard nothing at all. She uses her laser pointer to underline the point on the slideshow that she has projected onto the wall. I immediately wish I hadn't asked my coworker Victor to cover my shift tonight in order to subject myself to this. She turns back to her screen and purses her lips. "We need to be drumming up support for you within the student body, because they ultimately decide who wins."

"Okay, but I shouldn't be too behind, right? I mean, I'll do all the volunteer things, and I definitely have the highest GPA," I offer. "Madame Simoné made it sound very egalitarian yesterday."

"Jesus, Mary, and Joseph." Britt kicks her legs up in her leather seat and bites down on nacho-cheese Doritos covered in spicy hummus. "Don't tell me this is some electoral college garbage."

"Great questions, my friends." Gabi smiles. She has been studying this process her entire life. "You're easily in the lead on GPA, Lizzie, but that is worth the smallest percentage of overall scoring. So while the different events and your class rank get you on the court, the votes alone determine whether or not you win. So as important as the next few weeks are for how well you manage to show up and take illiterate ferrets for walks at the ASPCA or whatever, what matters is that you win over the people."

Gabi tells the Alexa to bring up the lights so that we're no longer lit only by the glow of the PowerPoint. It's always like being in that old Disney Channel movie *Smart House* when I come over to the Marinos.

"Stone, if you don't mind." Gabi waves her hand to the side as an invitation to have Stone join her in front of us.

"While I would normally be inclined to allow the universe to dictate its will to us, due to the dire nature of the circumstances at hand, I found it in our collective best interest to—"

"Stone, some of us have to get home at some point this century." Britt interrupts as gently as she can.

"I've devised an algorithm for evaluating where Liz is at in the rankings at any given point during the race." She hands me her phone. "I'm not particularly adept at coding, but this application should suffice for our purposes."

"Whoa. Seriously?" Britt leans over and gapes at the screen. I've always secretly assumed that Stone is so spacy because she's tapped directly into the motherboard. This confirms it.

"Stone, G, this is amazing. How did you do this so fast?"

Gabi polishes her manicure on her chic black sweater. "I told you to leave it to us. We'll take you far, my fierce and fantastic best friend."

"Be advised, it's an imperfect system. We're using the number of hits a candidate's name is getting on Campbell Confidential as a stand-in for projected votes to determine what type of traction you'll need to win the popular vote, should you make court." Stone says it as lightly as she says everything, like she's talking about her moon being in Venus, or Mercury retrograde incoming. "But our primary concern is calculating the other elements—GPA, community service events—to understand just how competitive you need to be in order to enter the top four."

"There are twenty-five girls in the race currently. And Liz, given our calculations . . ." Gabi starts.

Britt looks down at the app and back up at me with her expression pinched like she's just smelled something rank. "You're dead last, buddy."

"Wow, you should think about a future in investigative journalism." I roll my eyes.

"Well, yes, technically she's in last at the moment, but that's what *strategy* is for, Brittany Luca." Gabi rolls her eyes, and Britt throws a chip at her for using her full government name. "I'm *saying* that's exactly why we must handle this with precision."

"I think we should skip all of this and tell Rachel precisely where, exactly, she can shove a crown—"

Gabi pinches the bridge of her nose, clearly frustrated with the inability of the band of misfits she has in front of her to execute her intricate thirty-two-step plan, which so far has included nineteen points specifically aimed at sabotaging Rachel Collins. She sighs.

"Buttons. Britt, I'm saying we need buttons with Liz's face on them. Every successful campaign has buttons. Your parents are still willing to volunteer pro bono, right?"

Britt's parents own the biggest print shop in central Indiana, and G somehow roped them into volunteering an obscene amount of supplies for the campaign. They're honestly my favorite type of ally: the kind that puts their money where their mouth is.

"Absolutely. I've been waiting for a chance to have Rachel Collins canceled since she called me a Troll Doll on acid in the eighth grade. You just say the word, Liz, and I'll have one of the freshmen from the JV team take care of her." Britt moves a finger across her throat ominously, and I spit out my water. All my friends are losing it. "What? I'm not going to have her killed or anything! They'll just put sugar in her gas tank or cut her brake lines or something." She shrugs. "Nothing drastic."

I know that Britt is (mostly) joking, and I know that they all have my best interests at heart, but this whole discussion is making my chest feel tight and my stomach go haywire. All these steps and strategies just to make people like me, to make myself into someone worth paying attention to, makes me get that too-big-for-my-skin feeling.

I stand up suddenly, brush the stray Doritos crumbs off my jeans, and try to smile at my friends. My hands are shaking in the telltale I'm-getting-ready-to-have-a-panic-attack way, so I stuff them into my pockets. Gabi looks confused about my abrupt move to leave, but Britt just presses her lips together and nods.

"I think that's enough for today, don't you guys?" Britt asks. "Hell, we're not even plotting on my life, and I'm exhausted. I say we reconvene after Liz's first volunteer event."

Gabi points at the screen with a pout. "But what about—"

"Yes, I think our dearest friends have the right idea." Stone places a gentle hand on Gabi's arm. "Perhaps we should reassess after a brief respite."

Gabi visibly deflates, and I almost feel bad about taking the wind out of her sails like that, but I have to go. I grab my backpack from the floor and shrug it up onto my shoulders. I'm out the door before I even think to say goodbye.

When I get home from G's, I'm completely wiped.

I'm ready to crawl into bed for the next forty-eight hours straight. Which, okay, after homework and practicing the fingering for the new arrangement of one of our songs we got in class earlier, I don't have eight hours to sleep, let alone forty-eight, but a girl can dream, right?

But Granny is standing in front of the window with her hands on her hips, waiting for me, when I head up the walk, and I know dipping out to go to my room instead of going to the kitchen to check in is not going to be an option.

"Where you been, Elizabeth?" she asks when I open the door. I barely have a chance to kiss her on the cheek before she continues. "You missed dinner tonight, and you know that don't fly around here."

I would never tell my granny to dial back the attitude—I value my mouth too much to get it slapped off my face—but I wish I could.

"Gran, she's been at practice, remember? Long nights this week!" Robbie shouts from his place on the couch next to Grandad, and I couldn't be more grateful for the save. I don't like Ro lying to Granny any more than I like lying to her myself, but everything about prom has to stay under wraps until after I've gotten the scholarship. Because if they find out about the campaign, they'll find out about the scholarship I'm working toward and the one I didn't get, and if they find out about the scholarships, they'll start the process of selling the house.

I can hear Alex Trebek's voice from where I stand. They're watching *Jeopardy!*, and even though Robbie will beat him in final Jeopardy like he does every night, Grandad is confidently yelling out wrong answers along the way anyway. "Chill, Grandad! You're so far off it's not even funny. It's: What is the Treaty of Guadalupe Hidalgo?"

Granny ignores him and is right at my heels as I step farther into the foyer. I can see Ro from his spot on the couch, and he shoots me a sympathetic look.

"You don't get to just walk into this house whenever you feel like it, Elizabeth. I didn't play that when your mama was a little girl, and I'm not going to play that now."

And that's just the punch to the gut I needed after today. A comparison to one of the many ways I can't live up to the expectations set by my mom. But I can't say that to my granny either, because I don't talk back and because she's right. I know the rules. You don't miss dinner without a phone call, and I dropped the ball.

It's only been a day of this prom stuff, and I'm so over it I could puke.

"Sorry, Granny. It won't happen again," I mumble.

"I know it won't, baby." Granny's voice is soft as she holds my cheeks with both her hands. She examines my face and pats my cheek twice. "You look tired. Make sure you drink plenty of water. Last thing we need is you studying yourself into dehydration before we even get you to Pennington."

When she walks away, she pushes at Robbie's feet that are currently resting on the coffee table and tells him to quit acting like "some kind of heathen." I drop my bags off in my bedroom and sort of shuffle through the living room and into the kitchen. I know Granny is annoyed, but she wouldn't leave me without a foil-wrapped plate, ready to be reheated. When I open the door to the fridge, it's on the second shelf, right where I figured it would be.

I don't even bother throwing it in the microwave before dragging my feet into my room and falling onto my bed with a thud. I don't even toe my shoes off, because it would take too much energy. I still have to practice my music and review G's thirty-two-point plan again before I can call it a night, but for a moment I just balance my plate of cold chicken on my stomach and stare up at the ceiling. The notes from my arrangement practically dance across my line of vision, almost like counting sheep. For the first time all day, in the silence of my room and the almost-music of those imaginary notes, I feel close to relaxed.

And before I know it, I'm asleep.

eight

The thing about anxiety is that it looks different for everyone. I mean, yeah, of course there are some threads that run through all of us that mark us as, you know, anxious people: being restless, exhausted, just plain fidgety. But it's the nuances that change the game. It's my stomach-churning, gazelles-dancing-gracefully-across-my-abdomen feeling that always gets me the most.

It's why I toss my cookies (or *almost* toss my cookies, if I'm extra lucky) before nearly every performance, and why I'm clutching my bike's handlebars for dear life, breathing slowly through both nostrils like that counselor they made me see after my mom died taught me, as I psych myself up to go clean up trash in this already-clean park after school.

Granny is used to me going to work or having rehearsal after school, so as long as I'm home in time for dinner, at least I don't have to worry about that.

> Gabi Marino: **You've got this bb** 👀💕
>
> Gabi Marino: **Rachel is a barbarian with terrible cuticles. We can beat her**
>
> Gabi Marino: **Call me when you're done and we'll talk strategy**

I'm perched on my seat at the bike rack next to the parking lot, and from where I'm sitting, I can see everything as I scan the area: the group of ladies and their newborns doing Mommy-and-Me yoga in the freshly cut grass, the kids from the nearby community college playing Ultimate Frisbee in the clearing, the dogs chasing one another in the fenced-in dog park.

Across the parking lot, Jordan Jennings tugs at his black Nike hoodie and bends down to check his appearance in his side mirror. He runs a hand over his waves—the style he's been wearing since he cut off all his curls freshman year—and stands up straight. He must have decided that he's public-appearance ready. Nothing less than cover-model worthy for Jordan Jennings.

I remember that I have a job to do—one huge, my-entire-future-depends-on-this job to do—and hop off my bike just as his eyes catch mine across the lot. He doesn't smile when he sees me looking. Instead, his face flashes what is almost a grimace before it schools itself back into something more flawless.

"Hey, Lighty!" he shouts, and gives me the classic head nod. I lock my bike to the rack and steel myself for this interaction. We've successfully avoided each other for almost four years, but all good things must eventually end, I guess. "Still riding your bike, huh? Good to see some things haven't changed."

I bite back the urge to say something snarky to him about how all our families can't just buy us the newest Supercharged Range Rover because we remembered to tie our shoes or whatever. If we have to work together, the smart thing to do is to make this as bearable as possible. Bite my tongue, put my head down, and get to work. The Lighty Way.

"Looks that way." I tug my backpack higher on my shoulders and start in the direction of the park attendants' station.

"So, partners, huh?" He waits a beat, and when he realizes I don't plan to respond, adds: "Crazy they have us out here, right? It's not like they need our janitorial services."

"Sure."

"A woman of few words nowadays, I guess," he mumbles from behind me. The petty in me is a little bit happy about how frustrated he sounds with my short answers.

What? I never said I was perfect. He's had four years to make aimless conversation with me: in the classroom, in the hallways, over my grandparents' old landline using the number he used to have memorized. But he hasn't. So.

The park is bustling now, all our classmates who were also assigned trash duty today finally here and milling around. I see a couple of guys from the baseball team leaning against the swing set, the girls they're partnered with taking selfies.

A group of freshmen in matching denim jackets stand near the park attendants' station, posing in front of one anothers' phones

61

and adjusting their portable ring lights to make sure everything is ready to go. The Prom Projectioners also act as a sort of unofficial documentary team. We have one every year. A group of freshmen, usually girls, filming every step of the process for Campbell Confidential Live, because nothing—and I do mean absolutely nothing—about this race goes unnoticed.

"Last name's Lighty." I offer a smile to the bored college-aged park attendant once we reach the booth, my first since leaving school today. "Here for the—"

"Prom thing. Yeah, I figured. When your time is up, you'll come back here, and I'll sign off on your sheets. Capisce?"

Jordan reaches through the window and grabs the stuff. "*Capisce*, man."

I can hear the smirk in his voice without even turning to look at him.

"Who does he think he is? Al Capone?" he offers once we're out of earshot. "I swear everybody in this town that gets to be a part of prom stuff thinks they're the leader of the most powerful mob outfit in Prohibition-era Chicago."

I snort, before I think better of myself. I try to get stoic again really quickly though. I'm not going to give him the satisfaction of making me smile.

"How's Robbie? Haven't seen that kid in ages. He still some sort of mad genius when it comes to playing NBA 2K?" Jordan has never been great about periods of silence that last more than a few minutes at a time. I grab a stray Pepsi bottle from the grass in front of us and drop it into the bag without answering him. Maybe if I act like he's not saying anything, he'll get the hint.

"Soooo, are we ignoring each other, or are we going to at least pretend to like each other while doing this?" His voice has more bite to it than usual as he drops a Honey Bun wrapper into the trash bag. "Just let me know so I can adjust my expectations accordingly."

My answer comes quickly. "I don't think we should pretend to be friends just because we got stuck working together. You've been pretty good at ignoring my existence for a while now."

"Wow." He laughs with no humor. "That's rich."

My head snaps up. "What's that supposed to mean?"

"It means exactly what it sounds like. I'm not the one who—" He stops himself suddenly and takes a deep breath.

I know what he stopped himself from saying: *I'm not the one who couldn't just grow up and act like everybody else.*

He runs a gloved hand forward on his head. "Whatever, Lighty. Look. You're right. We don't have to be buddies or whatever. But maybe we could, I don't know, at least acknowledge each other's presence?"

I look away and mumble, "Fine."

"Yeah, *fine*," he scoffs. "It's actually perfect."

Perfect. There's nothing perfect about it, but that's how it goes sometimes. That's how it goes most of the time, I guess.

Something in his tone makes me clench my jaw to bite back a response. Jordan and his perfection. I almost want to ask him how things are going with his perfect girlfriend, Emme, and the perfect couple they used to be before she went AWOL. There have been so many rumors about where she's gone and why she left that are anything but perfect—I know it must be eating at him. But I

63

can't bring myself to be that petty. Outside of what happened with me and him, it's not fair to Emme for me to pry.

It's hard to believe that we were ever close. But I remember it all, and standing near him makes it even more impossible to forget.

The summer before freshman year, Jordan spent two months at some football intensive camp for the first time ever. He wasn't returning to band in the fall, we both knew that. But that wasn't going to change much for us. He'd always played football, and now he was just going to play it a little more seriously, like his dad had been pushing him to.

It was the longest we'd gone without speaking to each other in three years, but it wasn't unbearable. I spent the summer watching TV with Robbie and lounging around the Marinos' pool. Me and G read old issues from her mom's *Vogue* collection and spent hours on Tumblr reading about our favorite K-pop bands.

But by the time school started again, I missed my friend. I missed laughing with him and cracking stupid jokes in rehearsals and dancing down the hallways like no one was watching, even if they were.

On the first day of high school, I saw him standing by his locker, surrounded by guys I didn't recognize. They were smiling and joking, all their skin darker from a summer playing football for hours a day. Jordan looked older, his curly hair completely gone, replaced with a close-cropped haircut that made his ears stick out a little. He didn't have on mismatched socks and a ratty old T-shirt like he had on the first day of eighth grade. All of a sudden he was wearing new J's, crisp jeans, and a black Nike T-shirt. It looked normal on the guys around him but strange on Jordan.

I ran up to him as excited as we always were to see each other.

My hair was in its full form, big and curly, and fell into my face as I threw my arms around his neck. I knew something was wrong when he didn't hug me back.

"Jordan! You missed everything this summer. Gabi got poison ivy, and we made up a new dance for this year's talent show—she says she's *actually* going to do it this time. And—"

"Jennings, is this your girlfriend?" one of the older guys asked, elbowing him in the ribs a little too hard. I could tell because Jordan's face screwed up a bit as he did it. "You like 'em wild, huh?"

The guy reached out and pulled on one of my curls, and I jerked my head away quickly.

"Don't touch me," I said, looking between him and Jordan, waiting for Jordan to say something.

"Ooooh, so she's feisty too!" The guy was really going now. He narrowed his eyes and reached for me again. "Aw, you don't want to have some fun? I just wanna see how you get your hair like this. Come on, what's your secret?" He pitched his voice up and imitated a seventies commercial announcer. *"Nothing but a little Afro-Sheen!"*

"You're crazy man; I don't like her!" Jordan laughed. It was nervous but bitter. "I don't even know her. I wouldn't hang out with her."

It felt like I used to feel all the time after my mom died: scared, unsure, out of control. My stomach flipped, and my heart felt like it was in my throat. My chest got tight, and I knew what would come next. I didn't wait around for it. I ran to the bathroom as fast as my legs could carry me, and I cried through the first period of my first day of freshman year. Eventually, Gabi found me camped out in a stall between periods, helped splash some water on my face, and got me to my next class.

I couldn't even make eye contact with him the next day when I passed him in the hallway. I couldn't put a name to it, but I felt ashamed in a way I never had before. I was suddenly embarrassed about everything that made me, me. What memo had I missed that said everyone was supposed to change overnight? Suddenly everything came into focus for me: The outfits were cooler, the haircuts more Pinterest-worthy, the cars in the senior parking lot shinier than I'd ever seen.

And Campbell Confidential meant that all of it—the good, the bad, and the embarrassing—would be caught on camera. I learned what Jordan had figured out over the summer: He had his place in school and I had mine. So I started wearing my hair slicked back in a tight bun nearly every day. Switched from bright colors to quieter tones so no one would spot me coming. No one was going to make me feel that way again.

I figured out my place in the social hierarchy at Campbell, and I stuck to it.

I swallow the lump that forms in my throat at the memory. As annoyed as I am about standing around and pretending to clean a basically already-clean park, I'm even more annoyed by the fact that I have to do it next to Jordan. So the moment the alarm on my phone buzzes to tell me it's time to go, I'm out of there. I turn on my heel and power walk to the park attendants' station like my breathing depends on it, leaving Jordan holding the bag.

"Well, time flies when you're having fun, huh, kids?" The snarky park attendant holds our signature sheets in his hand and uses them as an impromptu fan.

I feel Jordan appear behind me at the same time as the urge to knock the attendant upside the head with the trash claw washes over me.

"Yo, just sign the papers, man." Jordan's voice is clipped, way less happy than it was when we started. I almost feel guilty that I had something to do with that. "We don't have all day."

"Well, not with that attitude, you don't." The attendant tucks a too-long, stringy bang behind his ear with a smirk. "I don't have to sign these, you know."

My body immediately tenses, and my heart rate spikes. My stomach starts churning. I can't redo these hours. I don't have time, I can't not get credit for this afternoon, everything depends on every one of these stupid volunteer things, I—

Jordan places two fingers on the inside of my wrist and holds it in place with his thumb on the outside. His grip is firm but gentle as he taps out the beat of my pulse with his foot. It's familiar. I settle without meaning to, without realizing it, and Jordan's voice drops an octave as he leans into the attendant's space. Into his tiny, glorified port-o-potty.

"Look, I don't want to have to do this. But I still have *that* video of you from my Fourth of July party last year, and something tells me you wouldn't want it to mysteriously end up on Campbell Confidential, would you?"

The guy's face drops its smug smile and goes slack. He reaches for a pen and signs the sheets quickly before pushing them into Jordan's outstretched hand.

"There. Okay? God, I was just joking." He shakes his bangs out of his eyes. "Please don't post that video."

"I was bluffing, man. I would never do that." Jordan lets go of my wrist and smiles as he hands me my sheet. "But it was nice doing business with you."

We're halfway to the parking lot before I get my voice back.

"You remembered."

Jordan slows.

"Yeah. Of course I remembered."

I rub my wrist where he held it. I saw a counselor for a few years after my mom died, back when my anxiety first got really bad. It was terrible. I was getting sick at the smallest changes: a pop quiz, having to pick my own partner for a project in a class where I didn't have any friends, you name it. My heart would start beating so fast it would feel like it was about to jump out of my chest. Until my counselor came up with a trick.

I would place two fingers on my wrist and try to feel my pulse, and if I could, count how many beats were occurring per minute. I kept time with my foot as I went along, just like I did when trying out a new piece's rhythm in band. It was supposed to ground me, help me find my center—and it worked. I still do it even now.

It was so embarrassing though, feeling so out of control that I had to start using little tricks to keep from completely losing it that I never told anyone. Not even Gabi. But then, one day before our first band concert as first and second chair, Jordan caught me doing it while I was trying to hide behind one of the massive velvet curtains backstage.

"What's wrong?" he asked as his big brown eyes searched my

face for something I knew I couldn't help but give away. "You look sick."

"I am sick," I answered, wiping at my eyes. I wasn't crying yet, but the tears usually came right before the puke. "Or I'm gonna be. I'm supposed to do this when I'm scared. It usually calms me down."

I could see the audience from where I stood, and my grandparents were front row center, Robbie playing with his 3DS. Granny already had a disposable camera out, ready to click away. It was a big deal, their first time seeing me play in front of a crowd. Even Grandad had put on a tie and a nice pair of slacks for the show. I couldn't stand the thought of messing up in front of them, not when they looked so proud.

"Okay." He looked out at the audience and then back to me. His parents weren't going to be there, he'd told me earlier that day. His brother had a big football game out of town, so his dad was there watching him play and his mom was at her Pilates class. It was just him. "What do we do?"

And it was that simple. I told him about counting the beats, about taking deep breaths, and he stood in front of me mirroring my moves like it was the simplest thing in the world. And from then on out, for the rest of middle school, he did the same thing. Finally this ritual that I'd had to adopt to keep from completely falling apart wasn't just mine anymore. I had someone to share it with.

I stop to look at him now, all tall and handsome and every bit as much of the all-American guy as his parents always wanted him to be. And I guess the guy that he wanted to be too.

"But, um, sorry about, like, touching you without your consent or whatever. You just looked really stressed when that guy started messing around. I know how you used to, you know . . ."

"Yeah. Well. You know. Um, thanks." I hold up the sheet and start tucking it into my backpack. "I, uh—every point counts. So I appreciate it."

He smiles, bright and brilliant and every bit the Jordan Jennings who I used to know. Like something has been unlocked, like whatever cool and collected attitude he's mastered over the past four years has suddenly fallen away. And for a second, all I can do is smile back.

I'm not forgiving him—not even a little bit. But I think it might not be the worst thing in the world to make the best of working with him if I have to. Madame Simoné assigns partners at these events how and when she sees fit, and if there's a chance we could get stuck together again, I should try not to be miserable when it happens. I don't know if people ever really change, but for the sake of this race, I think I might be willing to hope.

nine

"You're only a few days into the campaign, Lizzie." Robbie's voice is low as he hands me a sudsy dish to rinse and dry. "So what, Gabi's weird algorithm has you a little behind where you wanna be?"

Granny is getting changed into her scrubs for the night shift at the nursing home, and Grandad is already dozing in front of the TV, but Robbie and I are whispering to each other just in case.

"I'm not 'a little behind,' Ro. Out of twenty-five girls in this race, I'm currently ranked twenty-fourth. And that's only because Cameron Haddix has worn the same tracksuit for three years straight and is still trying to convince everyone that Maria Sharapova is her long-lost cousin." I groan. "It's not hard to beat her."

"Okay, first of all, that tracksuit is vintage Adidas. They don't even make those anymore! So I feel like you should put some respect on her look."

I roll my eyes. Four days into the race, and while Gabi and Stone's magical algorithm has had everyone else bouncing around in the polls, my name has remained firmly at twenty-four. I went up one spot, thanks to Cameron's tracksuit affinity and her already missing a community service event, but other than that, no luck. Yesterday I even tried on some of the pieces that G had sent over to my house in a moment of desperation.

The bright red cable-knit cardigan I'm wearing isn't exactly my style, but I have to admit that it's pretty cozy. It feels like a million bucks—literally. I didn't even bother looking at the price tag before I tore it off.

"Okay, seriously though, you and Jordan have been getting chummy, right?" He hands me another plate and looks at me like he knows something he shouldn't. "Campbell Confidential won't shut up about it. And some of it is . . . not flattering."

I wouldn't say "chummy," but Jordan and I were paired together for both our community service activities this week. It wasn't exactly easy, being around him again. But he's still charming, and still funny, so it was easy to halfway forget to be mad at him. Like earlier this week, for instance, we cleaned the art room, and for a second it was almost like old times.

We'd been working in silence for a while in the art room when he said, "It's kinda cool that you're running, you know." Jordan smiled at me over the basketful of rubber glue in his arms. We were tucked away from the rest of the candidates who got assigned to classroom-cleaning duty, and it was less intimidating to be honest with each other when no one else was around. "It's good to have you with me in the trenches."

"Trenches? You make this sound like we're going to war."

He scrunched up his nose like he was getting ready to sneeze and the diamond stud in his nose glinted in the art room's fluorescent light. Jordan is the only jock I know who could pull off a nose ring and have nobody say anything shady about it. But also, when you're hot enough to've been a *Riverdale* cast member in another life, and your dad played for the Colts for eight years, you can kind of do whatever you want.

"I think if you haven't figured out that this race is a little bit like going to battle, then you definitely have to pull your nose out of your sheet music," he said, his elbow nudging mine. "Don't worry, I'll be your personal Uncle Iroh, offering sage advice along the way."

"I'm sorry, did you just make an *Avatar: The Last Airbender* reference to me?"

"Of course I did! It's only the greatest animated television series about love, friendship, identity, and goodness triumphing over the ever-present force of evil in the history of television." He rubbed his chin like he was deep in thought. "You're very Book One Prince Zuko—all honor and determination and stuff. You could use some guidance from an old pro to ease you into Book Three Prince Zuko: more relaxed, more open to adventure, better hair."

My shoulders stiffened at the mention of "better hair," and Jordan immediately backpedaled.

"I'm just saying, we gotta make the best of an otherwise not-great situation. So we might as well come out the other side with more than just a plastic crown."

I didn't bother mentioning that if we won, we would come out

73

with a scholarship. And at that point, who cares about the plastic crown?

"If you think it sucks, why do you do it?" I asked, grabbing some empty glue sticks and dropping them into the garbage. I knew I was moving quickly, but I didn't really have time to waste cleaning out closets all afternoon. I still had at least an hour of homework left when I got home, and if my grades slid and Pennington revoked my acceptance altogether, all this would have been for nothing.

"Because it's who I am," he said simply, a little resigned. "Comes with the Jennings territory. My mom's been on the planning committee for eight years now, so I'm pretty sure she would actually murder me if I didn't run."

He stopped for a second before turning to me with a smirk.

"Besides, Lighty, didn't you know? Prom is the"—Jordan twirled his imaginary handlebar mustache like we were in old-timey London or something—"*social event of the season.*"

I laughed, some of the tension I'd been holding in my shoulders all day slipping away.

It was nice how friendly Jordan was being, but I tried not to let myself get caught up in it. Just because you're free to be one person in private doesn't mean anything when it comes to the person you are in public. I know that better than anybody.

"Seriously, Jordan, you mean to tell me that your mom has been on the alumni planning committee for the past *eight years*? That's, like, a med-school level of commitment." I shook my head as he tested out some markers on a piece of old construction paper to see if they were dried out or not.

74

"Yeah." He frowned a bit and scratched the back of his neck. "She and my dad are . . . dedicated."

"How are they doing?" I asked. I knew what he meant, even if he didn't say it. They were worse than dedicated; they were downright obsessive, like a lot of parents in Campbell.

"They're them. You know." He shrugged and then cleared his throat. "I can't wait for them to take off for the weekend in a few weeks though! It's going to be just like *House Party*. Me and you can reprise our roles as Kid 'n Play."

And then, without giving me a chance to prepare, he stepped back and brought his foot up, just like Kid 'n Play from the movie. He just sort of let his knee suspend there for a minute while he looked at me expectantly.

It was stupid. It was so stupid to do it, but I've known that routine like the back of my hand since I was eight. The House Party movies are hilarious, each of them about these two friends who keep getting themselves into trouble. They're super goofy—all colorful '90s outfits and old-school slang—but watching the first one, at the very least, is like a mandate of black culture. Robbie and I had been obsessed as kids, and I guess old habits die hard.

So when I lifted my foot to his, and then stepped back to do it again, it was like muscle memory. I narrowed my eyes like he was really inconveniencing me, but I followed his lead without complaint. And then it was like we weren't in some classroom tucked in the back of the art wing at Campbell County High School. We were back on that stage in our middle school talent show, listening to '90s hip-hop, moving like this was just something we did in our free time. Jordan was so good at it, and although I've never considered myself a dancer, I knew it well enough to hit those moves like a pro.

I was full-on, hands-on-my-knees cracking up by the time we finished.

And that's when I heard the applause. The Prom Projectioners had their phones trained in our direction from the entrance to the classroom, and I instantly wanted to crawl out of my skin.

Jordan stood up straight immediately to smooth his black T-shirt out, and he turned back to the closet like he hadn't been goofing around with me only a few seconds before. It was like as soon as we had an audience, I didn't exist. Just like he'd done that day freshman year.

I looked back at the Prom Projectioners, and they may have been smiling, but they were also whispering to themselves. I didn't have to hear them to know what they were saying: *Why is he hanging out with her?*

But now, in the kitchen, I want to tell Robbie the whole story, to unload all the details of hanging out with Jordan onto him in a way I can't with Gabi, Britt, or Stone. But Granny chooses this moment to stride into the kitchen to say good night, fully dressed in her bland blue scrubs.

"Robert, I know I didn't just hear something about no Campbell Confidential! You better get off them apps and social medias, or so help me you're going to be sending smoke signals to your friends instead of texts." She reaches into the fridge to grab her floral lunch box. "Y'all know I don't like that nonsense."

"How do you know I'm even talking about Campbell Confidential? I could be talking about good old-fashioned, ear-to-the-ground gossiping. You know, like the industrious and inquisitive young man I am."

"Industrious and inquisitive my foot, Robert. I pay your phone bill, remember?" Granny is where we get our height, so despite the fact that she's getting shorter with age, she can still kiss us both on the forehead easily on her way out the door. "I know how much data you're using."

When Granny says good night, she reminds Ro to take his medicine and reminds me to make sure to watch him do it. It's not that we don't trust him, but him forgetting or thinking he's healthy enough to skip a dose is a chance we're not willing to take. He's a smart kid, but sometimes he starts feeling good, and he gets so cocky and convinced he's invincible that he doesn't take his meds. He's done it before, and I'm terrified he'll do it again.

"How does she even know what data is?" Robbie whisper-hisses in my direction as the front door clicks shut behind her. I'm laughing as I drain the sudsy water from the sink. "The elders are evolving, and it's going to ruin us all."

ten

The week is so busy, I don't have time to meet up with Mack after school to help her learn the new music until Friday afternoon. Since she's also running for queen, her schedule is just as hectic. And even though I'm doing this as a favor to Mr. K, I'm kind of looking forward to it. There's rarely a time when I wouldn't choose to be in the band room over any other place, especially with everything else going on right now.

I'm only a little annoyed when she shows up fifteen minutes late.

"Hi! Sorry I'm—" She bursts through the door and immediately the book she's holding slips out of her hand and onto the floor. And when she bends over to pick it up, the drumsticks tucked loosely into her tiny half ponytail slip out onto the floor. She picks up her drumsticks and smiles at me apologetically.

"This is so not the impression I wanted to make on you today, but I somehow still manage to get lost finding this place even though I've been here multiple times this week. But my old school—I went to this super small art high school in Chicago—was not designed like this." She walks over to the kit and plops down onto the seat. She drops her bag to the floor with a thud. "I miss it—my school—but I'm glad to be here. This feels like the quintessential American high school, honestly."

"I—"

I don't think she hears me, because she just keeps going. I'm convinced she's on track to set the record for most words spoken without taking a break in the history of the universe.

"It's funny, because I've always kind of wanted to go to a school like this, but I just wish it hadn't happened this way. We moved because of my great-aunt Ida. She's pretty sick, and never had any kids of her own, so my dad moved us down here to help take care of her."

She looks up at me from her place behind the drums. It's almost like she's seeing me for the first time. She tightens the screw on the crash cymbal without breaking eye contact with me, and once again I'm sort of shocked by the way her eyes look. I know it's superficial, but I don't mind listening to her talk a mile per minute if it means I just get to keep looking at them.

Purely for, um, opposition research purposes, obviously.

"You know, you dress a little bit like her." She adjusts the seat on the kit. It comes out so quick—like everything she says—that I don't even think she realizes she just compared me to a woman who I'm currently imagining has a mouth full of porcelain teeth and smells a little bit like mothballs and the nearness of her own mortality.

I look down at the sweater Gabi had sent over to my house and cringe. "I love her. She's a real ballbuster. Kind of like Madame Simoné, you know? Very takes-no-nonsense-from-anybody."

She looks up at me and smiles. Her smile slips when she sees my face. I can only imagine I look shocked. Not only did she compare me to her denture-mouthed aunt Ida, but she also compared me to faux-French, takes-prom-way-too-seriously Madame Simoné. She's cute, but I wonder if maybe the part of the brain that keeps most people from blurting out their innermost thoughts just never developed for her.

"Oh my God, I did the thing, didn't I?" She bites at her thumb-nail and groans. "My dad is always saying that I put my cart before my horse, and most of the time I ignore it because dads, you know? But I'm beginning to see what he means, because I did just com-pare you to a seventy-year-old white woman from Ireland with a lopsided wig and cilantro perpetually in her teeth, so I—"

I laugh. I can't help it. This girl just keeps talking herself fur-ther into a hole. "I have to say I wasn't expecting the cilantro. But I totally called the lopsided wig." I pat the side of my hair like I would if I was wearing weave. I realize that it's the first thing I've been able to say since she walked into the room. "I can't believe you noticed."

She smiles back, obviously relieved. Something tells me this girl has chased away her fair share of new people thanks to her lack of a filter.

"What I mean is, your sweater. My aunt Ida has a really wide selection of cardigans." She shakes her head. "That probably doesn't make it any better, huh?"

"Not really."

"I ramble when I'm nervous. It's ugly. One time I told my English teacher that she reminded me of my childhood dentist because every time she came near me, I could smell that eerie doctor-y smell, and I was overwhelmed with the urge to cry, because it gave me flashbacks to getting my braces tightened when I was in middle school."

This girl is weird. Like, really weird. But I laugh anyway, because it's a weird that I understand.

"Maybe we should work on the piece before I put my foot in my mouth again?"

I nod. "That sounds like a good plan."

I stand by as I walk her through what the music sounds like with the entire ensemble. The places where she has a little more creative liberty to play around with a measure or two, though the sheet music may not have it marked. She's good. Like, *really* good. She's catching on to the arrangement way quicker than I expected, and it looks almost effortless. The way she plays, the ease of her hands and the subtle way she keeps time by moving her lips along with the beat, has me lost in a new, fresh version of the song.

I arranged it, technically, but with her playing, it sounds like something I haven't heard before. I feel a little guilty about it, but I send up a moment of gratitude to the gods above about Kevin's broken appendages.

I don't even realize that we've been here for over an hour until my phone starts ringing. It's Granny calling, no doubt reminding me that she needs me to get home early tonight to make dinner because she's leaving for her shift at the nursing home a little earlier than usual.

She doesn't usually miss family mealtime, but we're not really in a place for her to turn down extra hours.

"Oh, wow." I look down at the time on my phone and slide it back into my pocket quickly. "I'm sorry to take off, but I have to get home."

She sets her sticks down on the snare and stretches her arms above her head like she's just finished a workout.

"That was sick!" She grins and links her fingers together behind her head. "You're like a mad scientist or something. I've never gotten the hang of a piece that fast."

I close my sheet music folder and slide it into my backpack. I'm smiling down at the carpet.

"A mad scientist with a mean old-lady-sweater collection."

I'm gonna have to have a talk with Gabi about the clothes she sent over.

"Please don't hold that against me! I'd hate to have lost my first friend before we've even made it into each others' 'close friends' list on Instagram."

"Instagram, huh?" She's grabbing her stuff too, but she's not nearly as careful as I am about putting things into her bag. I can see old loose-leaf paper and a half-opened French workbook poking out of the top. It's not even my bag, and I'm stressed about its current state of disarray. "You mean the welcome committee didn't take your phone the minute you walked through the door and automatically download Campbell Confidential? CC is the gold star of social media around here."

She laughs, and it's not what I expect. The rest of her is so bold, but her laugh is a small thing, a little twinkle of a sound she tries to contain behind her hand.

"There actually was a girl! She works in the front office. She has very blond hair, these teeth that look like they should be in a Colgate commercial . . ."

"Quinn Bukowski." I've had the same thought about her teeth before while picking up a schedule in the front office, honestly. "She's one of the student helpers. Most of her friends are big advocates for the app—probably because it was sort of designed with them in mind."

The pretty, the popular, the people whose lives you want to press your face up against the glass of and watch from the outside.

"Yeah! That's her! She was in the prom meeting the other day, right?" She stands up and pulls her bag across her body. "I think I might have promised to vote for her when she was telling me where to find my classes because I was so mesmerized by her teeth?"

"If everyone were that easy to persuade"—she follows me to the door, and I flip the lights off behind us—"then that would suck all the pain and suffering—err, uh, fun—out of the process." I roll my eyes so she knows that I'm joking, and she snorts with her laugh this time. It's a cuter sound than should be legal, really.

"You're really funny."

I'm not blushing. I can't be blushing, because Liz Lighty doesn't blush. But my face does get a little warm.

"That's debatable. I don't think anyone is confusing me for senior class clown or anything."

84

She slips the drumsticks in her hand back into her hair and smiles. I shove my hands in my pockets because I'm suddenly feeling jittery and I'm not sure what else to do with them.

"Well, I, for one," she says as she takes a couple of steps backward toward the doors to the parking lot, "think there might be much more to you than meets the eye."

eleven

The Bake-Off is a time-honored tradition where candidates for prom court gather in the culinary-arts classroom at school on Sunday afternoon and bake different desserts to sell at a charity bake sale the next day. The competition part of it, though, is that the amount of money you make on your dessert is factored into your point total. And the public aspect is that the culinary-arts room looks like something from the set of *MasterChef*, with a long window where a wall should be.

"How is my gloss? Too glossy?" Lucy turns to Quinn and puckers her lips. Her crisp, white apron is already tied around her waist, and despite the super-glossy lips giving her definite covergirl vibes, she looks ready to host her own show on Food Network. "I just bought this online—it has real diamonds in it."

"OhmyGod, Luce! Is that the new M·A·C?" Quinn claps her hands together. "It's going to look so good on camera."

As the two of them gush over each other, I can't help but wish I were at least placed next to my new sort-of friend Mack, who's a row ahead of me, bobbing her head along to a beat no one else can hear. But instead I'm smack in the middle of the world's glossiest PomBot sandwich.

And as if on cue, the fifteen or so freshmen who have gathered all pull out their phones to record. They're pressed against the glass, smudging it with their fingers, which are no doubt sweaty with excitement. There is a live feed of today's Bake-Off scheduled for Campbell Confidential, and the thought makes me a little sweaty too. Although for way different reasons.

Everyone is situated at their ovens working on their dishes by the time Quinn dips a finger into her own batter and licks it off.

"Oh em gee, yummy!" The E. coli is going to be so strong at this bake sale, I can already feel it. "So good! Can I try yours?"

I can't believe that Quinn is speaking to me, but then again, this has been a week of unbelievable occurrences. She grins at me and cocks her head to the side, her blond ponytail swaying behind her.

"I don't think that's a great idea," I reply slowly, wondering when the other shoe is going to drop. "It's probably best not to try too much of the merchandise."

We haven't said more than two words to each other since the group project we did together in freshman Honors English. We were supposed to be unpacking the thematic elements of *Antigone*, and Quinn literally pronounced it "Ann-tee-gone" for the duration of the project, despite the fact that our teacher gently corrected her every class. That and her friendship with Rachel are the only things I needed to know about her to know to steer clear.

"You're so right. We *should* save it all for charity." She nods and wipes her hands on her apron. "I should have thought about that. Ugh, Liz, your *mind*."

Quinn goes back to humming whatever pop song she was humming before she accosted me with a spitty finger and hopes of desecrating my dessert, and Madame Simoné puts on some obscure jazz.

Jordan is situated by the row of ovens behind mine, his countertop neatly arranged with the ingredients to make authentic German poppy seed cake.

Jordan looks confident as he measures out some vanilla extract and pours it into the bowl. I wonder if he practiced at home before coming in here today, so that he'd look as at ease while baking as he does while doing everything else.

When I turn back to face my own dish, I barely get the chance to pour the batter into the baking pan before Rachel appears beside me. I can tell it's her without even looking up, because I can see the bright hot-pink apron she brought with her from home in my periphery. Most of us opted to borrow the plain white ones that were already hanging in the culinary-arts room, but she had to take it just a step further. Like she always does. It's definitely going to stand out on camera though, and that's the most annoying part. She's the worst, but the girl knows strategy.

"Good thing we're in here where everyone can see, huh? That way no one could buy some irresistibly tasty and very expensive gourmet dish." Rachel runs her hand along the side of the countertop where I'm standing. She's placed herself directly between me and Quinn. "I'm glad they do it this way, actually. It really levels the playing field, right, Liz?"

I look at her briefly and squint like I'm trying to figure her out. I may not like her, I may not trust her, but I'm not afraid of her. I've gotten very good at biting my tongue over the years, but something about Rachel Collins makes me want to be a little more reckless. I lower my voice and meet her eyes.

"Don't you ever get tired of being the biggest cliché in Campbell?"

Her face twists up in surprise. "You might've been able to sneak your way into valedictorian, but this? Prom is *my* territory. You know how this is going to play out. I'm going to win queen, Lucy, Claire, and Quinn are going to be my court, and that's it." She leans in and lowers her voice. Her smile is cloyingly sweet, something fake and bitter and mean, as she adds, "And in a year, no one will remember you, no one will walk past your face on the wall, and nobody will miss you."

She flips her hair, and her face resets to something more prom-queenly.

"Babe, come over here real quick!" Derek calls for her, and she straightens her apron before turning on her heel to walk to him.

I'm reeling after she leaves, but I do my best to settle my face into something like indifference. Because I know how to do that. I know how to make it look like I don't care.

I manage to slide my baking dish into my oven, despite the fact that my hands are shaking a little bit.

"Don't worry, Rachel's bark is worse than her bite." I look to my left, and Quinn smiles at me. It's bright and expensive-white, like her dentist father has personally cleaned her teeth every day of her life. She looks aloof, like none of this could possibly bother her. And maybe she is as oblivious as she seems to be. As oblivious as I imagine you'd have to be to be friends with Rachel Collins. "And you shouldn't frown like that. It'll give you lines."

She's wrong: Rachel's bark and her bite suck in equal measure, but I nod once like I agree.

"Your skin is so supple. I'm jealous—you won't even need Botox when you turn thirty, or anything." She's still trying to talk to me, but I'm distracted by a commotion behind her. Rachel is standing there, whispering fiercely to Derek and rubbing placating patterns into his back.

Lucas White, the cocaptain of the tennis team, is off to my right, and Derek is two ovens to my left. They keep mumbling insults to each other under their breath. "You wouldn't last a day on the court" is being met with "You couldn't make it five minutes without passing out on *our* court" over my head, and I can imagine a million better things I could be doing right now that don't involve being stuck on *SportsCenter Jr.*

But from the second row of ovens, I have a direct line of vision to Mack, who is currently mixing up some cheesecake batter right in front of me. And that's my saving grace. Every once in a while, when Derek and Lucas say something particularly ridiculous, she'll turn around to shoot me a knowing smile, like we're sharing a joke no one else in the room is in on.

It's weird. We've only ever really hung out in the confines of the band room, but I like having her around. She's late to every single class, which is annoying, but she always shows up with a smile and an apology. She's also an incredible drummer. She learned my arrangement in less than a week and—no shade to Kevin—is the best percussionist our band has ever seen. It's something magical.

Robbie and G always say that I have a serious problem with falling hard for talent almost as hard as I fall for people (see: my intense, lifelong crush on Kittredge's colead singer, Teela Conrad), but that's not what this is. Definitely not. Not at all.

"Hey, can you taste-test this for me?" Mack comes over, plastic spoon full of cheesecake batter in hand. She wiggles her eyebrows. Little does she know this offer is already light-years ahead of the last time someone tried to trade samples of our work (and, like, our DNA). I don't need convincing. "Please? I solemnly swear that I'm up to only good things and am not asking you because I think I may have dropped a piece of an eggshell in here and need someone to help me spot it before I offer this dish up to the masses."

"Wow, you sure know how to make a girl feel confident in your baking abilities." I lean in to take a bite and try not to think about the fact that I might seriously be blushing because I am practically being fed by this girl right now. Like full-on, one hand under my chin and the other spooning what is actually a ridiculously tasty bite of cheesecake batter into my mouth.

It's shockingly easy to let myself give in to the moment.

"You like it?"

"I more than like it. I'm fully expecting a VIP cheesecake just for me by the time this is over."

She beams. "That can be arranged."

Madame Simoné claps her hands twice at the front of the room to get our attention, and I'm more than a little bummed when Mack turns back around to face her. She announces before she steps out of the room that one of the reporters from the *Campbell Caller* needs to ask her a few questions for their annual prom cover story.

The door has barely shut behind her when I hear, "No way, babe. I'm tired of him."

My reflexes are pretty bad—I mean I've never played a sport or a video game in my life—but I duck out of the way just as a glob of cookie dough goes flying by my head. Lucas isn't quick enough though. It hits him square in his temple and just, like, sticks there.

Seriously, it doesn't even slide down his face. And if I wasn't so alarmed by what was happening in front of me, I might have been impressed by the density and viscosity of the dough.

"That's for last night!" Derek shouts over my head. "That's the last time you and your guys try and take over the weight room while we're conditioning."

The basketball team and the tennis team have some sort of beef, according to Britt. I don't get it, but something tells me this has everything to do with that.

"You sentient belly button crust!" Lucas reaches up and wipes the dough off his face slowly, sort of like he can't believe what's happened. "You're dead."

I have the good sense to take a step back and out of the way when he reaches for his own bowl, a mixture of what I think is supposed to eventually become chocolate cake.

"Oh yeah?" Derek laughs. "Who's gonna try me? That crew of

93

off-brand Lacoste models you call a team? You know where to find me."

All the eyes in the room are turned on the two of them now. Everyone has mostly been working on their own dishes and talking occasionally up until this point, but alliances are already beginning to form. The other Jacket Jocks—the ones who wear their letter jacket every day, mostly football and basketball guys (minus Jordan, who is looking between the two guys like he's trying to decide when to step in)—start chiming in from their ovens.

"Off-brand Lacoste models?" Chad Davis, one of the golf team guys—which makes him a non–Jacket Jock, stick with me here—snorts from the back row. "You Neanderthals couldn't even spell *Lacoste*."

Jaxon Price, two ovens down from him, snaps back, "Okay, well, how much you wanna bet I can spell *fight me* without a problem?"

I feel like I'm in an alternate reality, I swear. This whole thing is so outlandish, so laughable, I can't believe I'm in the middle of it. I can't believe people actually fight about stuff like this. I can't believe that we're actually going all Sharks versus Jets in the culinary-arts room.

"Yo," Jordan starts, rounding the counter and coming to stand between them. "I know you're not about to start a food fight in here, right? Even you two must be self-aware enough to know how corny that looks."

But nobody can hear him at this point, because in the back of the room, Ryan Fuqua and Chad Davis have already taken it there. Chad beams Ryan in the chest with a mixture of maraschino cherries, and Ryan starts going ballistic.

"Screw you, Chad! Now I have to have my housekeeper take this to the cleaners!"

And from there it's anarchy.

I hit the deck as the desserts start flying. The room erupts in shrieks of shock and laughter, and the debris is splattering my back as I start crawling to the front row, where Mack is hiding beneath a cookie tray. I'm watching her get pelted with chocolate chips from the onslaught above when I accidentally put one of my hands in a puddle of vanilla frosting, slip, and faceplant into the tile.

"Woman down!" Mack shouts, sympathetic but altogether amused. No one can hear her but me. "You okay?"

She reaches out to me, and I take her hand with the one of mine that's not covered in frosting. Her grip is tight and warm, and I don't let go of it immediately when I maneuver my way underneath her pan-shield. We're tucked so closely together—definitely closer than we've ever been—that I can smell her rich jasmine-scented shampoo through the overly aggressive sweetness of the culinary-arts room at present. Our shoulders bump, and I feel all weird and warm at the sensation.

"Is this all it takes to get them so fired up?" I manage to get out over the noise. I have to say something, anything, to distract myself from the sensation of her body against mine and her shampoo smell swirling around my head.

So, okay, yeah, maybe I am attracted to a little more than her talent.

I hear something shatter near the back of the room and a voice that sounds like Rachel's yelling, "Derek, please! You're going to ruin this for us!"

Mack doesn't answer me, just laughs as her eyes search my face.

But her hand—which she must realize is still holding my own—releases mine. And then, almost like she needs a new way to busy it, she reaches up and smears some now-spilled cheesecake batter across my cheek with her index finger. She must not have intended to, but she manages to get it dangerously close to my lips. So close, in fact, that before she pulls away, I probably could have kissed the tip of her finger.

Without thinking or breaking eye contact, I dart my tongue out and quickly lick away the batter. And suddenly neither of us is laughing. At once, I'm both terrified and thrilled about what that might mean.

But then, like a record scratch, a shrill voice devoid of any faux-French accent cuts through the air. And all bets are off.

"Holy mother of God," Madame Simoné shrieks. "What in Heaven's name have y'all done?!"

Mack

WEEK TWO

When the going gets tough,
the tough go viral.

Mack

Type here . . .

twelve

When I walk into school on Monday morning, I stop short as soon as I reach the Commons.

I can barely tolerate Rachel in human size, but the face in front of me is enough to make a nun curse God and walk backward into hell. A banner the size of a small Mediterranean nation is displayed from one wall to the other across the Commons. COLLINS FOR COURT is emblazoned across it in this gaudy hot-pink glitter font.

She didn't even opt for a clever caption, and that is, perhaps, the most devastating part about it. I mean, honestly, where's the effort?

But I get it. Rachel has to reassert herself as queen worthy since she can't sell anything at the bake sale today, thanks to her boyfriend's food fight debacle. Gabi was right. The devil works hard, but Rachel Collins really does work harder.

"This is incredible, but also a little terrifying." I turn around, and Mack is smirking over my shoulder. "You'd think that with a poster this big, she would have put a little more thought into her slogan."

She must be clairvoyant or something. I should have known that those eyes were a sign of being in touch with—what does Stone call it? The astral plane?

"Rachel Collins is much more flash than substance. It's sort of her superpower."

Mack snorts and bumps her shoulder into mine.

"I can't wait to try out the pound cake you made, by the way. My cheesecake was dead before I even had a chance to duck and cover yesterday." She crosses herself like she's in prayer. "We have to mourn a fallen soldier."

When the warning bell rings to remind us that we have three minutes to get to class, I hesitate to leave but know I have to get going. I've never received a tardy slip in my life, and I don't particularly want to start now. But I also sort of really want to keep talking to Mack.

"I'll see you at the bake sale later?" I say as I step out of the way of a kid running to class. "I'll, um, save you a slice of cake."

I couldn't sound less smooth, but Mack just smiles and salutes me.

"Wouldn't miss it, comrade."

And okay, I spend more time than I should in my next few classes thinking about her saying goodbye to me instead of conjugating verbs in French or finding symbolism in *Great Expectations*.

We have two lunch periods at Campbell, and since the bake sale is held during both of them, I'm given a pass out of my AP Stats class to staff the table. Madame Simoné makes sure that everyone is settled—latex gloves on and dishes retrieved from the culinary-arts room where they've been since last night—before bidding us farewell to get back to her classes. Before she goes, she offers a gentle warning.

"Like I said yesterday, there better not be any *drôles d'affaires* today. We've already lost a number of candidates to irresponsible behavior this weekend. I would hate for us to see other members of our *petite famille* removed before this is all over. *Comprenez-vous?*"

We all nod in unison. Derek and a couple of the guys from the food fight got kicked out of the race for causing such a mess, which no one expected. But when the whole thing was broadcast for all of Campbell to see, it was kind of hard to deny that they were the culprits.

Luckily, I've made that pound cake so many times, I have it down to a science, and unlike most people, I was able to get my dish in the oven before the desserts went flying. Me, Harry Donato, Lucy, and Aaron Korman—one of the tennis guys that managed to make it out of the Bake-Off debacle unscathed—all arrange our dishes on a long table in the Commons. Two freshmen have volunteered to supervise the cashbox so that none of us have to handle food and then handle money. We're mostly only here as smiling faces to hawk our goods.

I look at the other offerings and have to admit that my pound cake looks a hundred times better than anything the other three have cooked up.

Inside, I'm beaming. I can't seem to move the needle on the rankings by showing up to volunteer events or whatever, but my granny's signature pound cake recipe never fails. It's perfectly buttery and still fresh, even after a night in the culinary-arts room. That, paired with the fact that my competition in this arena seems pretty slim, might be the thing that moves me up in the rankings. Even if that just means getting me the hell away from Tracksuit Cameron and safely in the territory of candidates who haven't fabricated elaborate backstories that involve famous tennis players.

I have two cakes on the table, just like Granny taught me: "One for the goose and one for the gander." I'm not entirely sure what that means, but I know that come Thanksgiving, we always have twice as much dessert as we need, and I don't believe in putting a question mark where God put a period.

Gabi is the first to buy a piece, followed immediately by Britt and then Stone. Stone can't actually eat hers, because it's not vegan and she's "ethically opposed to any food product that required animal labor for our own selfish consumption," but Britt vows to donate it to one of the ravenous sophomores in her studio art class later.

"I'm stoked you managed to finish this before the melee started." Britt talks around the pound cake in her mouth. "This is the best. Remember when your granny sent you with some the first time you ever slept over at my house? My mom lost her mind when she tasted it. White people really don't know what to do with flavor."

She shakes her head sadly, and I laugh. She's right: Aside from Gabi's mom, I don't really eat anything that my friends' parents make, for the sake of my palate. Granny sent me with that pound cake in part because she has a thing about showing up places empty-handed but also because she wanted to make sure if worse came to worst, I'd have something to tide me over until she came to pick me up the next day.

You can never be too careful when it comes to eating white folks' food.

The three of them take their desserts back into the cafeteria when the lines for the table start getting a little long. There aren't many options to choose from, but I'm surprised at just how much my pound cake is killing everyone else's desserts.

The line is moving along, and before I know it, Mack is in front of me. She grabs her VIP slice and clutches it to her chest with a wide smile like it's the Medal of Honor or something equally valuable. As she walks away, she doesn't even seem to notice when Lucy glances over and huffs at the dramatic display.

"OhmygoshLiz!" Melly, one of the freshman flutes, nearly shoulder-checks Mack on accident as she rushes over and leans across the table to whisper to me. She's sweet, very enthusiastic, but has to work on not running all the words in her sentences together. "This*isamazing.*"

"Thanks, Melly, but you haven't even tried it yet." I shake my head.

"Notthecake!" She smiles and lowers her voice. Her light brown hair is shaved close to her scalp, and from up close it looks cute and fuzzy, like a tennis ball. "Yourunningforpromcourt. Peoplelikeus*never*makeitpastthefirstweek."

People like us. And that feels sort of good in a way that surprises me. She's right. High school is complicated, and the lines of demarcation that *The Breakfast Club* said divided us aren't quite so clean-cut. The athletes are also the smart kids; the theater kids are also the presidents of the student council. But there's still those out-liers. The people who are everywhere but fit nowhere. People who are involved but not envied—present but imperfect—so the scru-tiny pushes them out of the race. People like me, like G and Britt and Stone. And apparently people like Melly.

When lunch is almost over, I don't even need the freshmen to count the money out for me as I look over at my classmates' trays still covered in leftovers. I'm vibrating with an eagerness I haven't felt in forever. There's one clear winner, and for the first time in a long time, that winner is me.

thirteen

You'd think that moving up five spots in the rankings would be cause for celebration, but we're sitting in the Marinos' basement and no one is celebrating. It would be kind of hard to, given Gabi's relentless pacing and furious clicking through of her revised presentation.

"I was confident that you would move up more after the bake sale. I was absolutely sure of it," she says, underlining her previous projection of making an eight-spot jump instead of just five with her trusty laser pointer. "This simply isn't acceptable. I blame that absolute abomination of a poster hanging in the Commons."

I tug at the collar of the off-white wrap shirt I'm wearing. It's an upgrade from the cardigans, for sure, but I wish I were back in my favorite vintage Fleetwood Mac tour T-shirt instead. I don't feel like myself right now, but I'm willing to make sacrifices for

Pennington. If I'm serious about winning prom queen, I have to look the part. So I will, even if the part means I look more like a member of the cast of *The Real Housewives of Beverly Hills* than I do a normal, Midwestern seventeen-year-old girl.

"In all fairness, G, it only took her two-and-a-half seconds to come up with that slogan." I shrug. "We should be grateful for the gift that is her sheer lack of creativity and complete inability to put a remarkable twist on the English language."

Britt points the pen she's been using to draw on her bare knee in my direction. "Ten points for Gryffindor!"

I laugh and lean forward on my elbows. "But seriously, Britt's parents have the new posters finished, and we'll put them up tomorrow. That should get us a little more traction."

"We need more than just *a little* traction, my darling and dearest best friend. We need a massive jump, and we need it now." She taps her chin and gets the look she always gets before a big exam. Like she knows the answer but is almost hesitant to write it down just in case she's wrong. "We need to play Rachel's game bigger and better than her. We need posters twice her size. Buttons circulating through the entire student body, including the PomBots and their male counterparts.

"We need a full overhaul of your public appearance, Lizzie." She pauses for a second. "I'm talking full face of makeup before school, new hair—"

"Hear me out on this." Britt throws her hands in the air. "Maybe, just maybe, Rachel's posters and makeup aren't the things that have her in the lead. Has anyone considered that? Maybe it's something more insidious than that? Like the fact that this is a system designed to benefit people like Rachel Collins?"

Stone is at her acupuncturist, so it's just the three of us tonight. I'm hoping that for once no one will need to defuse a fight between Britt and Gabi, but it seems unlikely based on the way Britt's knee bounces up and down.

"Why won't everyone just leave the strategy to me? There is no one who wants to see Liz get to Pennington more than I do, okay?" Gabi crosses her arms. "While we're talking about strategy, I don't like how chummy that Mack has been with you lately. It's not good for your image."

"What do you mean?" I sit up straighter. "What's wrong with her?"

"Yeah, she seems cool," Britt says, reaching for the Doritos and chomping down. "You remember Billie, that junior from JV? She's in class with her, and apparently her dad does marketing for the company that makes our uniforms, or something? He's scoring us some free merch." She talks through the chip in her mouth. "So she's good in my book."

For whatever reason, I'm glad that Britt likes Mack too. Britt is usually a pretty good judge of character, and if she's endorsing her, then maybe my gut has been correct.

Gabi pinches the bridge of her nose in frustration. I feel like that expression is her permanent condition these days—a cross between exasperation and constipation. Or both.

"But the rumors about her? Have you two not been reading my evening briefing emails?"

My smile fades immediately, and I feel like maybe I've been

caught doing something I had no business doing, despite the fact that I haven't actually done anything at all. I wouldn't call us friends exactly, but every time I see Mack now there's something familiar about it. Every time we so much as pass each other in the hallway, her smile is bright and open, like we really know each other. And part of me feels like I do.

"Be realistic. Nobody has time to read those things, Marino."

"What rumors?" My mouth is dry, and my stomach starts to hurt. It's a sudden thing, the way it feels like all the air is sucked out of the room. "What could people possibly be saying about her? She just got here."

"Oh, you know, just that she's kind of, um . . . How should I put this? Giving definite Teela Conrad vibes." Gabrielle Marino, who spares no punches, is beating around the bush. And I know why.

Teela Conrad is one of the lead vocalists in Kittredge, and she has been pretty ambiguous about her sexuality over the course of her career. Tabloids are always snapping pictures of her leaving clubs with women or on the red carpet with men, and asking super intrusive questions about her life during press conferences.

She's even been rumored to be dating Davey Mack, the band's hot bassist slash colead singer and the closest thing to a real-life Finnick Odair anyone could ever ask for. But she refuses to come out and say what people already assume to be true about her, because, like she croons on their ballad "My Life, My Story," what she chooses to do should belong to her and the people she shares it with. She doesn't owe anyone anything.

Their entire last album was about those rumors, and in my

opinion, it was easily their best one yet. Because, okay, Teela Conrad is kind of my hero.

"I mean honestly, has she not thought about how this will affect her in the race? She has a *pride flag* hanging up in her locker and everything." She waves her hands around her face. "People love drama, a little novelty, but they won't vote for her if they think . . ."

She trails off, suddenly at a loss for words.

"If they think she's queer," I finish for her. I cross my arms over my chest and look out the window. "It doesn't go over well in small-town Indiana. Yeah, I get it."

"Jesus, Marino," Britt snaps. "This isn't the forties."

"Look, that's not what I meant!" Gabi tries to backpedal. "Like, Liz, it's different for you! Nobody would ever guess that you're into girls. I mean, you hide it so well."

But that's just it, I've never tried to hide it. Not exactly. I just . . . never made it a thing. Being into girls has never been a huge point of contention for me or my friends. Hell, when I came out to my grandparents, the only thing Grandad asked me was, "So are we giving up them waffle fries at Chick-fil-A now? Because, I'll tell you what, them things are the closest I've ever felt to Heaven."

No one baked me a cake, no one threw me a party. It just was. And a huge part of that is because I already know what it would be like for me to be out and proud in a place like Campbell County, Indiana.

Silence and shame aren't the same thing—not by a longshot. But sometimes silence is simpler.

"Well, good thing I canceled the order on my GIRLS JUST WANNA DO GIRLS T-shirt, then, huh?" I laugh, but it's empty.

I'm looking down at my shoes, a pair of Chelsea booties that used to belong to Gabi's mom, and holding my wrist like I used to. I can feel my heartbeat in my throat, and my eyes are burning at the rim like tears might be inevitable. Sometimes I'm convinced that it's never going to be enough—the good grades, the low-key clothes and hairstyles and attitude. I'm never going to be the type of person who makes sense to other people. I'm never going to be able to own every part of myself.

"Lizzo, I think what Gabi means is—"

I shake my head quickly and wipe at my nose. I gotta go. I gotta get out of here.

"It's fine. It's cool. I get it." I stand up and walk toward the door. "I'll meet you guys before first period to hang up the new posters tomorrow morning, okay?"

I say a hasty goodbye to G's mom, who's in the kitchen stress-baking some new vegan apple pie recipe, and rush out the front door. I hop onto my bike, which is leaning against the Marinos' garage. I've passed the homes in this neighborhood a thousand times before, pedaled down Gabi's street and thought of all the lives I could be living inside those big, beautiful houses if I wasn't me.

I've never felt quite like this though. Like I don't know if I'm running away from something or to it. All I know is that I'm tired, so incredibly tired, of having to run at all.

fourteen

Gabi has called me no less than ten times since last night, but I haven't been able to bring myself to answer. It's not her fault, I guess. Not really, anyway. She was right about Mack, and she was right about Campbell. There's just no room for any crushes like that for me, at least not now, when so much is riding on this prom thing working out.

But still, it stings that she would say it so frankly. Like my sexuality is a light switch I can flip on and off when it's convenient. I feel guilty for ignoring G's calls, but I know what would've happened if I'd answered. I would've accepted her apologies, and I would've pretended like I wasn't still burning up on the inside about what she said.

I show up to school early anyway though, so that we can hang the posters from Britt's parents. And it's a good thing I do, because we're not the only ones with that idea.

"What the hell happened here?" I ask as I meet Stone and Britt in the Commons. Britt has two venti cups of something hot from Starbucks in her hands and passes one to me when I walk up. I take it graciously. I'm never in a position to turn down good caffeine before eight a.m. "It looks like *The West Wing* and *Carrie* had a baby and named it *Pretty in Pink*."

I look around at the Commons and marvel at the sheer magnitude of campaign posters. It's like Rachel Collins's giant face on a banner yesterday was enough to kick everyone into overdrive overnight.

On one, Lucy and Quinn pose back-to-back in their pom uniforms on the football field. On others, Jaxon Price poses with the 3A state champion football trophy from last year, with the caption MAKE THE WINNING COCAPTAIN YOUR WINNING KING emblazoned across it—which is pretty bad but somehow still better than what Rachel has going on in her obnoxiously boring banner. And in the center of all of them, somehow managing to cut through all the noise, is Jordan's face. His posters are elegant; they look like masterful recreations of President Obama's official portrait in the National Portrait Gallery. Someone has done a very impressive Kehinde Wiley impression, with Jordan at the center where President Obama should be. There are no words, but then again, he doesn't need them. The imagery is enough. His message is simple: You know royalty when you see it.

"There's something truly energizing about the vigor of the student body in this moment," Stone sighs. She walks up with a green juice in her hand, and I'm thinking maybe that's what's making her so positive this early in the day. I take a sip of the caramel cloud macchiato Britt handed me anyway.

"You know what would energize me?" Britt asks. "If Marino would get here already. I would like to get these posters up before it's time for me to file for social security."

We go ahead and start hanging the posters without G, and even though the idea of my face being plastered all over the school makes me sick to my stomach, I have to admit they look pretty incredible. Britt designed them herself.

We took the photo a few days ago, but it looks so different now. What was originally just me holding my clarinet and standing in front of a white wall at the Marinos' house is now me holding my clarinet with a gold Basquiat-inspired crown photoshopped on my head, overlaid with a bright, Andy Warhol–like color scheme that reads: HIT THE RIGHT NOTE. VOTE LIGHTY FOR PROM QUEEN.

We leave some in the Commons, of course. But we decide to hit the band, theater, and choir hallways extra hard. If anybody can vibe with what we have going, it'll be my kin—the performing-arts geeks.

Time flies by. Gabi never shows, and I feel a little relieved. When the first students begin pouring into the hallways, we've hung every one of the posters and no one has gotten into a fight or had a panic attack. And considering our track record, I have to count this as a winning morning.

The show-choir kids are hosting a huge competition this week-end, and one of the volunteer activities this week is helping them set up for it. When I show up to the choir room after school, the director of the choirs, a short woman with a big voice and a black jumpsuit, is barking directions at the volunteers from behind a Clavinova. Everyone is already buzzing around like very frightened worker bees. Even the Prom Projectioners have been scared off.

"You two!" She points at me, and I turn to see Mack sliding down her headphones as she kicks up her skateboard into her free hand. "I need chairs stacked in the rehearsal room and pushed against the wall. Right now!"

Mack and I practically trip over each other to get out of the room before the ground opens up to an alternate dimension—one where I can't read music like the rest of those Broadway babies and am totally comfortable doing jazz squares in front of the entire student body—and swallows us whole. Once we're in the clear, we look at each other with raised eyebrows for a moment before bursting out laughing. It might be nerves, it might be relief, but I try to convince myself that it doesn't matter which one it is.

"I truly thought we might be the victims of a homicide back there." She reaches over and gently tilts my chin from the right to the left, like she's examining me. Her face is serious, but the way the corners of her lips quirk up a bit betray her, and I can't help but heat a little under her stare. "Luckily it seems like you made it out injury-free. What about me?"

She tilts her head up, and I think about reaching over to do the same to her. But I decide against it. I think about the spark that I could swear I felt at the Bake-Off as we cowered underneath that baking sheet. I remind myself that I'm not in this race for that.

So I stuff my hands into my pockets and laugh a little instead.

"You're good." I look down the hallway. She starts in the direction of the room, tucking her skateboard under her arm as she walks. "Let's go stack some chairs."

Her hair is in two knots on top of her head, and the wisps that are too short to make it into the buns are curling at her neck. It's the opposite of my own hair, every strand slicked down and tightly arranged so that my curls don't get too out of control. I like that about her—that she doesn't care about being so carefully put together.

Every time I see her, she looks like she either just rolled out of bed or spent an hour in the mirror before school doing her best to look carefree. But there's something about the way she walks, sort of bouncing on the balls of her feet like she doesn't really want to touch the ground, that tells me it's a little of both. Like she's here, but barely. Like she's already past this place and the things that are happening within it.

When we get into the classroom, Mack flips on the lights and turns back to smile at me as she leans her board against the wall. I take a good look at the bottom of it for the first time.

I realize it's decorated in stickers—one that reads GINGERS DO IT BETTER over an image of Princess Fiona from Shrek, one with a blue square and a yellow equal sign in the middle that looks familiar but I can't quite place, a bright pink GIRLS JUST WANT TO HAVE FUN . . . DAMENTAL RIGHTS banner, and a huge Kittredge sticker.

"Wait. You listen to Kittredge?" I ask, grabbing one of the chairs and pushing it against the wall to begin a stack. I'm smiling back at her, and I can't help it. "That's my favorite band."

I don't know anyone else who we go to school with who's into their music. I tried to get Gabi into them a few years ago, and after one listen through their first album in her car one day, she turned to me with an apologetic look and asked: "Can we please go back to listening to Beyoncé now?"

Since then, I've been on a Teela Conrad island all by my lonesome.

"Yeah, they're *my* favorite band!" Mack's face lights up. "Were you able to get tickets to their concert Sunday? I was the only person who was into them at my last school, so I thought that automatically meant my taste was better than all my classmates'. But you, Liz Lighty, have proven me wrong. I have officially met my match."

"No, I'm not going. I'm—" *Saving every spare dime I have to get out of this town.* "I'm sure your taste is great. If your drumming is any indication, you know music." I look away as I say it, and I'm not sure why. It feels a little intimate to tell someone that you have been thinking about the way they play, even after you've left the confines of the band room.

I keep stacking chairs, but I know she's stopped stacking hers because the sound of hard plastic meeting hard plastic stops.

Her voice is sort of quiet as she responds. "You really think I'm that good?"

"Yeah. Of course." I turn to face her quickly. "You have no idea what we were dealing with before the, um, incident. You were a godsend."

It might sound too earnest, but I mean it. There are very few things I take more seriously than band, and Mack's presence in it makes it better. That means more to me than she could know.

She doesn't say anything for a second. The room is completely silent except for the sound of me stacking another chair. Instead of replying, Mack just turns up the speaker on her phone and fills the room with the sound of "My Life, My Story"—my favorite Kittredge song. It feels sort of like kismet.

And then, in between slowly moving chairs, we're talking—not about prom or school or scholarships, but about the band. We're talking about their best album and Teela Conrad's best looks on the red carpet. We're talking about what Mack wants to do with music after high school and why arranging music is one of my favorite hobbies.

We've almost managed to stack all the chairs against the wall before I even realize we've been together for nearly an hour. I turn, and she's closer to me than I remember her being, but then again that could just be my nerves. It's kind of dizzying being this close to her, even though we're talking about nothing. Just music and the future and our collective crush on Teela Conrad, but it's been nice.

It's been exactly what I needed.

"I wouldn't have guessed you'd be someone who ran for prom queen," I say, thinking out loud.

"I could say the same for you." She leans an elbow against one of the stacks of chairs. "But here we are, stacking chairs together like a couple of real contenders. I don't know why they don't slap some tiaras on us right now, honestly."

"So you're in it for the hardware?" I shake my head with mock disappointment. "I thought you were a woman of principle. Someone dedicated to the scholarship and service that the crown represents!"

She laughs. "Can I tell you something kind of embarrassing?"

You can tell me anything, I think. I nod.

"You ever notice that one prom queen with the really bad bangs and that awful chartreuse dress with all the ruffles in the gallery?" She smirks. She's talking about the Royal Portrait Gallery— the wall that holds portraits of all the prom kings and queens dating back to when this whole thing started—that sits next to the front office. It's impossible to miss. From the moment you enter the school, there's no doubt about this town's commitment to the pomp and circumstance of the biggest night of the year.

I've walked past that picture a hundred times, so I know exactly who she's talking about, and I don't know why I didn't put the pieces together sooner. The freckles. The hair. The same smile.

"That's not your—"

"Yup." Her grin is wider than I've ever seen. "That's my mom."

"You've got to be kidding me!" I shout, more excited than I would usually let on. "So you're running as a legacy?"

"A legacy?" she asks, and I remember she's not actually from Campbell, even though she threw herself directly into Campbell's biggest tradition like it was her only mission.

"Oh, um, someone with a parent who's already won a crown. It sort of guarantees you a type of cache that running on your own can't really get you." I don't add that legacies are pretty much the closest thing you can get to a guaranteed crown without being a

Jordan or an Emme. I dig the toe of my bootie into the carpet. "Campbell is really big on tradition and stuff like that."

"Oh! Well, in that case not really? I mean, being a legacy only works if people know, right?"

"Well, yeah, I guess. But why wouldn't you be telling people about that?" I think about what Gabi would say if she were managing Mack's campaign instead of mine. The ranking formula that G and Stone cooked up would be thrown for a loop if this information was public knowledge. "You would be skyrocketing in the rankings."

"The rankings?" She laughs a little. "No, I'm not really worried about that. My mom used to tell me all about this amazing, incredible time she had running for prom queen in her hometown. I was raised on stories about how wonderful this tradition is and how many friends she made." She shrugs and bites at her thumbnail. "I thought that if I had to transfer midway through the last semester of my senior year, getting to have that would make it worth it."

"And has it been?"

She sort of smirks and cocks her head to the side.

"I'll say it has been an . . . experience so far."

I laugh. I definitely know what she means.

"I bet she's proud of you for taking the leap though."

"Oh," she starts, looking down. "She died a few years ago. Ovarian cancer."

This is weird, and probably a little messed up, but hearing her say that she's also in the Dead Mom Club makes me feel closer to her. Like the two of us are in on some secret—a deep, unrelenting trauma that you couldn't possibly understand unless you've been there—that can't be explained.

"Same." I answer, but amend quickly. "Not cancer though. Stroke. She, um, had sickle cell."

I don't talk about my mom, not ever. But for some reason Mack's admission has me wanting to be honest too.

"Would she have been excited about you running for prom queen?"

I freeze where my hand is reaching for the last chair. I realize I don't know how my mom would feel about prom. We never really got there. I was too young when she died to have gotten to most of the important stuff. Dating advice, how you deal with starting your period in the middle of gym class (which was mortifying, by the way), any of it. What I remember is learning how to love the people who love me with everything I have. I remember visiting Pennington for homecoming football games in my miniature Pennington Penguins cheerleading uniform. I remember knowing what it feels like to have someone be your entire world one second and them be gone the next.

My stomach churns, but I try to smile.

"I hope she would be."

fifteen

When someone in your life is sick, or could get seriously sicker, you're always waiting for the other shoe to drop. Even when things are going well, when it seems like everything is fine, some part of you is anticipating the worst. My palms are sweating as I read the text from my granny, and even though it's not the worst message I could have gotten, it's definitely among the ones I fear the most.

> Granny: **I picked Robbie up early today, was showing signs of a crisis**

> Granny: **Everything is fine. Don't worry about coming home**

"Lighty, you good?" I look up from my phone into the face of a very concerned-looking Jordan Jennings and realize that I've stopped walking in the middle of the hallway. His face looks almost as scared as I feel as he rests a hand on my shoulder. "You look like you've seen a ghost."

I open my mouth but shut it again immediately. Granny knew to tell me not to come home early because my first instinct is to leave, to go to him. Even though I know he's probably fine. Probably just pushed himself too hard in gym or something and needed to go home and rest before he had a flare-up.

Sickle cell anemia is in the blood. That's the way they explained it to me the first time I remember my mom being hospitalized long-term. It's a genetic thing. Where most people's red blood cells—the cells that carry oxygen—are shaped like circles, in people with sickle cell, they're shaped like moons. Sometimes when those moon-shaped cells don't move through their bloodstream properly, people with the disease can be in an ungodly amount of pain.

But they fail to mention when you're five years old that the median age of death for women with the disease is sometime in their mid-forties. And that for some women, it's even earlier. For women like our mom, it was the even earlier.

The pain they described is what people in the sickle cell community call a crisis. Robbie says it just feels like a cramp when it's not so bad, but it's something like being stabbed over and over again when at its worst. The switch can happen really quickly, and that's the scariest part. We can't really see it coming. So the days when his pain is at an eight on a scale to ten, when there's nothing I can do to help him but wait for it to pass and make sure he has his meds handy, those are some of the scariest of my life. I'm never not afraid of losing him.

Jordan's hand is still on my shoulder when I finally respond, and instead of being freaked out by him talking to and touching me in the middle of a hallway full of our peers, something about it is grounding.

"I'm fine. I, um, got some not-great news." I pull the straps on my backpack up higher. "Sorry for blocking your path or whatever."

He winces like what I said physically hurt him. I don't mean to be rude, but he set the terms of this non-relationship a long time ago. I'm just trying to respect that. Just because I've let my guard slip a few times during volunteer events doesn't mean I can trust him again.

"You didn't block my path," he answers. "You looked bad, so I stopped to make sure you were okay. It's not like— I was worried about you."

"You don't have to be worried about me anymore, Jordan." My palms are sweating, and even though going to class is the last thing I want to do right now, I don't know if I can stand in front of him and have this conversation. We may be in a cease-fire, but my nerves are worn too thin to be patient today.

"I'll always worry about you, Lighty," he says. "Us not hanging out anymore didn't change that."

He smiles, quick and easy. "But hey, you should think about switching volunteer things and coming to letter writing tonight. I got partnered with Rachel yesterday, and I'd take you giving me the cold shoulder again over her talking about her plans for world domination any day."

I smirk. The other mandatory volunteer activity I could have been assigned to this week was even more useless than normal—writing letters to elderly cats with acid reflux, which would be read to them by their caregivers. I'm so glad I spent my time preparing for Campbell to be overrun by show-tune fanatics rather than spend my night penning missives to gassy cats. Which is saying something.

Jordan leans against the nearest locker and crosses his arms, unconcerned about the fact that the warning bell just rang and the two of us should be heading to our classes.

"I'm convinced she's only writing these letters so that she can summon the cats to her altar of sacrifice under the next full moon."

"Hey, J! Let's go, man!" I turn around and see Jaxon Price waving at Jordan. Jordan waves him off, and Jaxon huffs before leaving him behind.

I put on my best Stone voice. "Pretty sure the spells only work when Venus is in its sixth house." Jordan shoves off the locker and begins walking in the direction of my AP Chem class with me. I know for a fact that he's supposed to be headed the other direction, like he was when he stopped me, but I don't bother mentioning it.

"Besides, aren't you and Rachel friends?" I can't help but ask.

The PomBots and the Jacket Jocks all seem to stick together. They go to the same parties, join the same extracurriculars, date one another.

Jordan laughs as he walks backward. People sort of move out of his way as he passes, so he doesn't even have to worry about running into someone.

"We're not friends, Lighty. We just know the same people." He shrugs as he rounds the corner effortlessly. "Let me know if your weird news gets any weirder, okay?"

I just nod as he gives me a quick salute and jogs the rest of the way back to meet Jaxon.

I look down at my phone one more time, hoping that Granny has sent me another text. An update, anything. Even though I know it's probably not serious. Even though I know he'll be better tomorrow. Sometimes I worry less, but I never stop worrying altogether.

Jordan gets it. Or he used to get it. But that limbo, the space between the people we used to be and the people we are now, feels like it's always going to hang in the air between us.

· ♛ ·

The first time I see Gabi in two days, she's marching around the corner into the band hallway, phone pressed to her ear and a small cardboard box in her hand.

She waves as she walks toward me, hanging up as she reaches me.

"Hello, my amazing and altruistic best friend."

"Wait. Are we just not going to address the fact that you dropped off the grid for like"—I check my wrist for a nonexistent watch—"two days straight?"

"Oh, don't worry about that. There were some things I needed to handle during business hours, and school was getting in the way of that." She smiles, like that's the end of that discussion. And I guess it is. Gabi is good at only talking about what she wants to talk about at any given moment. "Here. These are for you."

She places the box in my hands, and I look down. A variety of buttons with my face on them are scattered inside.

"G, this seems—and I really mean no shade, because I recognize that you're a prom-operative genius—but this seems absurd," I say. "There's at least a hundred of these things in here."

She reaches in and grabs one to pin to her blazer. And then she does the same to my top—some weird, flouncy thing that I never would have selected on my own.

I can't believe what I've reduced myself to in the name of a scholarship.

"You have to trust the process, Lizzie."

She pats the button where it sits over my heart. I realize that I never actually heard an apology or a retraction from her after the other night. Not even in her voice mails and text messages did she ever say she was wrong. Just different variations of "My therapist tells me that my tone could use some improvement" or "You know I love you for who you are, right?" None of which smooth over the way that conversation made me feel.

G nestles her snakeskin purse into the curve of her elbow.

"Please believe me when I say this is the only way for you to win, okay?" She pulls out her phone, checks the screen, and then frowns. I want to ask her what's so bad on there that it's got her wrinkling her forehead so hard, even though wrinkles are her number two biggest fear in life (second only to the robot band at Chuck E. Cheese, obviously). "The numbers aren't good. We really have the deck stacked against us here."

"Us?" My eyebrows shoot up. "Yeah, sorry, but last time I checked it was my face on these buttons and on the posters and on the bumper stickers you're having the Lucas make." I can feel myself getting more frustrated. "I'm the one who has to do all"—I wave my hand around at everything from the poster with my face on it on the wall next to us to my ridiculous country club–esque outfit—"this."

"Lizzie, please." She sighs, her small hand resting on my arm. I hate when she uses my nickname like that, like I'm some sort of toddler who needs to be placated. "You know what I mean. I'm just saying, I want me and you to do everything we can to give you the best shot at winning."

"Well, if you wanna help so bad, *you* carry this ridiculous box." I shove the box back into her hands as we approach the band room.

Melly and her friend Katherine Evans, our best cellist, rush up to us before we can even walk in.

"Lizwe*never*getbandgeeksonthese!" Melly comes up to me holding out her phone. My poster is the wallpaper on her lock screen. The sight throws me off for a second, and Gabi elbows me in the ribs, like, *See, I told you so.* "You're*famous!*"

Gabi loves that Melly and Katherine have become two of my biggest supporters. The two have practically made me a trending topic in the nerd circles thanks to how much they've been talking about me. I appreciate it—I really, seriously do—but I guess I'm still not used to having attention trained on me, especially not attention that I've purposely invited on myself.

Katherine lowers her voice like she's sharing some forbidden information. "This makes us look almost *cool.*"

"You guys are already cool." I nudge them inside the band room and laugh when they both roll their eyes. "But feel free to grab a button. We have a fully obnoxious amount."

I direct that last part at Gabi, but she's pretending not to hear me as she goes to the back of the room to grab her clarinet. When we step into the room, the band is in that sweet spot right before practice, where everyone has gotten done with their catching up and is tuning their instruments, adjusting their music stands, and getting into rehearsal mode. It's one of my favorite moments of practice days.

She hands me another button as we sit down.

"I still think this is overkill, G. I already have this face on twenty-four seven." I gesture to my head. "What do I need to wear two for?" I roll my eyes and pin it to my shirt anyway. My fight is half-hearted. As long as we're getting ready to play, none of this other stuff matters.

"All right, group!" Mr. K waves a hand in the air to draw all the attention in his direction. "Let's do this."

I set my music on the stand in front of me and breathe deep, my nerves settling instantly. And for a second, buttons, prom, over-bearing best friends are forgotten. Because this, right here, always makes sense.

sixteen

"Okay, one-for-one. You ask me something, and I'll ask you something," Mack says as we set up some tables in the Commons. There's an entire stack of them on a cart that we're expected to unload before our volunteer shift is over.

Some of the groups for the show-choir competition will start arriving tomorrow night, and the school is gradually transforming into something even worse than Prom Wasteland: Jazz Hand Junction. On top of the already-ridiculous layer of campaign posters and flyers with prom court candidates lining the walls and the lockers, we now have to deal with music note decals and glittery handmade signs welcoming groups with names like Park Meade High School Panache and Valley Glen Vocal Velocity. I'm getting nauseated just looking at it.

"Hmm, sounds dangerous. What if you ask me something I don't want to answer?" My arms feel especially Jell-O-y as we unfold the legs of the plastic table and tilt it upright. "Nobody needs to know that I shot a man in Reno just to watch him die."

"Okay, ten points for the Johnny Cash reference." She laughs.

I decide to start. "How do you feel about Campbell now that you've been here for a grand total of three weeks?"

"Sometimes I can see why my mom and dad liked this place so much. Other times I'm not sure how anyone can breathe in this town."

I sit on the table and close my eyes for a second. If there's one thing I understand, it's feeling stifled by the place we live and the people who live here. But I also understand the other part, the part of Campbell that is charming and beautiful, though I feel it less often.

"What about you?" she asks when I don't respond. She looks at me and bites her thumbnail. "I know it must be tough being one of the only black students at Campbell. And it doesn't help that Racist Regina George, Rachel Collins, has it out for you."

Instead of answering her question, I ask one of my own. "You've noticed that?"

"Of course I have. I notice a lot about you." She smiles at me softly before hauling one of the tables off the cart by herself, like she didn't just Hurricane Mack my entire world with one sentence. "You can actually make me shut up and listen for a minute. And if you ask my dad, that's next to impossible."

"Hey, you wanna go somewhere else with me?" I surprise myself by asking. I press forward when she turns around to look at me, eyebrows raised. "I mean, if they want us to do community service, we might as well help the community."

We've only been working for, like, fifteen minutes, but I find that I'm ready to go already. Well, ready to go somewhere with *Mack*. The only aspect of the campaign that makes any sense to me at all is the community service, honestly. But it feels empty to give back in a town like Campbell, a town that already has all the resources it needs. If I'm going to do this, I want to serve in a place that actually needs our help.

It's a risk.

We might lose the points for the day.

But sometimes it's worth it to do what feels right.

"Um, yes. Absolutely!" She nods quickly and wipes her hands on her overalls. She reaches down to grab her board from where it rests next to the cart full of tables. I swear her green eyes sparkle as she looks up at me. "Where did you have in mind?"

· ♔ ·

We pull into a spot on the street next to an unassuming brick building. Mack is too down-to-earth to act squirrelly about the neighborhood that I've brought her to, but I can tell she's wondering what we're doing here.

"Are you good with kids?" I finally think to ask as she trails after me across the street.

"Um, yeah." She nods. "I haven't been around any in a while, but—"

"Miss Lizzie! Miss Lizzie!" She's cut off by the sound of kids screeching my name as soon as we step through the doors. There's no chance to prepare her for the mass of rug rats that barrels toward us, wrapping themselves around her legs and pulling my hand toward the rec room. "You're back!"

"Liz, uh . . ." Mack is frozen in place, pinned to her spot by Peanut Parker sitting on the floor in front of her tying her shoelaces together. "A little help here?"

I shake my head with a laugh. Peanut's a fiery six going on twenty-six and has loved giving newcomers a hard time since the day she was born. "Peanut, leave her alone! This is why I don't bring people around anymore—y'all don't know how to act."

I brought Gabi once, two years ago, when I was volunteering over the summer. And Peanut—then just a four-year-old terror in the day care—finger painted all over the prized pale pink leather Givenchy tote G's grandmother had gotten her for her sixteenth birthday. Honestly, I've never seen my best friend cry the way she cried that day. It was a tragedy the likes of which we dare not speak.

Needless to say, I stopped bringing guests to Bryant House.

But I feel like I can trust Mack with this part of my life. And if the way she's suppressing a giggle while she imitates a giant's voice as she stomps around with Peanut wrapped around her left leg is any indication, I made the right choice.

"Lizzie." Dr. Lamont surprises me by putting her hand on my shoulder. She's a tall, slender black woman in her mid-fifties. She moves so gracefully, sometimes I barely even hear her coming. "Why didn't you tell me you were coming by?" She tilts her head in Mack's direction with a smirk. "And bringing a *friend*."

"Yes, Dr. L, my *friend*." I turn to wrap my arms around her neck in a tight embrace. "Mack and me were out doing some service in Campbell today. But I thought you all might need us more."

Bryant House is always looking for people to come by and help. It's a cornerstone of the Indianapolis community—a day care, a summer camp, a refuge for neighborhood kids with nowhere else to go. But beyond all that, Dr. L has been organizing support groups and events specifically catered to the kids getting treated at the children's hospital down the road and their families since I was a kid. It used to be a part-time pet project, something she did to help the families of her patients, but since she retired, she's gone full-time at the house.

She treated Robbie when he was still really little, before she left medicine, and watching her work is one of the reasons I decided I wanted to become a hematologist.

"Well, come on, then. The littles need someone to read to them for a while." Dr. L kisses me on the forehead and nods to the rec room. "You better come on too, Red the Friend."

I look over my shoulder at Mack, whose face has gone completely pink.

"Um, yes, ma'am." Mack whispers something at Peanut, and the little girl giggles and runs ahead into the rec room. I couldn't quite make out what she said, but no one ever gets Peanut to follow an order on the first try. Not even me.

We walk down the short hallway that leads to the rec room. Normally the kids would be outside, but I heard on the news there was a shooting in the neighborhood last week. Dr. L is always extra careful with letting the kids on the playground after news like that.

While Dr. L reprimands some of the six-year-olds—the oldest in this particular age group—for roughhousing, Mack comes up beside me. "Okay, please tell me who this magnificent Amazonian woman is and why do I feel like offering up my firstborn child to her?"

I shake my head, and my laugh bubbles up from that place in my gut where only the most honest laughs come from. I realize I've laughed more with Mack this afternoon than I have in a long time. "Well, first of all, you should offer up your children to her because she is a better parent than any I've ever seen, and she doesn't even have kids.

"And second," I continue, "her name's Dr. Leanne Lamont, but you can call her Dr. L. She rules this place with an iron fist and a heart of gold."

Mack nods and bites at her nonexistent thumbnail, clearly taking in the information. She does that, bite her thumbnail, when she's processing new things or situations or people. I find it weirdly adorable. But, like, adorable in the type of way that will absolutely not lead to anything else between us ever because we're just friends and I have too much other stuff on my plate right now to start worrying about cute girls and—

"Iron fist and a heart of gold, huh?" Dr. L appears behind us again, and I actually yelp this time. "I should get that copyrighted." She puts two fingers into her mouth and lets out her infamous whistle to get everyone's attention. "Y'all know what time it is! Who wants to hear Miss Lizzie and her friend read some stories?"

Peanut is the first to dart away from the jump rope station that she'd commandeered and join us where we've formed an informal circle on the floor. She climbs into my lap, where I'm sitting crosslegged, instead of finding a seat of her own.

"She's white," she whispers in my ear conspiratorially.

"I know she's white, P." I smile, amused. "There's all kinds of people on the earth who look different than us."

Bryant House is smack-dab in the middle of an almost entirely black neighborhood, so it's not often we get a white person strolling through these halls. I can't blame her for being a little curious.

Unsatisfied, she looks at Mack as she sits across the circle, currently in deep conversation with a five-year-old named Troy. "Okay, well, why's her hair like that? She looks like that scary girl with the arrows."

It's worth mentioning that Peanut absolutely did not like *Brave* when we showed it during summer camp last year.

"She was born with that hair. Just like I was born with this hair and you were born with your beautiful curls." I tug at one of her pigtails, and it immediately bounces back into place. "Why are you so nosy anyway?"

"I dunno." She shrugs. "I like her. She smells good, and she said she liked my shirt."

And listen, an endorsement from Peanut Parker goes a long way in my book.

When everyone is finally nestled into their spots, Dr. L hands Mack the stack of books instead of giving it to me.

Dr. L never so much as asked G to pour a glass of juice when she visited, so this feels something like an endorsement too. Albeit a little less passionate than Peanut's, but still.

But Mack takes the stack and asks Troy to pick a book. He pulls out *Whistle for Willie* by Ezra Jack Keats. My chest gets a little tight as I listen to Mack read it, her voice fluctuating perfectly with each scene. She looks so comfortable with the book in one hand and Troy leaning against her shoulder. As she flips to the last page, Peanut leans up to whisper in my ear again.

"Miss Lizzie, why are you looking at the white girl like that?"

"Like what, P?"

She rolls her eyes and tries again. "Uh duh, like Tiana looked at Naveen?"

Because okay, Peanut didn't buy into *Brave*, but she really freaking loved *The Princess and the Frog*. And— Oh shoot. I just got called out by a six-year-old about my ridiculously inconvenient, now-impossible-to-ignore crush.

So as Mack reads the final line and is met with an enthusiastic round of applause from her captive audience, I finally realize something major: Dr. L has to stop letting the kids watch so many Disney movies.

seventeen

Jordan seems to have a way of finding me when I am at my most frazzled.

I'm powering out the front doors of the school when Jordan spots me. He's leaning against Jaxon Price's car, laughing with a few of the other guys from the football team.

"Yo, Lighty, wait up!" he shouts. He shakes up with his boys before walking in my direction. I look down at the time on my phone. I'm late for work because I decided to stop by and talk to Mr. K after school. I had to tell him about not getting the scholarship. It was beginning to feel too much like lying. And I couldn't make him one of the people I'm not being completely honest with.

When he offered to do whatever he could to help, I told him that I was working on a solution and that everything would be fine. He nodded, but his face told me he didn't quite believe that. And I couldn't blame him. I wouldn't believe it either. I'm not sure I believe it now.

"Where you headed?" Jordan asks once he finally reaches me. "Work? You need a ride?" He nods toward his car. "You still at the music shop? I'm getting ready to head out that way."

I hesitate. And look over at the bike rack where my bike is locked. I would really prefer not to have to pedal all the way over to work.

"Um, yeah actually. That'd be great."

I jog over to grab my bike, and he lifts it easily into his trunk. I hop into his passenger seat, and I'm sort of surprised by how clean the inside of the car is.

I'm jittery, unable to focus. After talking to Mr. K, a part of me feels lighter. But still, the weight of all the things I'm not saying is starting to feel almost crushing.

"Lighty, you may not be my second-in-command anymore, but something is off." He looks over at me as we pull out of the parking lot. "You're doing that thing you do with your eyebrow."

"I'm fine!" I rub at my eyebrow quickly because I know exactly what he's talking about. It's one of those anxiety tics. My left eyebrow has a tendency to get all twitchy when I'm stressed. For instance, it got so bad last year before the SATs, my granny seriously considered having me see a doctor. "Okay, so I'm a little stressed. But nothing I can't handle. Nothing I can't figure out."

The drive from the school to Melody is a short one by car, and he rounds the corner to the plaza without any directions. He puts his car in park and turns to me.

"Look, if you need me to handle anybody, I got you." He tries to put on an intimidating face, but his soft brown eyes and very unconvincing growl give him away. When I laugh, he softens. "Just like old times."

"Well," I start, picking at a thread on the uncomfortable Saint Laurent straight-leg pants G had sent over, "it's not exactly like old times. You know. Given the circumstances."

There isn't really a good way around this. That there was a time, whole years of our lives, when our friendship meant everything to us, and he threw that away in one day.

"You're right." He looks vulnerable and honest. "But it's been nice to be around someone who really knows me again."

And yeah. I get that. I get the comfort that comes with being near people who know who you are, deep down, when no one else is watching. I used to feel that way with Jordan, and up until a few weeks ago, I felt that way with Gabi.

Jordan did what he thought he had to do to survive high school freshman year, and I did the same. It sucks not to get the apology I've wanted so badly for the past few years, not to ask how he could give our friendship up so easily, but I've missed him. I've missed *us*, and it seems like he has too. And that's enough for now.

I hold out my pinky in a promise that I'm halfway terrified to make.

"Truce?"

He links his pinky through mine, and offers his usual half smile.

"You bet, Lighty."

eighteen

It's the day of the annual prom powder-puff football game, which always takes place right in the middle of prom campaign season, and thanks to my nerves, I've been halfway to hurling all morning. I'm getting ready in our state-of-the-art field house, and Robbie's words from breakfast this morning that, if all else fails, I should just "play dead" once I get on the field, are ringing in my ears. We're not actually supposed to tackle, but he has a valid point—nothing is off the table with these monsters, and all options for self-preservation should be explored.

To distract myself from my impending humiliation, I turn back to my bag and pull out my phone one last time to check for any missed messages. Mack hasn't shown up yet, and my chest gets a little tight. I hope she doesn't miss this event. Spending time with her is one of the only good parts about this whole thing.

I need to relax, but none of my usual coping mechanisms are working. This game is everything I hate—super public and involving physical activity, with no practice to speak of so I could at least try and develop a strategy—and I feel like I'm about to shake out of my skin with anxiety. Even worse, the members of the winning team get extra points in the race, and I could really use the bump. According to Gabi, while my posters and buttons have helped my standings, and since GPA is the smallest part of the score, I'm still well away from making court. Six spots away to be exact. That's light-years from where I started, but still not where I need to be.

"Liz!" A pair of bony arms wraps around my waist tightly, and I jump a smooth foot in the air.

"Quinn." I turn around, and Quinn is beaming at me. I crack a slight smile at how excited she looks, sort of like a puppy who just got let off her leash at the beach for the first time. "I want you to know that I'm not really a physical-affection type of person."

"Ohmygosh, Liz, I totally forgot! You're absolutely right; consent is crucial." She nods her head vigorously, but her smile never fades. "I just wanted to tell you how excited I am we're going to be on the same team! It's going to be great. I'm thinking we could run a—"

"Wait. Who else is on our team?" I ask, realizing suddenly that the only thing worse than competing against Rachel Collins would be having to help her win.

"Oh, you know, the usuals!" She waves her hand like that answers everything. "It's ten on ten. Me and you are together, which is great because I know for a fact Rachel and Luce can't tell the difference between a linebacker and a cornerback."

She laughs like that's the most obvious joke in the world, and I laugh too. Not because I have any idea what she's saying but because Quinn Bukowski is the living embodiment of a person who contains multitudes.

"Come on! Let's rally the other girls and get a game plan together." She starts walking toward the mirrors where the stragglers are still getting camera ready, and I follow her lead. "I'm thinking we'll do a handoff for our first play, since we want to save Becka's arm for later—the girl has a cannon on her, and we don't want to waste it."

"Quinn, how do you know this stuff?" I ask as she begins gently directing the other members of our team to huddle up. She doesn't have to ask them twice either. They seem to snap to attention as soon as her bubbly voice gives them an instruction, like they know something I don't. "You're, like, scaring me a little."

"Oh, I thought everyone knew already." She cocks her head to the side and smiles bright as ever. "My dad is the official dentist of the Colts!"

• ♔ •

The minute we exit the locker room, I'm hit by the sheer magnitude of this game. The stadium is fuller for this game than it is during football season. People from all over the community are here, ready to take part in one of the parents' favorite parts of this race. I even spot Robbie posted in the front row, flanked by Gabi, Stone, and Britt. They're all waving their arms in the air as I run out, and I grin back at them in response. I want to laugh, so I do. This feels wild, a little absurd. But also kind of exciting. The hum of anxiety is still here, thrumming under my skin, but this is kind of . . . fun?

Everyone is cheering, and even though it's not nighttime, they have the stadium lights on at full blast. It's like a cross between *Friday Night Lights* and *Gossip Girl*: mothers in pearls and crisp blouses next to dads in Campbell County Cougars sweatshirts, holding signs to cheer on their precious daughters in a fake football game.

The guys are all in cheerleading uniforms, and they're doing a really bad (but well-intentioned) version of the "Boom! Dynamite" cheer that involves a lot of Jaxon shaking his butt and Harry doing the worm.

We're getting ready to line up on the field by the time I finally see Mack. She's in uniform, nodding quickly at something Madame Simoné is saying on the sidelines. Madame S shoves a white bandana into her hand and shoos her out onto the field.

Our team is huddled up again to go over our game plan. We have the ball first, thanks to Quinn's excellent coin-toss skills. Mack slips in right next to me and throws her arm over my shoulders like everyone else is doing. I want to ask her what's up, but she just smiles at me and says, "What'd I miss?" like everything's normal.

"Well, apparently Quinn is Peyton Manning incarnate and currently shaping this ragtag bunch into a real team." I shake my head. Quinn is talking, and I don't want to interrupt, so I add in a low voice. "I was sort of hoping I could just ride the bench and, you know, be a water girl. But she wasn't buying it."

"You would have been a very attentive water girl." Mack nods with fake solemnity. "This is a true loss for our team."

"And Liz will take it from there! Our secret weapon." Quinn is putting one hand into the center of the circle, and everyone else does the same.

"Wait, what?"

"Cougars on three, ladies!" Quinn shouts. "One, two, three, Cougars!"

Now I'm stressed. I was too busy flirting to listen to the plan, and I have no idea what I'm supposed to do. As everyone else manages to find their spots on the line of scrimmage, I sort of just find an open space near the middle and crouch down, because it looks like the right thing to do. After all, you don't get the GPA I have by knowing *all* the answers. Half the battle is correctly interpreting context clues.

"Well, look what we have here, ladies. Little Miss National Merit Scholar has decided to grace us with her presence." Rachel puts her hands on her hips and grins angrily. I know how weird that sounds, but it's true. Rachel Collins has mastered the art of the angry grin.

Claire and Lucy are on either side of her, and Claire giggles while Lucy rolls her eyes. "Rach, can't we just play already? Some of us have nail appointments after this, and you know how hard it is to get Lila to make house calls."

Rachel gets into position directly across from me and sneers. "I hope you're ready to get destroyed, sweetheart."

Rachel's team has red bandanas around their heads, and there's something fitting about the imagery of the ends of the knot sticking out like horns on her forehead.

The booming voice of the announcer they use for football

season gets things started. "Hello, hello, hello, Cougars fans. Who's ready for a little football?"

The crowd reacts instantly, erupting into cheers. I want to correct him and remind him that we're not even wearing the Indiana High School Athletic Association–sanctioned protective gear, so legally we shouldn't be calling this football, but as soon as the thought enters my mind, the people around me explode into a flurry of activity.

And when Becka—our quarterback, apparently—tucks the ball into my stomach suddenly, I look around frantically, trying to figure out what the hell I'm even supposed to do with it. I can hear Mack shouting from somewhere behind me, "Go, Liz, go!"

And suddenly I'm pumping my legs, channeling one of Robbie's barbs from earlier: "Lizzie, your legs are longer than anybody else's out there. All you gotta do is take one stride, and you've made it from midfield to the goal line."

Out of the corner of my eye I can see girls chasing me, hands reaching out to grab at my flags, but I just make longer strides until my calves burn, until there is nothing in my periphery but the green turf and the crowd. The sound of their cheers urges me on, and before I know it, I'm crossing into the end zone.

"That's a touchdown for white, and the first score of the game comes from Lightning Lighty!" The announcer's voice booms over the intercom, and the stands are shaking with the sound of feet stomping against the metal stands. I'm breathing hard, still clutching the football to my chest, when Quinn runs up to me, clapping.

"I knew it, Liz, I just knew it!" She looks so happy, and the way my cheeks are burning tells me my expression probably matches hers. I can't believe it! I scored! Me, Liz Lighty. Tall, gangly, awkward Liz Lighty has scored a touchdown in the powder-puff football game. Quinn grabs the ball from me to take back to the line but smiles as she adds, "Jordan told me you'd be our secret weapon."

Jordan?

I look to the sideline, where Jordan is pumping one fist in the air while shaking his pom-pom everywhere.

"You love to see it, folks!" He shouts.

I wave at him as I jog back to the line. I'm tired from the sprinting, but feeling strong—finally, biking everywhere has paid off! I never considered myself a team-sports kind of girl, but the way everyone pats me on the back and offers me their fists to bump as I pass them feels pretty freaking good.

We go for the extra point after that, and Quinn is the kicker. The ball soars perfectly through the air, and she turns to smile at us like she had no doubt it would.

It's almost halftime before Quinn decides it's time for us to try our luck and run the play again, only with me running to the left instead of the right. The red team is down by eight, and I can see Rachel getting visibly flustered. She snaps at Kaya Mitchellson, one of the poor souls currently ranked below me: "Stop dragging your gigantic, tragically uncoordinated feet and play the game already!"

When the play starts, I manage to get the ball and take off down the field again. I feel unstoppable as I run. I look into the stands to see Robbie jumping up and down, Britt pumping her fist in the air, and Gabi screaming as she records the whole thing on her phone.

Even Stone actually looks excited. I'm soaring, I'm coasting. Nobody can touch me. I'm like a bird, graceful and—

"Ouch! And that has got to hurt!" the announcer shouts. "An illegal hit by Rachel Collins has taken out Lightning Lighty!"

"Uhnnnnnnn," I moan from the ground. I open my eyes but close them quickly. I can feel the brightness of the stadium lights, and everything hurts. I feel like I've been hit by a semi. I think about sitting up but immediately decide against it. My body aches, but worse than that, I know every eye in the stadium is on me. I'm living through one of my biggest fears.

And then I remember what Robbie said, and I decide I will lay on the ground forever. I will play dead until everyone decides to go home. I will play dead until prom is over, and then maybe they will give me a posthumous scholarship for being ruthlessly maimed in the line of duty.

"OH MY GOSH!" I can hear Quinn's gasp from above me as she grabs my face with both her hands. They're incredibly soft and somehow not even a little bit sweaty even though we're in the middle of a football game. "Why are you celebrating, Rachel? She's dead!" I open my eyes when her voice raises to an octave only small dogs and people under thirty can register. "You killed her! Oh, Liz, you were so young!"

I tilt my head slightly to the left to look into the crowd.

"Quinn," I manage to say quietly. The moment she hears my voice, Quinn's tears stop, and her smile returns.

"Liz, you're back!" She throws herself over my body, and I yelp in return. She sits up quickly and winces. "I'm sorry! I forgot about your fragile body and how you don't like being touched."

When she stands, I take a couple of calming breaths. I can move now that the initial shock has worn off, but I don't try to get up just yet. I'm not maimed, as it turns out, but I can tell I'm going to have some wicked bruising where Rachel tackled me.

I see that the rest of the team has taken a knee down the field, and I'm shocked by how official this all feels. A ref is standing to the side with his hands on his hips, reprimanding Rachel. I can't hear what he's saying, but from the way her face is turning red and her foot is tapping on the ground, it can't possibly be good.

As I look at the crowd, frozen and waiting for my reaction, I think about what Gabi would do.

I decide to give them a show.

"Lighty, you good?" Jordan is kneeling next to me now, his face a picture of concern. His skirt looks shorter now that his hairy knees are right beside my face. He puts a hand on my arm and squeezes gently. "You took that hit like a champ."

I motion for him to lean in and he does.

"I'll be fine," I whisper. "But I need you to carry me off the field right now in the most dramatic fashion possible. I'll explain later."

His eyebrows knit together, but he doesn't hesitate before scooping me up into his arms. As he does, the crowd erupts in cheers.

"Lighty Strong! Lighty Strong! Lighty Strong!" I don't chance another look at the audience, but something tells me Gabi is at the heart of the cheering. Call it best friend telepathy, but I'm also sure she hasn't put down her phone once throughout this entire ordeal.

Jordan whispers in my ear as we approach the field house. "What kind of tricks do you have up your sleeve, Lighty?" He's got his half smile on as I look up at him.

I smile back.

"Just keep walking, Jennings."

nineteen

Jordan doesn't set me down until we're inside the field house. It's so much quieter now; I feel like I can think clearly again. He gently lowers me onto one of the treatment tables, and I look to where a trainer would normally be if this were a real football game. I don't think anyone was anticipating a full-fledged gladiator-esque battle out there today. And all before halftime, no less.

I ask him to grab my phone from the locker room, and when he comes back, he's full of boundless energy. He hands it to me with a flourish.

"Lighty, I must say, you did not disappoint out there today!" He pushes my shoulder, and I wince. Between him and Quinn, my real injuries might be sustained just from, you know, people liking me too much. "My bad, my bad! But seriously, I wasn't expecting you to bite it like that, but up until that point? You were moving. Nobody could catch you."

"How'd you know I'd be able to do it?" I mumble. I think about what Quinn said about me being their "secret weapon," and I suddenly feel weirdly shy. Weirdly *seen*.

"You've always been unstoppable, Lighty." Jordan smiles, one of the old smiles. One of the ones I recognize. "Consider it intuition."

"Anyone call for a doctor?" Mack appears in the doorway with a small smile and red first aid kit in her hand.

Jordan looks back and forth between the two of us and I can't quite place his expression. An even-wider grin spreads across his face as he claps his hands once.

"All right, Strawberry Shortcake, take care of my friend. I gotta go get my squad together. I'm sure that crowd could use a little pep right now."

When Jordan disappears, I look back at Mack, and my heart beats a little faster. I'm happy to see her, of course, but it's something else. Like I'm excited and relieved at the same time. I was wrong when I said her presence could calm me down. If anything, proximity to her makes me way too aware of how I feel. Not even in the height of my friendship-that-may-have-also-been-a-crush with Jordan did I ever feel like this.

"Where'd you get that?" I ask as she moves toward me.

"You happen to be looking at a professional, ma'am." She sits down next to me on the treatment table and sets the kit on her lap. She pops it open and pulls out what she's looking for: an antibacterial wipe. "I try a lot of tricks on my board that I probably shouldn't. I've gotten pretty good at patching myself up."

Mack gently dabs at a small cut above my eyebrow where my face ate turf. I flinch, and she immediately pulls back.

"No, it's fine," I clarify. "Distract me. Tell me about what's going on out there."

"Madame Simoné is having a major meeting with both teams right now. A lot of switching back and forth between French and English, so you know she's serious." She smirks. "But on the bright side, I've never seen the freshmen so concerned. I heard one of them shout 'Liz Lighty is stronger than the US Marines!' on my way in here."

I can't help but laugh. One day someone is going to do a documentary on the baby paparazzi of Campbell County prom, and it's going to be a hit on all the streaming services.

"It's that bad, huh?"

"In all fairness, 'There is only one thing in the world worse than being talked about, and that is not being talked about.'" Her smile is something worth putting in magazines, I swear. "Oscar Wilde could be super out of touch sometimes, but I'm convinced he wrote that line with Campbell in mind."

Mack moves to put a bandage over my brow, and I'm positive I look like one of those old rappers who used to wear those oversize T-shirts: goofy as hell.

My phone vibrates with texts from Gabi.

Gabi Marino: **You're up three spots already! From 10 to 7!!! CC is going CRAZY**

I close my eyes and wait. No text ever comes asking if I'm okay. I need a distraction.

"One-for-one?" I ask suddenly.

"Always."

"Why were you late today?"

"This isn't how I envisioned asking you out, in a sweaty locker room when you might very well have a concussion." She bites her thumbnail. I let out a sharp breath, somewhere between a laugh and a gasp. "But I was talking to a friend of mine about getting us into the Kittredge show tomorrow night. You know, if you want to go?"

And I know people say stuff like this all the time—that the world stops spinning or their whole life flashes before their eyes or whatever, but I feel all of that and more. The way she's looking at me—smiling like she's not sure if I'm going to say yes, green eyes searching mine—makes me forget for a moment that I don't date. That I'm not exactly "out." That I have to stay focused to win this race and get the scholarship. I forget it all.

"I'd love to."

twenty

Mack asked if we could leave earlier than we'd planned and offered to come pick me up instead of meeting at the concert. Maybe it was the fact that I was still riding the highs of the win at the powder-puff game and our moment in the locker room, but I couldn't even find it in me to say no. I'm actually going to let her see my house. I don't want to hide things from her—part of me, a big, scary part of me, wants to tell her everything.

Since there won't be anyone from school to see me stepping out of my newfound character, I decide to wear a pair of my mom's old overalls, complete with the requisite patches over the knees and bleach stains from twenty years of washes; a cropped black sweatshirt; and a pair of cool red booties that I found on sale at a thrift shop a couple of months ago. My hair is pulled up into two puffs on top of my head, with a few stray curls making their escape near my edges. Normally I'd be annoyed at my hair's inability to follow simple directions, but today I actually kind of really like it.

It's my first time in weeks wearing something I'm totally, completely comfortable in, and I can't take my eyes off myself in the bathroom mirror. I snap a selfie for posterity and laugh when I review it. My smile is goofy, and the framing isn't great, but I don't delete it. I want to remember everything about this night.

My phone vibrates with two texts from G.

> Gabi Marino: **Strategy sesh at my house tonight?**
>
> Gabi Marino: **Mom's baking vegan tres leches :))))**

I hate lying to my best friend even more than I love when Mrs. Marino stress-bakes, but I know how she'd react to this. I reply with some weak excuse about catching up on my homework tonight as Mack parks in front of my house. G's response comes almost immediately.

> Gabi Marino: **Ugh gotta <3 my studious and steadfast bff**
>
> Gabi Marino: **Text me later to talk plans for next week, k?**

When Mack starts to bound up the front walk, I shove my phone into my pocket and shut the door behind me. I meet her outside before she has a chance to come and knock. My stomach swoops a little when I realize she was probably going to do the whole "date" thing: ring the doorbell, greet my grandparents, promise to have me home before curfew.

"Oh, wow." She stops suddenly as I rush out to meet her. I smile, because I honestly can't help it. Not when she's looking at me like I'm something really and truly special. "I don't think I've seen you wear an outfit that makes you look like you're in high school. You look, um—"

"Yeah. Well, you too."

Because, like, wow. She looks amazing.

She looks like she does every day, but with a twist. She's got on a tie-dyed KEEP INDIANA WEIRD T-shirt that she's cut into a crop top underneath her oversized camo jacket, which looks like it came straight from an army-surplus store, and over some black denim high-waist shorts with black fishnets underneath. She also has on a pair of those high-top Chucks with the rainbow platforms that Miley Cyrus designed for Pride forever ago. It may not be much in other places, but here, it makes Mack a beacon—drawing attention and making a statement wherever she goes.

When I get into her car, she turns to me and bites her thumbnail.

"Okay, so I lost all my cognitive skills for a minute back there. What I meant to say is that you look amazing. And you changed your hair."

I reach up to touch my puffs. It feels strange, even to me, to be touching curls instead of a tight ponytail. "Yeah, I thought it might be a little too Princess Leia."

"No way, I think they're awesome!" She looks over at me quickly. "And if Princess Leia were a black girl from central Indiana with amazing taste in music and even better taste in shoes, I have to say, I think the franchise might actually then be worth all the sequels and prequels and reboots."

My cheeks sort of hurt from how hard I'm cheesing.

"Well, you look like you're a pro at this. I feel outmatched by how seriously concert ready you are."

She bites at her lip before replying. "You have a standing invitation to come to any concert with me from here on out. You'll have me beat in no time."

And I don't know if it's a real invitation or not, but God I want it to be.

"Mack," I say, sort of quietly under the sound of Kittredge playing over the speakers. I'm almost surprised when she looks at me, eyes bright. She reaches for the volume and turns it down immediately. "You should know that nobody outside of my best friends knows I, um. Well, that I'm . . ." I motion between us wordlessly.

Mack eases the car onto the highway that leads to downtown Indy. I can't make out her expression. Her face flashes between surprise and disappointment and then settles on a simple nod.

"I get it. I totally get it. This isn't the most tolerant place on Earth, for sure. And I bet it's even harder for you because you're not only queer but you're also black, and I've been reading a lot of Kimberlé Crenshaw, so, like, *intersectionality* and all that definitely makes it harder. I mean, it's not ideal, of course, but your safety—"

"Mack," I interrupt, and she looks at me again. She hasn't rambled like this since we first met, and it scares me a little, makes me think that with one sentence I've undone all the good that's been building between us for the past few weeks. She laughs nervously.

"Sorry, wow, yeah, sorry. I thought I was cured. I figured I'd suddenly stopped putting my foot in my mouth every couple of minutes, but nope. Apparently not."

I don't even think about it, I just reach over and put my hand on hers where it rests on the gear shift. She thinks I'm worried about my safety, but that's not entirely the truth. I don't think I'm at risk of any hate crimes in Campbell or anything, but it would ruin my campaign, just like—judging by her current ranking of nineteenth—it's currently ruining Mack's. It would ruin my chance at Pennington and at saving my grandparents' house, and that is unacceptable. So instead of the truth, I keep asking questions.

"Are you really okay with keeping this between us? I don't want to, um, push you into anything you don't want."

She flips her hand over in mine and squeezes.

"I don't want to be back in the closet, you know? It took a long time to be able to feel confident in my sexuality." I swallow a lump in my throat. If this setup doesn't work for her, I convince myself that it's good to know that now. "But I'm not going to ask you to come out before you're ready if it means you'll be unsafe. I would never do that to you."

And there it is again. *Unsafe.*

I don't correct her. I just nod.

"On another note, I think after you meet the guys, you might not want to see me anymore anyway," she adds after a beat. She smiles at me again. "They're a little hard to handle."

"Yeah, I mean—" I look over at her. "Hold on. Are we meeting the band? Is that what you meant when you said you needed to pick me up early, because you had a surprise?"

I'm not one of those people who gets super weird about meeting celebrities, but I'm just saying, a girl could use a little warning before something like that.

"If that were the surprise, would you still have come with me?" She raises her eyebrows, and I can tell she's aiming for a joke, but something about her tone tells me she's genuinely curious. That she really thinks I might run if she makes a wrong move tonight. Like I—too lanky for my own good, more awkward than not Liz Lighty—am the one who would ever consider walking away from this.

The thought is so wild, so backward, that I almost laugh.

"If there's one thing I can promise you"—I look out the window because suddenly the thought of making eye contact with her as I say this makes me so nervous I feel like puking—"it's that I'll probably follow you wherever you lead me tonight, Amanda McCarthy."

twenty-one

The show is general admission, so even though there's two hours left until the doors open, the line is already beginning to wrap around Old National Centre. But Mack parks at a meter across the street and gestures for me to follow her, past the line and up to a side door. A tall white guy in a black T-shirt and black jeans stands stoic with a cigarette in his hand until Mack walks up. When he smiles and waves us inside, it's so unexpected, I almost take a step back from the sheer force of surprise.

I have so many questions as he leads us into the building and down a set of hallways, I barely even know where to begin.

"Wait. Am I currently on a date with a rock star double agent without my knowledge?"

Mack blushes and reaches down to lace her fingers through mine like it's just totally natural. And for some reason, I'm not even thrown off by it. Like maybe, in this weird alternate universe in which the girl I like might also be an undercover rock star, and I'm totally the type of person who hangs out backstage at concerts, this is the sort of thing we do.

"Not a rock star." She grins. The guy from outside is talking to someone through his walkie-talkie as we wind through the halls. "More like a junior roadie. The band was cool enough to let me tag along on a couple of the Midwest dates last summer."

"You still haven't explained how—" I don't get to finish, because as soon as the security guy pushes open a door to some dank-smelling room, people rush us quicker than I can keep up with.

"Baby coz!" Someone shouts and lifts himself out of his chair. And—

It's Davey Mack, the skinny and scraggly but somehow un-believably star-worthy bassist of Kittredge, doing a convoluted handshake with my date. When they're done, he turns to me with the same goofy smile he had on their cover of Billboard two months ago. "And baby coz's girlfriend. She told us you were a crazy-good musician, but she failed to mention how cute you are."

More people come over to hug us and say their hellos, and I realize just how many people are in the room. The entirety of the band, and maybe even a couple of crew members, are sitting around talking and eating and plucking at their guitars.

"Davey, do you have to flirt with literally every human being on the planet?" Mack groans. I notice she doesn't correct the part about me being her girlfriend, and I try not to think about the but-terflies in my stomach at the thought. "Liz, I'm sorry my cousin doesn't know how to turn off his rock star anymore."

I freeze midway to another handshake. She has got to be kidding me.

"Cousin?" When I look at his curly red hair, it clicks.

She and Davey throw fake punches at each other for a second, and I feel, not for the first time tonight, that I am out of my depth with this girl.

And as they go at it, the rest of the room resets, going back to whatever it was they were doing before we arrived.

"Is this okay?" When she's done fake fighting, Mack leans in and whispers in my ear. I can hear her smile without seeing it. "These guys are a bit . . . much. Todd—the guy you met at the door—taught me all the best ways to shut them up though, if need be. And only two of them involve brute force."

I laugh, something light and airy and altogether un-me sounding. We stay in the green room for about an hour, talking to the band about their tour, all our favorite artists and influences, and our upcoming concert band performance.

"Mands says you're wicked with arrangements, Liz." Davey grabs a pair of drumsticks from a nearby table and drums a distracted beat into a tabletop. "That's dope! You majoring in music performance in the fall?"

"Davey is too curious for his own good, sweetheart."

And that's it. That's the moment when I'm sure my heart stops.

Because there, in faux-leather pants (she's a devout vegan), hot-pink platform boots, and newly dyed jet-black hair slicked straight back, is Teela Conrad. She breezes through the door and turns to Davey. "Not everyone goes to college for music, David." She softens and squeezes my shoulder as she passes before

163

falling into the couch. "I actually majored in Lit at Northwestern."

"Really?" I squeak out.

"Yeah." She smiles at me and she looks so much like the poster I had hanging up with her face on it from sixth through tenth grades that I want to throw up a little. "The best education is one you get in the world. But you can always jam with us when we're in town—if you think you can tolerate being around these guys."

"Or they could jam with you guys on tour this summer." Todd chimes in from his position leaning against the doorframe.

Mack pushes past that, says something about how we'd need all the time we could get to recover after this prom thing is over. Davey says that the offer is always on the table though. And that means for me too. Not that I have plans of going on tour with a hugely successful rock band or anything, but the offer feels huge. Like maybe things don't need to be exactly as I've imagined them. Like maybe in this universe I've suddenly found myself in, things could be different. *I* could be different.

Before long, the band pulls their stuff together and heads toward the stage. Todd offers to escort us to a VIP booth, but we both opt for being in the mix of things down on the floor. And it's the best choice we could have made. The concert is amazing, the energy of the audience palpable. Kittredge fans are die-hard, know-all-the-words, can-mimic-every-guitar-riff types. Mack, obviously, is right there with them—singing at the top of her lungs and grabbing both my hands to dance along with her during the breakdowns.

Kittredge is everything every magazine profile of them has described: electric, charismatic, authentic artists. Davey is the perfect front man to have alongside Teela, his energy onstage practically tangible as he sings and jumps from the drummer's platform down to the stage. He and Teela work so well together, so symbiotically, it's no surprise people think they might be dating.

At one point, when Teela has taken over on lead vocals, she even dedicates a song to "two girls making big noise in Campbell, Indiana" and winks down at the two of us in the crowd. I think I might be dreaming.

"Do you feel that?" Mack shouts over the music. Her hand slips into mine gently, bringing me closer.

"Feel what?" I don't know what she means, not exactly anyway, but I want to stand still and allow whatever is happening to completely wash over me.

She pulls back to smile at me. "Everything."

· ♔ ·

"Why didn't you tell me your cousin was your cousin?" I ask once we step out of Sub Zero on Mass Ave with two milkshakes—one chocolate chip cookie dough and the other white chocolate with dulce de leche.

She takes a sip and looks at me over her eyelashes. "Honestly?"

"Always."

"I didn't want it to seem like I was trying too hard to impress you, you know?"

We're walking in the opposite direction of the venue and the car, and I don't even mind the fact that it is absolutely too cold outside to be drinking these milkshakes. I'm not ready for this night to be over yet. I smile into my straw.

"Well, did you want to impress me?"

"Hell yes!" She laughs, bumping my hip with hers. "But I didn't want you to *think* that I wanted to impress you. See, it was all part of my master plan."

"Oh really?" I lick some whipped cream that's started to slide down the outside of the cup. "Is this where you take all your dates?"

And okay, I'm mostly joking, but part of me feels weirdly jealous of some other girl who may or may not even exist.

I gotta get a hold on myself.

"Nah." She empties her shake faster than should be possible and tosses her cup into a recycling bin. "Just you."

I suddenly feel all weird and fuzzy again.

"I really do love the band, and what they do, and I thought you would love to see it up close. I wanted to share that with you," she adds with a shrug. "I probably would have gotten tickets whether I was related to the colead singer or not. And then I just hoped and prayed that you would agree to come with."

I have so many things I want to ask her, so many things I want to know. I thought I had Mack all figured out, thought that I knew how this night would go and what would happen at school on Monday and how I would find a way to walk away from this after just one quick hit of being with her. But I realize that this isn't going to be so easily navigated. She's not like the SATs or the AP French exam, reliant on formula and structure. Everything is so much more magnificent and complicated than I had initially budgeted for. I can't be distracted by dating right now, but I can't not get to know her better either.

"Well, for what it's worth," I start, finishing my own milkshake and dropping the cup in a bin, "I think that no matter who we were going to see, I would have had a great time with you tonight. I don't think I would have been able to stop myself."

She smiles down at her feet and grabs my hand again. "Is this okay?"

I nod. No one is watching us here. We talk about the show (we both agree that it was amazing) and about the city (we both think it might be a nice place to settle down one day way way wayyyyy after college) and about Sub Zero versus Ritter's Frozen Custard (Mack says Sub Zero wins every time, and I think seriously about calling off the rest of the evening because, honestly, how can I trust a person who doesn't love Ritter's?).

"I liked it when you called me Amanda earlier," she says quietly. "I don't use it at school, because a nickname gives me some distance from everything, you know?" She smiles at me softly. "But with you, it feels like it's supposed to feel. Right."

And okay, wow, my stomach won't stop flipping. Amanda. *My* Amanda. There's something I like about being the only person who calls her that.

She moves toward the edge of the sidewalk. She balances there, one foot in front of the other like she's walking on a tightrope. In more ways than one, it sort of feels like that's what we are. On the edge of something neither of us is bold enough to put a name to.

"One-for-one," I say, following her lead and hopping onto the curb at the corner of Mass Ave as well. "I know what it is about music that keeps me coming back to it. What is it for you?"

"I'm not a writer like my mom was. But musicians are the best storytellers in the world," she says, talking quickly and waving her hands around like she's conducting an erratic choir. "That's the thing that's always drawn me to it—how much *life* is in it, you know? Like Kittredge, for instance. It's chaos, right? The songs all start out big, so much sound you can't begin to process it all, but it comes together in this wild, magical way. The beauty is in the imperfection. The way they control and navigate it.

"Maybe it's like practicing medicine too," she adds. "Like out of something complex and dark, like illness, you'll produce something incredible, like a cure." She looks at me and cocks her head to the side. When she smiles at me, sort of shy and majorly adorable, I realize I've been staring. "Sorry, I get kind of caught up in this stuff."

"Don't apologize for caring," I say, shaking my head. She's silhouetted under a streetlight, and we both stop walking.

"What?" I ask as I catch her looking at me like she can't believe I'm really there. Instead of wilting under the scrutiny like I used to—like I did just a few weeks ago when people would look at me too intensely—I stare back, chin up, just a little defiant. "What is it?"

I'm no longer walking beside her. We step down into the street, and I turn to take her in.

Amanda's not quite as tall as me, but with her platforms we're at eye level when she takes a step toward me. Her eyes search my face, and I think briefly that she might be about to do the thing that I want her to do. My heart beats quicker, and I realize it's not just because I'm excited, it's because I'm afraid. Afraid she might not want what I want, that this may have all been some elaborate ruse, some Rachel-esque campaign strategy to sabotage my run. That I might be bad at this. That this might ruin everything.

"I've never met anyone like you before," she says.

"I'm sort of terrified of you," I respond, swallowing down my fear. I say it now, regardless of what may or may not be happening between us, because I don't want to hold on to it anymore. I'm tired of holding on to everything all the time.

We're so close I can feel a gentle puff of air as she speaks. "I'm scared too."

"I don't," I start quietly and close my eyes for a moment before looking back at her, "usually do stuff like this. With anyone."

"Okay." She nods, her smile widening slowly. "That's okay."

"I might not be good at it." Her hands are gentle as they slide around to the back of my neck.

"Me neither."

"I don't even know what to do with my hands."

"I'm not an expert or anything, but . . ." She reaches down to where my arms are hanging uselessly at my side and puts them on her waist. "Done." She pushes one of my flyaways back behind my ear and cups my cheek with one hand. "Anything else?"

"Well, not exactly, but—"

"Liz."

"Yes?"

"I'm going to kiss you now, okay?"

I nod, probably acquiescing a little too quickly. "Uh-huh."

And it's not perfect, a little eager, our noses bumping momentarily before we settle into an angle that works for both of us. I can feel it everywhere, the way the warmth spreads through my body, the way my heart feels like it's no longer the right size for my chest.

I urge her closer to me, my hands slipping under her jacket and tightening in the fabric of her shirt.

She sort of stumbles into me—because, okay, I apparently don't know my own strength when hormones are involved—and our teeth clash together in a horrible way that is definitely not the makings of a movie-moment kiss.

"Oh my God!" I throw a hand over my mouth. "I am so sorry! This is really not how this was supposed to go."

But Amanda can't hear me, because she's doubled over in laughter. Seriously, full-blown, can't-catch-her-breath, hands-on-her-knees laughing.

"This is truly, truly mortifying. Like, #LightyStrong levels of embarrassment."

She stands up straight again and cocks her head to the side, confused.

"What? You grabbing me like that was kind of the hottest thing anyone has ever done." She shakes her head. "I'm laughing because I think I may have finally found someone as clumsy as me."

"It was only *kind of* the hottest thing?" I smirk. When she looks back up at me, the only expression I can find is relief, followed by excitement.

"No." She shakes her head. "Definitely. It was one hundred percent the hottest thing that's ever happened to me. Ten out of ten, would recommend."

"Kiss her again, sweetie!" someone shouts behind us. When I turn, a lady from the patio of an expensive pizza place is standing with her hands cupped around her mouth to amplify the sound of her voice. "It isn't a kiss without a little teeth!"

Amanda and I both laugh then, and she looks at me with her eyebrows raised—a question I don't have to think about to know the answer to. This time, it's me who kisses her. And it's *everything*. The fireworks, the butterflies—all of it. I get it now. And I can't believe I lived in a world where I didn't get to kiss her whenever I wanted.

"Can I ask you something crazy?" She pulls back, and her hands are still on both my cheeks. She is smiling this heart-stopping smile, and I'm convinced that this is how I die. Kissing Amanda McCarthy on a sidewalk in front of a pizza place. I nod anyway, because honestly, if I'm gonna die, I want to die having said yes to her as many times as I can. "Do you want to be my girlfriend?"

I don't even answer her. I can't. My lips find hers before I can even get the words out. It's hurried and excited and a little messy, but just like a great arrangement of the right song, the beauty is in the imperfections.

WEEK THREE

Necessity is the mother of resistance.

twenty-two

Rachel is a human good-PR tornado from Monday through Wednesday to make sure she remains on top of the prom court food chain. She manages to recruit all the PomBots—even girls who have their own campaigns to worry about, like Quinn and Claire and Lucy—to help her atone by passing out hot-pink miniature footballs that say CONSENT IS SEXY as people walk into school.

"It's for charity, Liz!" Quinn titters as I try to maneuver to first period. She shoves a ball into my hand with surprising strength. "I know what you're thinking: Is it overkill for the Collinses to donate a thousand dollars to the ASPCA after all the ticket sales from the powder-puff already went to them? But the answer is no! We have to do what we can for those poor, defenseless animals."

That most certainly was not what I was thinking. But Quinn deserves points for her boundless positivity.

I mean, really. The messaging doesn't even make sense, even though I do support it. It's just, like, why on a football? And what does it have to do with the charity from the game on Saturday? Rachel Collins never fails to both shock and disappoint.

On Tuesday, her massive banner in the Commons has somehow gotten even bigger but has a different photo. This time, instead of whatever department-store glamour shot she had before, there's an image of her holding three tiny dachshund puppies. Puppies! With no caption!

Wednesday she stops into half the upperclassmen homerooms to drop off collection boxes for a canned food drive she made up called: (Non)Perishables for Prom. So although part of me is still flying high from my date with Amanda over the weekend, Rachel is impossible to ignore. It's like my sympathy bump from the game no longer matters. Because in just three days, Rachel has managed to use her resources to convince everyone that she is somehow a magically good person even though she nearly concussed me not even four days prior.

It's truly amazing.

By Wednesday afternoon, she's back at her number one spot, and I can't help but wonder what it's going to take to make someone like her fall out of favor enough to give me a chance to ever catch up. I'm down to ninth, and the more I yo-yo between getting to the zone where I might make court or not, the worse my stomach hurts when I think about prom. It's a different game when no one thinks you stand a chance, but when all eyes are suddenly on you as some sort of underdog story, things suddenly feel more intense.

I'm trying to remember my deep breathing exercises at my locker when—

"It's been three days, and I can't believe you're still holding out on me, Lighty."

I somehow link up with Jordan at least once each day, and he seems to be able to talk about anything—his family, his college plans, the weird rash he recently got from switching to a new brand of deodorant—anything but his girlfriend, Emme, who the rest of us still haven't seen or heard from in weeks. The rumors about her are still swirling, though, but despite my curiosity, I refuse to ask what happened.

"Looking good, Lighty!" Some guy with shaggy blond hair and a scraggly White Jesus beard that I've never spoken to but had one class with sophomore year walks by and holds his hand up for a high five. It's so fast, I bring my hand up to his before I even know what's happening. "Woo!"

I look at his backpack as he walks away like that was a totally normal thing to do. A button with my face is right next to his Green Day patch.

I laugh, a little nervous. Like I said, it doesn't stop being weird.

"You have to tell your coach to give you more breaks during practice. I think the lack of proper oxygen intake is affecting your brain," I say, turning back to Jordan and dropping my AP Lit textbook into my backpack. This is my one day of the week free from prom duties, and I can't wait to get to band rehearsal. A few prom-free hours is going to do my heart good, I can feel it.

Gabi has gone into full-blown Campaign Monster-Manager—*Monsterger*—mode. She insists on upping our strategy, wants me to be seen with Jordan more often, and had additional flyers with my face all over them plastered everywhere. As if I'm not already swamped with all my volunteer events, she wants me to give a speech at the next student council meeting stating my qualifications for queen, and to broker peace between the Manga Club and the Anime Club so that I can get their collective endorsement.

I'm willing to do a lot for this race, but it's going to take some definite mental fortitude to make that last one work.

I smirk at Jordan and start down the hallway.

"The minute I have anything interesting to share, you'll be the . . . Well, you'll be the last to know."

The final bell rang five minutes ago, which means the halls are still full of people running to the buses and the parking lot.

"You wound me!" He clutches his chest and walks backward next to me. It never stops making me nervous when he does that. Jordan lowers his voice as we round a corner. "You weren't going to tell me that you went on a hot date this weekend?"

"Jordan!" I grab his arm and pull him with me into the alcove where the vending machines sit. It's a pretty tight fit, but I find enough room to pull my fist back and punch him in his bicep. "What do you know?"

"Whew, girl, who knew you had such a strong right hook?" He rubs the spot on his arm like I really injured him. "Nobody knows anything, okay? Your girl just posted a snippet from the Kittredge concert on CC, and my Lighty Senses told me you wouldn't miss a chance to see that Teela chick."

"Sorry for punching you," I say as I reach out to rub his arm where I hit him. "It was a reflex."

"Some reflex." He grimaces. "But who cares? Tell me about Molly Ringwald."

"Jordan."

"Sorry, Jessica Rabbit."

"Jordan."

"My bad, Kim Possible."

"Jordan!"

He holds up his hands with a laugh. "Okay, I'm being serious now. Please don't punch me again."

"You can't tell anyone." I don't want to hold this like some secret shame anymore, and something in me still trusts Jordan, especially after the past couple of weeks. So I tell him everything. About the concert, the agreement to keep whatever is happening between us super under the radar, all of it.

Jordan shakes my shoulders. "Don't look so terrified! A girlfriend is not the worst thing that could have happened to you. Enjoy it! Make out with her some more. Go to prom. Whatever." He wraps an arm around me, and I lean into his frame. "Whatever you do, don't let this place take it away from you. Campbell ruins good people."

His voice is sad, sadder than I've ever heard before. I wonder if he's thinking about Emme, about whatever it is that drove her out of Campbell. But her life has always seemed so flawless, so shiny to me, I can't imagine what could have happened. When I pull away to look at him, his face has rebounded to the Jordan Jennings everyone expects. Bright, confident, collected.

"But, we gotta get you to practice!" He shakes his body a little, like he needs to wake up. "Come on."

We duck out of the alcove and almost run right into Cruella the Pill herself, flanked by her trusty sidekick, Claire.

"Jordan, we missed you at lunch today." Rachel's voice is dripping with a sugary sweetness that I know well as she looks between the two of us. It's the voice she uses when she knows she's got you where she wants you. "It's funny we should run into you. I finally heard from Emme a few minutes ago.

"Yeah, she said she misses the love of her life and wishes she were with him." She clicks her tongue. "It would be such a shame if she knew you were ducking into dark corners with the likes of the help while she was away."

"Watch it, Rachel," he says, voice low.

Rachel narrows her eyes.

"You don't want to get mixed up with her, Jordan. There'll be no saving your reputation when she's finished with you," she says. As she walks away, Jordan and I look at each other. He finally deflates as she rounds the corner.

"God, she gets under my skin." He leans back against a locker with a thud and breathes out. "Always has. Her *and* her idiot boyfriend."

I lean on the lockers too and bump his shoulder with mine. For all his posturing and prom kingliness, Jordan is still so much like that kid I used to know. He's still soft in all the places that this school, this town has tried to make rough.

"I just don't get it. I thought she was just like that with me because I'm, you know, a pretty easy target," I say. "But you're untouchable. And Emme is one of her best friends. What is her deal?"

"I keep trying to tell you that it's not that simple, Lighty." He rubs his brow with the back of his hand. He looks at me seriously. "There are only two people I've ever trusted in this school, and one of them might not ever come back."

I'm silent for a second as I take him in.

"I wish more people like you won prom queen. Then Rachel wouldn't get to live out this little fairy tale where she rules the kingdom and the rest of us are her little serfs," he adds. I shake my head at him with a curious look. He rolls his eyes. "I'm an athlete, Lighty, not a slacker. I only slept through, like, ten minutes of the feudalism unit in AP World History—max."

As surprised as I am by Jordan's knowledge of the class system in medieval Europe, he has a point. This whole race is set up to mimic some twisted fairy tale. The queen is supposed to be the best among us: the smartest, the most beautiful, the worthiest. But the people who win are rarely the people who deserve it. Like with any monarchy, they're just the closest to the top. You don't earn queen; you inherit it.

People like Rachel don't have to do much at all as far as campaigning. They can run with the same tired strategies and tactics year after year and still eke out wins. As for the rest of us, we can do everything right—go above and beyond, maybe even make court—but we never, ever win. It's practically an unspoken law of nature. So even though I'm focusing my tactics on getting the votes of the outliers of Campbell's student body, it's not moving the needle enough.

"You know what? Forget her fairy tale." I realize then what Gabi—and even Britt, with her threats of physical violence against Rachel's person—keep failing to recognize in our campaign strategy. We don't need posters and fliers and speeches. That's for people like the PomBots. We may never have whatever it is that makes people like Rachel feel like they own everything on God's green earth, but we have something else. We're smarter, scrappier.

We don't have to play dirty; we just have to play different.

"Jordan, I need a little time to work out an idea"—I look down at my phone to check the clock—"but when I'm ready, if I asked you to help me make sure that no one like Rachel wins this year, would you?"

"You know what?" His nose crinkles up as he smiles. "I thought you'd never ask."

twenty-three

I know that for most people, walking down the hallway with someone they like is not a big deal. I know it's a totally normal, healthy part of growing up. It's something that people write songs and diary entries and Campbell Confidential posts about. It's supposed to be easy.

Amanda and I could just be friends, friendly competitors, gently bumping into each other's shoulders as we walk down the hallway and toward the parking lot. If anyone saw us, this wouldn't be Campbell Confidential worthy—it wouldn't even be conversation worthy. So I try not to think about the way her knuckles are brushing mine and the way my entire body feels a little electric at the fact that my girlfriend—my *girlfriend*—is right here. That she's real. That, even if this is not the way I want this to be, it is happening.

"You want me to give you a ride home?" she asks as we approach my locker. We had a check-in meeting with Madame Simoné tonight given that the end of the race is quickly approaching. She reminded us that crunch time is upon us and that everything—our scores, our scholarships, our ability to make court—hinges on what happens in the next couple of weeks. The thought, as usual, made my stomach ache.

But I nod at Amanda, shoving those feelings somewhere I can't reach.

"Cool." Her smile is shy. "Is it too much too soon to say that I want to be alone with you again?"

She lowers her voice a little and bites her thumb. "This low-key thing is harder than I thought it would be, especially when I already know what it's like to kiss you."

And whoa. If I wasn't already feeling off-kilter, that just did it.

We haven't had time to be alone together since the concert on Sunday, and I'd be lying if I hadn't been thinking the same exact thing. But we barely even see each other outside of class. I've spent nearly all my time bouncing between rehearsal and homework and my job and prom events, and the only time we get to talk is via text. We write back and forth in all my open windows of time. Most nights that's usually right before my head hits the pillow, and only for a few minutes, but they're easily becoming the best minutes of my day.

With no hesitation, I pull out my phone to fire off a text to Gabi and let her know that I can't make it to our scheduled strategy session tonight. That I'm doing some opposition research of my own instead. Which isn't, you know, a complete lie.

Her response comes quickly.

Gabi Marino: **We don't have time for you to change plans like this** 🌴

Gabi Marino: **But we WILL talk tomorrow! I expect a full report at lunch!**

I see Jordan standing near the door to the parking lot. He's out of earshot, talking to Jaxon and Harry, but he catches my eye with a questioning, raised eyebrow. His look tells me to throw bros before hoes out the window and just go for it. Or, that's what I intuit from it anyway.

When I wave him off, he grins and does this weird body-roll thing that is definitely also a sign for something, but I'd rather not even think about that right now. I gesture for him to stop, because Jaxon Price is literally standing right there and even though he's not the brightest crayon in the box, I don't want him to put two and two together. But I also laugh, because Jordan is a hilarious, overgrown child.

Amanda has an amused expression when I finally answer her.

"Yeah, yes, sorry. Er, um, I'd like that." Jordan's shimmying like Shakira in my peripheral vision, and I shake my head, attempting to clear the image from my recent memory. I grab her hand without thinking and pull her in the direction of the parking lot. "Oh my God, can we just go? Let's just go."

When we step outside, I reluctantly let go of her hand. The parking lot is mostly empty by the time we reach it, but I feel like it's better not to chance it. Still though, our knuckles brush as we walk, and while neither of us says anything, the moment is heavy with something unnamable.

Amanda drives the long route to my house, a way that takes us down a road lined on both sides by cornfields. Granny thinks I'm working late at Melody Music, so I have some time to kill before I need to be back home. I tell Amanda to pull over into the off-road dirt path between a line of trees and a field that will be tall with stalks of corn in a few months. It's a tight squeeze, but it's private— no streetlights, no prying eyes of classmates—so it's perfect.

The sound of Kittredge fills the car as she kills the engine.

"I've always wanted to come out here, but I've never really had a reason to," I say, not nervous exactly, but definitely trying to talk myself away from the way my stomach is Simone Biles–style front-flipping at the thought of being alone with Amanda. I look out at the way the sun is disappearing behind the farthest edge of the field and practically setting the whole thing fire, and I am reminded that there are some things in this town that will never cease to take my breath away.

"One-for-one?" she asks, and I nod.

"Do you actually like running for prom queen?" she says, and I have to admit I'm a little surprised. I wasn't expecting that. "I thought this experience was going to be one thing—one big, very cool thing—and it's actually just ridiculously stressful." She looks as me and winces. "Is that horrible?"

"No," I start. "You have no idea how completely un-horrible that is."

Her fingers slip between mine in my lap, and my heart does that thing it always does around her now. Like it can't decide

186

whether or not to expand five sizes in my chest or, you know, bust out completely.

"You're the best part about all of it." She looks down at where our hands are linked. "I would deal with the long hours and the bad volunteer gigs and the diatribes by Madame Simoné all over again if it meant we would end up here."

I stop breathing. I almost don't know how to be with her like this, completely alone, completely vulnerable. I just know that I want to be. I just know that there's nowhere else I'd rather be, in fact, than in this car with Amanda McCarthy as she leans forward and holds my face in her hands. I close my eyes, because it's almost too much, looking at her and feeling her breath on my lips and smelling her shampoo as her hair brushes my cheeks.

Since we're covered by the confined space and the near-darkness of the early evening light, it's the only place me and Amanda have ever been allowed to be this close. And, God, are we close right now. But when her lips barely graze mine, every thought gives way to the very real sensation of this *thing*—of how much I needed this. Having her like this is every bit as great as I remember, probably better since we don't have an audience.

I look at her as she pulls back, and I know my eyes must be just as wide as hers. She waits—always waiting for me to tell her what I want—until I nod once, maybe a little frantic, before her lips meet mine again. And it's urgent, more urgent than it was the night of the concert.

When I open my mouth, everything happens so fast—the way I can feel her everywhere, the way my hands steady instead of shake where they tangle in her hair because I've maybe

187

never felt so grounded before, so rooted in a moment.

"I want," she sighs as she pulls back slightly. She's leaning her forehead against mine. I think about kissing every one of the freckles that are sprinkled across her nose. "I want so much with you."

That we can't have. She won't say it, but I know she's thinking it.

"Come to prom with me," I blurt out as I break away from her. I can feel the rest of my word vomit before I even open my mouth. "Sorry, I know people do promposals and stuff, and I know things are weird with us competing against each other and the fact that it's technically against the rules, and nothing is how it should be really, but—"

"Don't say sorry for any of that." She shakes her head and gives me a quick peck on the cheek before easing herself back into her seat. I hadn't even realized that she'd practically been in my lap. "I'd love to go to prom with you, Liz. We deserve good things too. No matter how we have to get them."

I nod, sort of stunned silent by it all. I didn't imagine that we'd be here when Amanda offered to drive me home, but I'm so glad we are.

"Can I tell you something?" she asks as she leans back against the headrest and sighs.

"You can tell me anything."

"I don't want to take you home yet," she whispers. "I wish we never had to leave this car."

"Okay." *We deserve good things too,* I remind myself as I look at the clock. I have some time. *No matter how we have to get them.* "Then let's stay in it for as long as we can."

twenty-four

"Liz, since you skipped our strategy session last night, maybe you don't know that Rachel is *still* at number one." Gabi taps her fingernails against the tabletop. It's lunchtime, but she hasn't touched her plate all period. "And you're stuck at number nine. It's time to do something drastic."

I was feeling good, enjoying pizza day in the cafeteria, a little high on last night and my amazing girlfriend and being able to think about something other than prom, until this very moment.

Stone sighs. "Perhaps now is the time we let Mother Universe lead us in the direction—"

"Not now, Stone!" Gabi snaps.

"Whoa," I start. I look between Stone and Gabi and wonder what, exactly, is going on with my best friend. She never snaps at Stone. No one does. Stone's, like, not capable of reciprocating anger. It's like yelling at a newborn kitten. You just don't do it. "G, relax. Maybe we need to take a break from prom talk today. I think the whole crew is a little burned out."

It's like she doesn't even hear me. She just shakes her head.

"We've run the numbers, and the fact is that you poll better when you're seen with Jordan," she says. "So you need to leverage that relationship."

"Leverage . . ."

"Yes, leverage. Be seen with him. Maybe make it look more than friendly." She runs a hand through her hair in an attempt to smooth down her flyaways. Gabi Marino never has flyaways. "He had a huge crush on you in middle school." She waves a hand around. "Rekindle that."

I'm flustered and more than a little shell-shocked. I mean, there's so much wrong with what she's saying that I don't even know where to start. On what planet did Jordan Jennings ever have a crush on me? And why on earth would Gabi ever think I could pretend to date him—when we just now got back on speaking terms—for potential *votes*? I want to do what it takes, but there has to be a line somewhere. There's a bitter taste in my mouth, literally, and I'm convinced she's officially lost it. The last of her good sense, gone.

"You literally called him a Great Value Odell Beckham Jr. the other day—you can't even stand Jordan!" I shake my head and laugh, but it's nervous, short. "I can take wearing these *Stepford Wives* clothes and brokering peace between the manga and anime factions or whatever, but I have to draw the line at stealing someone's boyfriend!"

"Stealing someone's boyfriend?" I look up and see a smiling Amanda standing over the table. She looks so cute in her yellow jumpsuit and pigtails that I almost forget that she isn't even in this lunch period. What is she doing here? "Do I have something to be worried about?"

Oh my God. Oh my God. Oh my God. My brain is full-on malfunctioning. My mouth doesn't move, and my palms start getting sweaty. Gabi is staring at her like she wants to rip her face off with her bare hands, and Britt and Stone are just wordlessly watching the standoff. I wish I could turn to dust right here and now.

"You shouldn't be here," I blurt out. Her face falls immediately, and I realize what I've said and how it sounds. I try to backtrack. "Sorry, what I mean is—"

"What she means is you should go back to wherever you came from." Gabi folds her hands under her chin and cocks her head to the side.

"Okay, Marino. Let's dial it back a little, huh?" Britt says.

Whatever smile had been on Amanda's face before, whatever joy or fondness or excitement she'd had when she walked up to the table, is officially gone now. My heart is practically pressing against my ribcage, the way it's beating. This isn't how I wanted her to meet my friends. This isn't how any of this is supposed to go.

Gabi the Guard Dog is off her leash, and I know she needs to be corralled. But I don't know how to do it. I look to my left, and a freshman is eyeing the situation curiously. She doesn't have a phone in her hand, not yet anyway, and I take that as my cue to step in before this becomes a scene.

"I'm just curious about what this one's intentions could

possibly be with my best friend." Gabi's tone sounds so aggressive that I cringe.

"Gabi, relax," I say quietly. This can't go any further. I turn to Amanda and try to apologize with my eyes. "Amanda, maybe we can catch up later? After school?"

I hope beyond hope that she understands what I'm really saying. *I'm so sorry about my friend, who I haven't told about our relationship yet and probably never will. Can we go back to our bubble now? Where it's safe and chill and there's no one gawking at us like zoo animals?*

But her answer tells me everything I need to know. It sounds so harsh coming out of her mouth that I know I've messed up. Bad.

"Sure, Liz. *Later*."

· ♛ ·

I text my coworker, Victor, to see if he can cover my shift the minute I step out of school.

> Victor Ferrer: **Of course mama!**

> Victor Ferrer: **You good?**

I thank him for covering my shift but don't answer his second question. I'm not good yet. Not really, but hopefully I will be soon.

I look around the parking lot to see if I can spot Amanda's Jeep, but it's nowhere to be found. I practically flatten three different freshmen on my way to the bike rack, I'm moving so fast. I can't remember the last time I felt so guilty. Gabi really stepped out of line today, but so did I. I should have been a better girlfriend, a better *person*, and instead I just froze.

I owe her an apology at least. I owe her . . . a lot.

"Liz!" I hear Gabi before I see her, and I cringe inwardly. I've never had that reaction to her before, but then again, a lot of things have been different lately. "Where are you going?"

"Gabi, I seriously don't want to talk right now." I unlock my bike and shove the key back into my pocket.

"I can tell. You rudely ignored all my texts during sixth period!"

"Are you seriously complaining that I didn't respond to your texts today? After that scene you made in the cafeteria, you expect *me* to apologize to *you*?"

I would say that I can't believe her nerve. But I absolutely can.

"Elizabeth Audre Lighty, are you *drunk*?" She steps closer to me and lowers her voice. "What was your plan, huh? You just thought you were going to get all cozy with the new girl and no one was going to notice? It's not rocket science, Liz. It's only a matter of time before people figure it out."

Her face is pink, and I know it's a mixture of rage and embarrassment that's fighting for real estate inside her. I know because I feel it too.

"It's not . . . It doesn't matter what people—"

"It does matter!" She's so suddenly so loud that I think even she is surprised by the volume. Her eyes go a little wide at the sound, and she pinches the bridge of her nose. She's quiet again when she speaks. "Liz, it *does* matter here. You know that. I just want— I just want what's best for you."

I don't want to fight with my best friend. I really don't. All this has had the two of us going back and forth for weeks, and I am tired of it. Gabi has always been there for me, even when her methods are questionable, so I want to believe her. But, I definitely don't have to like it.

"You can't snap on her like that, G. I don't care what your reasons are."

And I didn't confirm anything, not really. But there it is. My line in the sand. Gabi has to know that even if she doesn't agree with me, she can't come for Amanda like that again. She is off-limits.

"Fine. Are you at least coming to Jordan's party tomorrow night?" She puts her hands on her hips and stares me down. "You need to be there, Liz. Everyone is going to be there. If you care at all about this campaign—"

"Yes! Okay? I'll be there. I'll do it." I click the lock shut around the frame of my bike and hop onto the seat. "Is that it? I'm late."

Instead of answering, she just steps aside and waves an arm out in front of her like, *Be my guest.*

· ♛ ·

I'm grateful for the years I've spent biking everywhere in this town to build up my endurance, because I ride to Amanda's neighborhood in ten minutes flat. I don't know which house is hers, but I have a vague idea because the Marinos live in the neighborhood. G had a conniption the first time she saw Amanda's Jeep parked in the McCarthy's driveway a few weeks ago and called me immediately afterward.

It doesn't take more than riding around two blocks in The Oaks before I find it. Amanda's house isn't as obnoxiously big as some of the others in the neighborhood, but it's still at least two of mine stacked on top of each other.

I drop my bike on the driveway behind a new-looking black Jeep Wrangler and run to the front door. I don't want to waste any time. I ring the doorbell once, and not even fifteen seconds later, the door is opening to reveal a smiling man in a black Joy Division T-shirt, a pair of ratty jeans, and bare feet.

I guess I expected Mr. McCarthy to also have red hair and freckles, but he doesn't. He has Timothée Chalamet brown, curly hair that is teetering on the border of too long.

"Hi, Mr. McC—"

He pulls me into a hug before I even get the words out.

"You must be Liz!" He leans back to look at me and wags his finger. "I did not think I would be meeting you today, but I am so glad you're here! I've been trying to get Mandy to invite you over for dinner ever since she told me about this Very Important Girl that she met while running for prom. She hasn't talked about anything else over a meal in days—"

"Dad!" Amanda shrieks from the staircase, and rushes to the door. She grabs my hand and urges me inside while laying into her dad just a little bit. "Wow, this is much more mortifying than I thought it would be, and that's after knowing you for seventeen years. And you say I have a big mouth!"

"Sorry, daughter of mine!" He laughs as Amanda walks us up the stairs and into her room.

She shuts the door behind us and flops down onto her bed. I stand near the door and don't move. I'm not sure where I would go, even if I were feeling comfortable enough to move. I mean, Amanda's room is . . . a mess.

It's clear that she hasn't unpacked everything by the boxes still stacked against her walls, but there is stuff all over the floor. Old issues of *Ms.* magazine and dirty clothes and skateboard decks without wheels. There's a desk that's covered in stacks of records, and the only thing that looks completely set up is the drum kit in the corner.

"I wasn't really expecting company." She looks at me looking at her room. She bites her thumbnail. "This isn't exactly how I wanted you to be in here for the first time."

"Yeah." I slide my hands into the pockets of the plaid chinos I'm wearing. "What did you imagine it would be like?"

She smirks. "Well, for one, I imagined more kissing."

Maybe she hasn't forgiven me for what went down today, but I'm taking that as a good sign.

"About lunch today. That was screwed up six ways to Sunday. I just panicked because I haven't told them yet and then Gabi was going feral and I just . . . I'm sorry. I was a terrible girlfriend, and it only took me five days."

"Was?" she asks. She stands up and crosses the room to me. "Girlfriend in past tense?"

I swallow hard because she's right in front of me and for whatever reason, my brain just doesn't seem to function around this girl.

"Not past tense." I shake my head. "I mean, not if you don't want it to be past tense because I was an idiot."

"Okay. Not past tense then." She stops for a second to think. "I know you said we were keeping things quiet, but I thought at least your best friends . . ."

I shake my head. Of course she thought I would have told my

best friends. That's what I should have done, but I didn't. I haven't.

"Are we going to be okay?" I ask instead of offering an explanation.

"I'm just glad you're here. I'm glad you said sorry. It was only four hours of radio silence and I already missed you."

And then we're kissing. And it feels better than I remember. When you thought you might never have something again, when it comes back to you, it's somehow a hundred times better than you remember. She pulls away and looks up at me.

"I came to tell you that I quit. Today at lunch, I had just come from meeting with Madame Simoné. After last night I realized there was no point for me to stay in the race." She smiles, and her eyes do that sparkling thing and my stomach flips. "I got what I came for."

She got what she came for. Me. I am that thing. And I know this is the moment to tell her about the scholarship, the real reason I'm running, the real reason people can't know about us—all of it. But I don't want to ruin it. So I just smile back and wrap my arms tighter around her neck.

"Me too," I say. And it almost doesn't feel like a lie.

twenty-five

Standing outside Jordan's house reminds me that Indiana rich is a different kind of rich. It's not like New York wealth with fancy penthouses on Park Avenue, or LA rich with garages full of luxury SUVs and sprawling ranch houses in Hollywood Hills. Indiana rich is a little quieter but no less impressive to me.

"Just how much money do retired NFL players bring in these days?" I mumble and pull at the hem of the little black dress that Gabi masterfully outfitted me in this evening. She designed it herself and has been waiting for an opportunity to get me to model it. It's a simple A-line with pockets, a deep V, and a red-and-black faux flannel at the waist. Unlike the clothes she practically banned me from wearing to school, it turns out something I'd actually want to wear is, for once, prom-queen worthy. "I mean honestly. Is this Campbell County or *Keeping Up with the Kardashians*?"

Jordan's front porch is massive, and his front door is flanked by two large white pillars. They don't even have neighbors directly on either side of them; the neighborhood is designed to give everyone plenty of space and privacy between their lots.

"Stop pulling at your clothes!" Gabi swats my hand away and ignores my comments about the house. "You look great. I've done some of my best work on you."

She rings the doorbell and shakes her hair so it falls perfectly even on both sides of her black off-the-shoulder blouse. Her outfit and the way her hair is parted straight down the middle make her look like a '70s French movie star. She straightens her spine and pushes a hand against my shoulder to get me to do the same.

"And walk tall. We need people to think you're queen material, remember?" She smacks her lips together once to make sure her bright red Fenty lip paint is evenly distributed.

I roll my eyes but decide to follow her instructions. I pull my shoulders back so I stand at my full height and run a hand through my hair to shake out my curls a little. I never wear it down, but after a lot of cajoling from G and a frankly ungodly amount of water, leave-in conditioner, Eco Styler gel, and Cantu curl-defining cream, here I am. And to my surprise, it doesn't look half bad. It's full, with all my natural curls on display, but it still looks styled instead of like I lost control of it. It's . . . nice.

"I can't believe you seriously haven't considered a future in politics."

"I've considered everything." She smiles. "Don't count it out as a possibility: The first White House chief of staff with her own haute couture collection at fashion week? Sounds totally doable."

I'm still laughing as Jordan opens the door. He's beaming, and little beads of sweat are dotting his forehead.

"Welcome, ladies!"

I blink when I realize he's completely shirtless. And honestly? Forget laughing. I can barely remember how to breathe. I mean, seriously. How is it fair that God gave one person that many freaking abs?

"Jordan." Gabi hikes her purse up on her shoulder and feigns complete disinterest in the guy in front of her. But I know it's totally fake when her voice sort of hitches as she says his name. Like I said, he's unfairly attractive. "Are you going to let us in or are you planning on doing a striptease in the doorway all night?"

He smiles even wider and steps aside, motioning us in. "Well, by all means, please enter my humble abode."

I know he's being ironic by calling the place humble, because Jordan's house is anything *but*. It seriously looks like royalty lives here. And I guess that's because it's not entirely untrue—royalty sort of does live here.

As soon as we step into the foyer, there's an enormous spiral staircase that leads to the second floor. And on the wall directly to our left, there's a huge painting of the entire Jennings family. His mom and her long, platinum blond hair. His dad, the only black guy besides his oldest son to ever win prom king in Campbell, whose huge linebacker form is just as impressive now as it was when he played in the Super Bowl. And Jordan beside his older brother, Jalen, back when their dark curls were grown out long. It's the picture of a flaw-free family.

When we step into the kitchen, Jordan grabs me a bottle of

water off the cluttered center island and shoves it into my hand. When I hold it up in question, he shrugs.

"You're not getting all loosey-goosey on my watch, Lighty. Consider this my expert advice to you: Keep your head clear at the pre-prom party. I've seen many lose their dignity and shame at this yearly bash."

I laugh, and G sighs like she's fed up with Jordan already.

"Oh!" Gabi spots Britt and Stone in the backyard and waves at them before turning back to me. She lowers her voice so Jordan can't hear. "Don't mess this up, Liz. Remember what I said about strategy." She jerks her head at Jordan before disappearing to catch up with our other friends.

"What was that about?" he asks, his eyes following Gabi out onto the lanai. (I barely even know that word but there's no other way to describe the massively beautiful situation Jordan's family has in lieu of a regular backyard and porch.)

I change the subject. "What's the shirtless thing about? You don't have to convince us you're training to be the light-skin Idris Elba. We believe you."

"For your information, I took it off to prove to Jaxon that I could eat more hot wings than he could in three minutes. I might be a cliché, but I refuse to get buffalo sauce all over my brand new Yeezy hoodie."

"You really are a caricature of a high school jock from a bad '80s movie sometimes, you know?"

"Oh yeah? Well, if I'm the stereotypical jock, then that makes you our reluctant protagonist, the hot nerd with a heart of gold." My face heats, but he either doesn't notice or doesn't care. He grins and tilts his head to gesture behind me. "And there goes the love interest with the boom box, ready to stand in your front yard."

I cut my eyes out to the patio, where Amanda is standing near the swimming pool. Or, I would be looking at Amanda, I guess, if I wasn't so distracted by who she's talking to. Some girl I don't recognize (with ridiculously long, glossy brown hair) is laughing at something Amanda said and placing a hand on her wrist. My stomach starts to hurt a little.

"Who is that?" I ask.

Jordan looks back outside like he forgot who we were talking about already.

"Oh, um. Not sure. A lot of people are here from Park Meade. Word spread fast on Confidential today, so we've got a big crowd." Someone calls to him from outside, and he smiles at me quickly. "You gonna be good, Lighty? I know this isn't your scene."

There are so many people in the house and outside, my skin feels like it's a little too tight for my body. I know how important this party is, how crucial it is to put in the work tonight to get more people on my side, but the thought physically pains me. Suddenly, the same old anxieties that I thought I'd wrestled into submission bubble up. What if I say the wrong thing to one of Jordan's teammates and make a fool out of myself? What if any misstep I make is caught on Campbell Confidential for everyone to see?

But I have to be good—I have to be on—if I want to make this work. Anything for Pennington.

I nod, and he ruffles the top of my hair before taking off, yelling at Harry Donato to get the hell away from his mom's hand-painted Grecian vase.

"Liz, come outside!" G waves at me from her spot on the deck.

When I step outside, Amanda's eyes catch mine, and she offers me a quick, thin smile before turning her attention back to the girl with the perfect hair.

The rational part of my brain tells me that Amanda is doing exactly what we agreed to do—keep it cool and casual in public. But the other part of my brain, the part that isn't governed by logic and reason, is a little annoyed. I guess I expected her to act happier to see me, and it stings that she doesn't.

"Lighty!" I turn, and Jaxon Price has his hands cupped around his mouth, shouting for me. "Come over here a second!"

I look around, half-convinced there's another Lighty in the building, before finding my way over to him. He's sitting around the firepit with some people who I only know because they're so hard to ignore—real joiners, the lot of them. The type of people who I would've avoided at all costs three weeks ago.

"Lighty the Mighty, you gotta tell these fools about that sick touchdown you made at the powder-puff game!" Jaxon takes a sip from his red plastic cup and points it at me. "I swear to God, if we'd known what those legs could do, I would have tried to recruit her for the team a long time ago."

Everyone laughs a little, and my shoulders come down from where they've been all tensed up. One of the girls from the cheerleading squad moves over to make room for me in one of the oversized wicker chairs. So far, this isn't so hard.

"I rewatched the whole thing on Campbell Confidential like a million times! It was amazing." The girl nods. "And when Jordan carried you off the field after that hit? Ohmygosh, so romantic."

Wait. Romantic?

"Oh, no. Me and Jordan are just—"

"Lighty, seriously, where did that talent come from? You are a BEAST." Jaxon starts pumping his fist in the air. "Ligh-ty Strong! Ligh-ty Strong!"

The sound of it reverberates around the space outside, and suddenly other people are joining in. I'm shocked that I don't immediately ask the universe to create a black hole in the middle of this patio and swallow me whole. I'm sort of . . . liking it? Jaxon's tone is so genuine, his smile and energy so excitable, I know this isn't at my expense. We're all laughing together, and I'm not feeling like the butt of some stupid cosmic joke.

The sound of my name spilling from so many mouths, knowing that the girl I more-than-like might be watching me, fills me with something like confidence. I feel like a different person. I figure Amanda will come over any second now—this is too good for her to miss.

I spot the PomBots playing cornhole in the yard at the same time Rachel sees me. Her glare is enough to cut through glass, but even that doesn't bother me.

Jordan walks over and perches himself on the arm of the chair I'm sharing. He starts talking about how we used to battle for first and second chair in middle school and how, even then, I was relentless. I never let him get away with anything.

"Admit it, Lighty! You may be quiet, but you're lethal." He laughs.

"Silent but deadly!" Jaxon chimes in, and we all laugh because apparently fart jokes never stop being funny, no matter how old you get.

I sit around the fire with them, talking about nothing and everything, and as the night settles in around us, I don't even realize how much time has passed. For the first time in, well, maybe ever, I'm feeling something better than being cool—I feel like I *fit*. I'm smiling what I'm sure is a cheesy, self-satisfied smile, and the tightness that usually takes up residence in my chest slowly fades.

My face isn't pressed to the glass, wondering what's going on inside with all my classmates. I'm right here, right in the center of it all. I'm not just The Black Girl or The Girl with the Dead Mother or The Poor Girl. I'm Liz Lighty, and I'm all of that, but suddenly, that doesn't seem like such a bad thing.

I'm cracking up at some story Jordan is telling about how he and Jaxon accidentally switched cleats at practice one time (which absolutely should not be as funny as it is), when I see Amanda out of the corner of my eye. Amanda, *my Amanda*, and the random girl with the hair—who probably, by the way, doesn't even *belong* at this party—head inside the house, laughing at something between the two of them.

When I look down at my phone, I realize it's well past eleven. I'm suddenly indignant that she still hasn't said a single word to me. I asked her to not act like we're girlfriends in public, but I didn't ask her to pretend I don't even exist. Every good feeling I was collecting immediately evaporates and is replaced by the burn and bitterness that accompanies rejection. It's like every bit of rationale for staying away from her all night disappears, and all I can think to do is follow them. I'm out of my seat and halfway there when—

"Where are you going?" Suddenly Gabi's hand is tight around my wrist, holding me in place. I'd lost track of her before, but now

I wonder how I ever could have lost her. Her presence in front of me is so *big*. "You need to keep mingling. I'm going to try and get the theater troupe president to endorse you. You could have the show choir kids tied up by the end of the night if you sweet-talk Chrissy Shelley about getting into AMDA."

"You can do that, G. But I'm not interested, okay?" Gabi is a force of nature, but she's been wrong more times over the course of this campaign than I can count. The clothes, the tricks, using people as just a means to an end—it's all messed up. It makes me think of Amanda, the only person at this party I really want to talk to right now but have been avoiding to toe the line. I pull my arm out of her grip calmly but firmly. "I have something else I need to do right now."

· ♔ ·

When I make my way into the kitchen, I see Amanda and Perfect Hair near the fridge, their heads close together like they're sharing a secret. I get this feeling in my gut like I've eaten something expired, like I can't trust it to just calm down and stay settled.

"Liz!" Amanda waves me over. It's the first time all night she's said my name. "Come here really quick. You have to meet Kam."

Amanda reaches for my hand as I approach, and I shove it into my pocket quickly. I try not to look at her face as it falls. I can feel disappointment radiating off her, and I hate myself for it. I have to be realistic. No matter how badly I wanted her to talk to me, being physical is too risky. There are too many eyes around. Too many people waiting for something juicy to happen that they can put on

Campbell Confidential, consequences to the people involved be damned.

"I wanted to introduce you to Kam. She's from Park Meade." Perfect Hair—Kam—holds out her hand for me to shake. And damn my Midwestern manners, I take it even though I don't want to. "Kam, this is my—"

"Hi, Kam, I'm sorry. Will you give the two of us a second?" I cut in before Amanda can finish her sentence. I'm suddenly even angrier in a way I don't think I've ever been angry before.

I'm cutting through the living room fast, trying to get to the front door, and my stomach swoops a little as I go. I'm not even entirely sure Amanda is behind me until we're out on the front porch, which, now that the party is in full swing, is completely empty.

"So, Kam from Park Meade, huh? She seems nice. Is she your type?" I cross my arms. I feel petty and ridiculous, but I can't stop myself. It's like my brain has a brain of its own.

"My type is— Whoa. Wait a minute. Are you . . . jealous?" She cocks her head to the side. "You can't possibly be jealous, right? I'm following your lead here."

"That was before you didn't talk to me all night and then deigned to introduce me to your new *friend*."

I feel petulant, childish. But I'm annoyed. This is all so annoying.

"Well, this feels very pot calling the kettle black," she mumbles.

"I don't know what that's supposed to mean."

She sighs. "I don't want to fight with you."

"This isn't a fight. We're not fighting. I just want to know what you mean."

"You barely want to be seen with me in public, meanwhile you and Jordan are all over each other tonight." Her voice is low but quick. "I just don't know what you want from me anymore. I'm okay with not being the poster children for healthy, transparent queer teenage relationships, but I have to know what we're doing. It's like your best friend is doing everything she can to—"

"Gabi doesn't have anything to do with—"

"—keep me from you. And you and Jordan keep getting closer and closer—"

"Me and Jordan used to be really close. That's not really—"

"And meanwhile, you snatch your hand away from me in public like I have some sort of communicable disease when I dare to interact with you! Which is what you just said you wanted me to do!"

We stare at each other for a moment, breathing hard. I'm frustrated, so freaking frustrated. She doesn't get it. She couldn't possibly. She doesn't understand that the stakes are always higher for me, that I don't get the option of not being in control. Joining the race and then dropping out or going to a party without a game plan and strategy are decisions that have no consequences in her life. Amanda gets to do things because they're fun or easy or sound good, not because she has something to lose. But that's not how things work for me. That's not how they've ever worked.

My eyes are burning a little, and I know it's because I'm not too far from crying. "I told you I had to be cool about this. You don't understand. It's . . . it's different for me."

"It's not different, Liz! You like girls, so do I. So what? It's 2020." She shakes her head. "Campbell is backward, but it's not as bad as you make it seem. I'll be there to support you through your coming out. This is only this hard because you're making it this hard."

Now it's my turn to be indignant. "You don't know what you're talking about! You didn't grow up here, so you don't know how people can be. If people knew that I . . . that I, um, whatever. If they knew, I wouldn't have even the slightest chance of winning—"

My hand shoots up to cover my mouth. I didn't mean to say it.

I know what it sounds like. I know how it feels when I hear Gabi say it, and I know how it feels to believe it myself. I don't want Amanda to see me that way, but it's the truth. No queer girl is ever going to have a chance at winning prom queen in Campbell. The race is hard enough for me as it is without adding the fact that I'm queer to the mix.

"Wait." She takes a step back toward the sidewalk. "This is about *prom*? All these secrets? All this hiding has been about you wanting to win that stupid crown?"

"It's—it's complicated! You don't understand—" I wave my hands around as I try to find a way to explain it to her. Explain everything—that every time I tried to tell her the truth about the scholarship and the secrets, it felt like bursting the bubble where things between us were simple and light. But I'm coming up short. My stomach flips instead.

"I do understand, Liz. I understand that you are not who I thought you were." She pulls her keys out of her pocket and starts walking backward toward her car. She stops for a second and just looks at me in a way she never has before. Like she's seeing me for the first time. I hate it. "You can do low-key all by yourself. Because I'm not interested anymore."

She turns and runs the rest of the way to her Jeep without

stopping to look back at me, and I want to scream. I want to cry. I want to kick myself for not just saying "Who cares?" and doing this the right way from the beginning. And worst of all, I wish I knew what the right way would have been.

I feel terrible. Sweat is beading at my brow, and my heart is beating faster than it should be. I haven't felt like this in a long time, like I can't control my breathing. My stomach clenches, and I wrap an arm around it. God, it's just like elementary school again. I feel like—

"Lighty," Jordan's voice comes from behind me. "What's going on—"

And he doesn't even have a chance to get it out, because as I turn to face him, I puke all over his precious Yeezy hoodie.

twenty-six

"Up and at 'em, Lighty!"

I jolt upright and immediately wish I didn't. My mouth tastes disgusting. I don't know where I am.

I look down at the oversized Ohio State crewneck I'm wearing, bleached and threadbare from years of washes and wears, and then around the room I don't recognize. Sunlight streams in through the curtains and across the huge flat-screen on the wall connected to the Xbox with its cords knotted together and strewn about. The pile of dirty clothes overflowing in a basket in the corner. Framed pictures of the Jennings men in different football jerseys from peewee to professional.

My eyes finally settle on a smirking, shirtless Jordan Jennings in the doorway, and I remember how I ended up here. I've become such a cliché.

"You look like hell, my friend." He pushes off the frame and sits on the side of the bed. He grabs my hand from where it's clutching the blue plaid comforter close to my chest and drops two aspirin in it. He sets a bottle of water on the end table. "You did your anxiety-vom thing. You looked so pitiful afterward, I just brought you upstairs to relax for a second, and by the time I came back, you were asleep."

I look at the time on my phone and see it's just past nine o'clock.

"If you think I look bad"—I pop the pills in my mouth and swallow them down dry. I can't even muster up the will to open the bottle—"then you should see the other guy."

He snorts. "Don't be too hard on yourself, killer. We've all had our nights. I peed on Lawson's dad's cop car last summer after the Fourth of July bonfire."

He stands up and crosses the room to his dresser. He grabs a fresh T-shirt for himself and a pair of sweatpants, which he tosses to me. He's smiling again as he heads to the door.

"Come on, sunshine! What you need is some good ol' greasy cheer-up food."

· ♛ ·

I'm in Steak 'n Shake looking like exactly what I am: a pitiful heartbreakee in a pair of Jordan's old Ray-Bans from his glove compartment. As we drove, Jordan wound through the streets of Campbell like someone who owns it, window down, tapping his hand on his door and nodding along to the new Cardi B song on the radio. He drove in silence, exactly the speed limit, never going above or below except to slow to a stop at a red light and accelerate at a green one.

We passed the main strip of shops that make up the center of Campbell: A Ritter's Frozen Custard that me and Robbie used to beg to go to for cookie dough glaciers when we were kids, a Speedway gas station with a bold window decal advertising eighty-nine-cent Speedy Freezes, the nail shop where every girl in town will find herself the day before prom. So many stores Gabi and I have drifted in and out of on boring summer Saturdays, the restaurants that we dreamed we'd get hostess gigs at when we were old enough to get the jobs that'd fund our way out of Campbell.

All the pieces of the place that have made up my life fly by outside the confines of Jordan's brand-new SUV.

Inside the restaurant, everything looks as it always has: the fifties motif dripping through every bit of the design, from the checkered floors to the waitresses in slightly stained white button-ups to the buzzing, red cursive sign above the counter telling customers to "Takhomasak."

Even though there are only a few people milling around the small restaurant—a couple girls I recognize from school giggling over shakes by the huge picture windows that wrap around the whole room—I still prefer the anonymity of wearing shades.

"You look like you had a great night, and I look like I just finished an all-night bender at Club Monaco." I grab his straw paper off the table and roll it into a ball between my thumb and forefinger. I'm exhausted in the worst way.

The aftershocks of a panic attack aren't like a hangover, even though they probably feel physically similar. I didn't black out last night—I remember everything. My stupid jealousy. Amanda's face. The puking all over Jordan's hoodie. Oh my God, the Yeezy hoodie.

I put my hand against my forehead and groan.

"I am so sorry about your hoodie, Jordan."

"First of all, Club Monaco is a store, not an actual club, Lighty. Bless your innocent soul." He nudges my foot with his underneath the table. "Second, it's just a hoodie, man. I can get another one. I'm more worried about you. You haven't been that bad since, what? Before we even met?"

"Yeah." The glasses slip down my nose a little, and I have to push them back up. "Yeah, it's been a while."

No matter how much time has passed, my body acutely remembers the shame that follows a panic attack that severe. I feel like I'm in fourth grade again, barely making it to the trash can in time after hearing that we would be having a math quiz that I hadn't had time to study for because I was in the hospital with my mom the night before. Everything aches; my face burns.

"What's going on with you, Lighty?"

"Me and Amanda broke up." It hurts to say, to admit so plainly. "I wasn't honest with her about why we couldn't be, um, out together."

He leans both elbows on the table and waits. He doesn't push me until I'm ready to be pushed. Exactly like the old days.

"I'm not running for prom queen because it's fun or tradition or whatever. I'm running because I need that scholarship money. I didn't get as much in financial aid from Pennington as I thought I was going to get, and now I'm screwed. I've been too embarrassed to talk about it." I shake my head. "I just knew that if people found out about my relationship with Amanda, my chances of winning would be absolutely shot."

"That sucks," he says simply, a little insulted on my behalf. "The breakup and the scholarship. And the whole lying to your cool, goofy girlfriend. That part is also bad. You definitely fumbled the ball there."

He's smirking when I look up at him, and I throw the straw paper ball at his face. But I'm smiling too. A little.

"Can I ask you something?"

"Shoot."

"How come you never talk about Emme? I've been broken up for less than twelve hours, and it's all I can think about. I don't know how you can stand it."

He hesitates.

"Because I love her, and her secrets aren't mine to tell." He crinkles his nose in that way he does sometimes, and the diamond stud catches the light. "But things got bad. And I think I didn't do enough for her, you know? So it hurts to talk about."

I nod. There's a heaviness in what he's saying that tells me I have to tread lightly on how to proceed, like he's entrusting me with something major. The whole conversation suddenly feels surreal and deeply personal, but somehow it makes sense for us to be having it. Me and Jordan may not be who we used to be, but we still fit together. Like Snoop Dogg and Martha Stewart: Freaky, but it works.

"I'm gonna miss this," I say after some silence. I take a sip of my water. I really am going to miss Jordan when this is all over. Having him in my life again for the past few weeks has been amazing. It's almost like the past four years didn't happen. But the reality is they did. "Me and you sort of balance each other out."

"Miss this? Lighty, there's FaceTime, Campbell Confidential DMs, snail mail. Just because you're going to Pennington and I'll be at THE Ohio State University doesn't mean—"

"No," I shake my head sadly. "I mean when prom is over. You'll go back to your people, and I'll go back to mine. Like before."

When the waitress drops off our meals, Jordan pushes my plate closer to me since I don't immediately reach for it.

"It doesn't have to go back to that. I told you that freshman year! I'm still sorry about being an asshole that day in the hallway. You don't even know— I never stopped being sorry for that day." He shakes his head. "I shouldn't have stood by while those idiots said that stuff. I don't even have a good excuse. But I wanted to talk afterward, and you never responded to my letter, so I figured that meant you—"

"Wait." I freeze as I bring a fry to my mouth. "What letter?"

"The letter, Lighty. My apology letter. I didn't know how to just come out and say sorry to your face because I was convinced you would tell me to never speak to you again—which I would have totally understood. You didn't have a phone yet, so I couldn't even text you, and I felt weird about calling your house, so I gave the letter to Gabi, and—"

"I didn't get a letter." Even though the reasons are different than last night, my heart is beating too fast and my mind is all over the place. There was no letter. Gabi would've told me . . . She wouldn't lie like that.

"Lighty, I definitely gave her one. I never would've just—"

My brain is working so fast to process what's going on, I can't even listen to him. But my thoughts are interrupted by giggles from somewhere behind us, and a group of underclassmen girls by the window keep cutting glances in our direction and then looking away. I recognize two of them from the Prom Projectioners. They couldn't have heard our conversation—both me and Jordan are too far away for that—but they keep glancing over at us anyway.

"Ugh, I'm not in the mood for this. I always forget that being with you makes me famous by association." I bring my hand up to my head to check my own temperature. I have to be in some kind of fever dream right now.

"Oh yeah," Jordan says quickly. "Those girls probably think we're on a date right now because of some stupid thing on Confidential." He reaches into his pocket to pull out his phone. He holds it up so that Face ID unlocks it before he swipes up. "We've apparently even got a hashtag."

There's a couple of pictures of Jordan and me sitting next to each other by the firepit last night posted from an account with a weird, random handle and a default avi, and if you didn't know any better, they might look like something else is going on. My head leaning against his side, his hand squeezing my shoulder, the two of us looking at each other and smiling. I know it was totally innocent, and he knows it was totally innocent, but the hashtag doesn't seem to know that.

"#ReplacementEmme?" I whisper-shout. "Are they kidding me?"

"Creepy, right?" He shakes his head, like this is more of a minor inconvenience to him than anything else. Meanwhile, I feel like the walls are closing in around us. "It feels like a bad reality show."

A reality show is an understatement. This feels like *1984*.

And that's when it clicks. There's only one person nosy and sneaky and strategic enough for something like this. Only one person who has apparently been manipulating my relationship with Jordan since the very beginning.

"Let's go." Jordan doesn't hesitate to toss a crisp twenty onto the table to cover us both. I scoot across the seat and out of the booth, faster than I thought possible an hour ago.

"There's somewhere we need to be right now."

twenty-seven

The walk to the Marinos' front door has always been super long—
their house sits so far back from the sidewalk, it looks like it
should have a moat or something—but today it feels even longer.
Jordan stays in the car as I make my way to the door.

The houses in The Oaks are all different, custom floor plans
designed for people who wanted homes so new no one had so much
as sneezed inside them before they moved in. I used to be amazed
when I came over to Gabi's for a sleepover, awed by the sheer size
and luxury of it all. And I guess sometimes I still am—jarred by
the difference between her world and my own.

I've barely taken my finger off the doorbell when Mrs. Marino
appears in their high-ceilinged foyer, apron around her waist and
shiny dark brown hair pulled back in a tight ponytail. She's
dressed in a casual outfit, but one that still reeks of old money:

pearls around her neck (which, honestly, who bakes wearing pearls?) and a crisp white button-down blouse tucked into jeans that fit so well you know they must be tailored.

Looking at Mrs. Marino is like putting Gabi's school picture in one of those Facetune apps that make you look older and collect your data—they look so similar.

"Liz." She steps aside to motion me in. "Gabrielle didn't tell me you'd be by today. But when does she ever tell me things?" She laughs, but it's hollow. She adds distractedly, "I should call my daughter down."

When she calls her name, Gabi comes bounding down the stairs.

She stops midway down the staircase when she sees me standing near the door. "Oh, Liz! I hope you're here to discuss strategy because—"

"I didn't come here for prom." I cut her off quickly as I follow her up the stairs. "We need to talk."

When we get to Gabi's room, things look exactly as they always have, but everything feels different. The air around us has shifted.

"*Okay.*" She drags out the word as she sits down on her bed. I shut the door behind me with a click. "What's going on?"

"What is wrong with you?" I say quickly. "Were you ever going to tell me that you're the reason Jordan didn't talk to me for four years? Even though you knew how bad losing his friendship messed me up?"

"Nothing is wrong with me. I should be asking what's wrong with *you.*" She points at me defensively. "Do you know how much damage control I had to run after Jordan came back inside with *your vomit* all over his hoodie?"

"Don't do that thing where you try and turn everything back around on me. I deserve an explanation."

"I'm not turning anything around on you! You are behaving completely out of character!" She stands up and throws her hands in the air. "You have secret girlfriends, you're not listening to anything I'm saying, and getting to Pennington is the furthest thing from your mind! For someone so concerned with her privacy, you sure are getting messy."

I can't tell if she's trying to throw me off her case or if she really is as flustered as she looks. She's always in full hair and makeup by this time of day. But now she's wearing joggers, and sure they're the stylish kind from H&M, but she never wears sweatpants.

"Why didn't you tell me that Jordan was trying to reach out to me freshman year? And why did you start that stupid hashtag on Campbell Confidential last night even though you know nothing is going on between us?"

"I started the hashtag because you needed help, Liz. If I was able to see how close you and that girl were getting, anybody could have seen you! You needed to throw people off before rumors got out of hand and tanked your chances at winning."

Which, okay, absolutely sucks but is sort of reasonable in a twisted, catastrophically unethical way.

"What about Jordan, Gabi? Explain that."

She looks away. "That was a long time ago."

She's not denying it. She's not denying that she had anything to do with the letter. Oh no.

"Yeah, well, it's new information to me, so let's talk about it anyway."

"You used to be so obsessed with each other," she hurries out.

"Don't tell me this is because you were jealous of our friendship? You can't be serious."

"You don't get it! You were my best friend, my *only* friend for our entire lives. When my parents used to fight, I could always turn to you." She crosses her arms over her chest. "And then what? Jordan Jennings comes along in middle school, and all of a sudden, it's like you didn't even care anymore. My family isn't great like yours, Liz. You were my family. And I thought I had lost you!"

She stops pacing to look directly at me. Her eyes are wet like she's trying and failing to keep herself from crying.

"And then he embarrassed you like that freshman year, and you were so crushed. I hated seeing you like that. And when he came to me to apologize, I just knew you would forgive him and then I'd be alone again and he would eventually hurt you again. It just seemed like the only . . ."

But I'm not listening anymore. I can't hear anything else she's saying. Not after that. My best friend sold me out, kept me from being able to repair one of my most important relationships, and lied to me about it for four entire years. Four years of fear of ever being humiliated like that again, of forcing myself to the fringes, hiding in the tiny protective bubble of my friends and band and my family. Four years of tanked self-esteem, when I was afraid to wear my hair a certain way for fear of standing out and making myself too visible. Four years of second-guessing myself every time I answered a question in class, because I didn't want to seem too smart or too bold or too much of *anything*. Four years of shrinking away and thinking that I wasn't good enough, thinking that Jordan ran away because he wanted to be in the realm of people who are everything that I'm not.

I'm fumbling with the doorknob, trying to get out. But Gabi is still talking.

"Lizzie, please! You have to forgive me. I—I tried to get you and him back together, didn't I?"

I stop. Because isn't that just the icing on the cake?

"You didn't do anything but screw me over, Gabi." I whip around quickly and can't even find it in myself to feel bad about her red cheeks and runny nose. I'm so angry, so tired. And I'm crying too, because none of this should be the way it is. It's not fair. "All this time, you made me feel like being me was something to be embarrassed about. Like it would take all kinds of tricks and strategies and changes to who I am and the way I look to get people to vote for me. To *care* about me. And I deserve better from my best friend than that."

I finally pull open the door and step through it. I've learned all the ways to keep my head down, to hide, to make myself scarce. But I never really learned how to say when enough is enough. Until now.

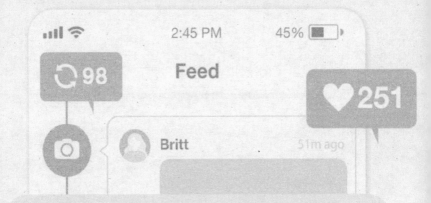

WEEK FOUR

She who hesitates is lost.

twenty-eight

When I walk into school on Monday, things feel different. There's an energy in the air that excites and terrifies me.

Robbie is standing at my locker with a smile when I show up.

"Sis," he starts, shutting my locker door for me after I grab my AP World History textbook. "You're gonna want to see this."

He pulls me toward the Commons. Just like we'd hoped, like I'd planned, a huge crowd has gathered in front of the glass wall. And they're completely buzzing, talking and snapping photo after photo. My first instinct is to run, to hide. But my second, the one that's even more dominant, is to look for Amanda. My heart sinks when I can't locate her face in the crowd.

The crowd breaks just enough for me to see what everyone is staring at, and Britt's handiwork is even more incredible now than it'd been last night. It looks like it could be right on the glass, but in an effort to save the janitorial staff undue stress, Britt's managed to do it all on a series of those massive papers that come on a roll you find in art classrooms.

After I left Gabi's, I told Britt I was ready to shake up my campaign, and she was immediately on board.

Jordan kept his promise to help however I needed—it was practically three in the morning when he met us at the school with his key, courtesy of being the trustworthy and almost-famous D1 recruit and football team captain—and Britt and I got to work. I didn't do much but help her hang the paper and hand her a new brush when she asked for it. But somehow, Britt created something Banksy couldn't have dreamt up. You know, if Banksy was invested in doing vaguely anarchist prom displays instead of anti-capitalist, anti–state surveillance street art.

In Britt's signature style, there's a huge, eerily realistic black castle, one that looks like something out of a horror movie instead of a fantasy. And right in the center, in loopy white script so perfect the words seem almost comically out of place:

Fuck Your Fairy Tale

She finished it all with a gold crown hanging off one of the turrets. The same gold crown that adorns all my posters and fliers.

Last night, as she finished it, me and Jordan stood by and marveled at what she'd managed to do.

"Whoa, Luca!" Jordan whistled from his place leaning against the wall. It was pretty dark in the Commons that late at night, but the flashlights on our phones offered just enough light for Britt to get to work. "This is dope."

"But won't that be too obvious?" I asked as she finished with a flourish. I was hesitant about using the crown imagery, worried that any misstep might bring Madame Simoné and Principal Wilson knocking down my door and pulling me from the race, but in the end, there was no other option. "I know we need people to connect me to this somehow, but I don't know . . . Is this not just asking to get me booted?"

I rubbed my forehead, leaving behind some stray black fingerprints from the paint.

"All guerilla art needs a calling card, Lizzo." Britt looked at the display and then back at me. "But we do what you want here. You don't want the crown, I'll scrap it and start over."

Jordan came to stand next to me, looking up at what we'd managed to do. He bumped my shoulder with his own.

"You're scared because this is different," he said so that only I could hear him. In an instant I was backstage with him again at our last concert together, our faces close and hearts beating loud. "But this"—he gestured between our bodies and then to Britt— "this is the same. We got your back, Lighty. Whatever goes down, it goes down with all of us."

And now, in the light of day, I'm grateful for the decision to let the crown stand, because as one person notices me standing next to Robbie, so does another. And another and then another, until it seems like the dull roar of conversation has all but disappeared. The people who had been taking pictures of the mural for Campbell Confidential have turned their cameras in my direction. A mix of surprise, annoyance, and respect plays across the different faces.

As they're looking at me, I look down at my phone. I take one deep, calming breath, and I press send on the Campbell Confidential post that I've been drafting since last night.

Robbie crosses his arms and smiles at me.

"You still worried about that ranking?"

And I feel it, that explosive and dangerous sensation of hope that I've been afraid of. Maybe I do have a chance, a real chance, to be queen. Without the games, without trying to mold myself into the box of what a queen has always been.

I hate that it took me so long to realize it, that I've let all the garbage like popularity and Campbell's antiquated ideals keep me from understanding the truth.

I never needed this race or a hashtag or the king to be a queen.

I was born royalty. All I had to do was pick up my crown.

· ♔ ·

I've only been to Principal Wilson's office once before, to collect some donations for Key Club junior year, but it feels almost familiar as I look around the space. It's so stereotypical, I've seen it a hundred times: three framed pictures of his wife and kids beside his iMac, a shiny brass nameplate perched on the edge of his big wooden desk, two degrees from Purdue University on the wall. And to top it all off: the pinched expression of a man who hasn't had his morning coffee or taken a poop in days. The thought almost makes me laugh as I ease into one of the two chairs in front of him.

Madame Simoné perches on the edge of her chair, opposite mine, like she can't bear to get comfortable.

"Elizabeth, you have really made quite the scene, haven't you?" She crosses her legs and uncrosses them promptly. "You have really made a mess of things."

I've always liked Madame Simoné. I've always respected her level of earnestness, even though I don't quite understand channeling that earnestness into something as ridiculous as prom. But in this moment, I sort of want to reach across the space that separates our chairs and slap that fake accent out of her mouth.

"Campbell County has built a system that benefits the privileged. Prom court shouldn't be for the same kind of people every year." Principal Wilson reads from his phone, nostrils flaring. *"A fairy tale for some, and a nightmare for the rest of us. Enough. #EffYourFairyTale."*

He even says *hashtag*—the full word, broken into two parts, like he's sort of confused by it. Hash-tag. I try to fight back a smile. Hearing him read my words back to me is strangely satisfying. It's made even better because I know since I posted it this morning, it has been shared more than five hundred times. #EffYourFairyTale has collected more posts on Campbell Confidential today than any other tag. I don't know if people agree with the point I'm making, but at least they're paying attention to it.

"This is what you think of Campbell, Elizabeth?" Principal Wilson shakes his phone in the air. His face is damp with perspiration. "This is egregious!"

"The paper will come down. It's just stuck to the wall with double-sided tape." I ignore his question altogether. I want to get to the point of this conversation. I'm not interested in lying, or pretending. Not anymore. "It's probably gone already, actually."

Credit my GPA, credit Robbie and Gabi and their incessant interest in all things prom, but I know the rules inside out. According to Campbell guidelines, Jordan has a key and is permitted to use it as he sees fit, so we didn't technically trespass on school property to put up the mural. And according to prom codes of conduct, if the display is campaign related, we're permitted to hang it in any common space on campus, given that the candidate is in good standing.

It's not my fault no one thought to make a rule about profanity. For people so serious about a tradition, they sure don't look too closely at their own fine print.

"You should know that we could take you right out of the race for something like this, Miss Lighty. That language was just plain offensive." Principal Wilson's ruddy race somehow gets . . . ruddier? He must really not like the f-word. "Do you kiss your mother with that mouth?"

My mouth suddenly tastes metallic. My chest gets tight. But I straighten in my seat anyway. The Lighty Way.

"My mother is dead."

Principal Wilson visibly recoils and tries to find his footing. "Um, well, you know. I'm, um, sorry to hear that. But, um, the point stands."

"It doesn't, actually." I'm frustrated, and in my opinion, rightfully so. They can't do this to me. They can't threaten me if I haven't broken any rules. "I'm in good standing. I haven't so much as missed a volunteer opportunity yet. And Madame Simoné, if you check your records, I think you'll find that I'm not only the student with the highest class rank—which by your own admission is

234

a portion of the formula used to determine court—but I'm also the only student who has attended not only all the mandatory events I was assigned to but more volunteer events than anyone else as well."

I've done the events; I've gone above and beyond the set requirements. If there's one thing I'm good at, it's following rules.

Madame Simoné sputters in her seat.

"Well, that may be the case but . . . this is just . . ."

Principal Wilson cuts in. "That language is not befitting of what we believe our potential queen should embody, Elizabeth. And we don't like it one bit."

"With all due respect, Principal Wilson, if you don't have a specific violation for me, I'd really like to get to first period now."

"Elizabeth, I don't want to see any more stunts like this out of you. You were doing so well. I'd hate to see this not work out for you." Madame Simoné sits rod straight in her seat and looks over the rim of her wire glasses like she knows something she shouldn't. "Did you know you have the chance to be the first black queen in Campbell history?"

I swallow. I did know that. Of course I know that. But I don't like it being held against me. I don't like the implication in her tone.

You could make history if you just follow our rules.

You could be a real credit to your people if you just straighten up and fly right.

You could actually be worth something if you would shut up and take what we give you.

And I know then what I've always known: Campbell is never going to make a space for me to fit. I'm going to have to demand it.

twenty-nine

Every year, the week before prom, the administration puts on a drunk-driving simulation in the school parking lot starring the prom court hopefuls in borrowed and bloodied prom attire. It's a dramatic display. Streets are blocked off and firefighters come to pretend like they're responding to a multicar accident, the result of a drunken night of teenage merriment. And like everything in this race, it's a *massive* deal.

The fifteen of us who still haven't dropped out of the race, despite the outrageous time commitment and absurd amount of stress, are dispatched to different dressing rooms in the theater hallway and given our selection of shoes and tuxes and dresses to choose from out of the theater department's costume closet. Everyone is buzzing, a strange excited energy that feels like a definite precursor to what prom will be like.

I get ready quickly, throwing on one of the dresses in my size from the closet and picking a pair of heels that I seriously hope don't make me topple over and break my ankle. The dress is beautiful but decidedly not for me. It's a floor-length gown, strapless, with gold sequins all over it. The sequins are scratchy under my armpits as I pull it on.

The dressing room has mostly emptied out. All the girls rushed in and put on their makeup and clothes in a flurry of activity, but I hung back in the costume closet until I figured everyone would be taking their places out in the parking lot.

I know everyone is out there. I know *Amanda* is out there. And I'm still not ready to face her.

"I know she's being annoying about not being able to be crowned with Derek, but it's so *sad*." There's a muffled voice coming from the other side of the vanity mirrors and the swish of moving taffeta.

I'm tucked behind the folding partition that's up in the girls' dressing room, trying to zip myself into my dress, so I can only assume that whoever remains has no idea they're not alone. I peek around the side of the partition and am surprised I couldn't place the voice faster. Quinn and Lucy stand nearby applying makeup that looks like dirt to their faces. Rachel is nowhere to be found, so I assume she's already outside and in position. They don't notice me from my spot, and I don't make any move to be seen.

"Derek is such an idiot." It's Lucy. "He knew how bad she wanted this, and he just had to make a scene at the Bake-Off to show off for his boys. It's such . . . What's that thing we learned in sociology?"

Quinn responds. "Toxic masculinity?"

"Yes! Ugh, so totally toxic. I get why she had to break up with him." Lucy groans. "And now she's so worried about what it must look like for her to be single right before prom, she's being even worse than usual."

"You think she'll actually go through with her plan to—"

I bump into the partition as I try and slide on the strappy pair of heels I pulled from the costume room, and the whole thing falls to the ground with a boom.

Quinn and Lucy immediately rush toward where I'm just barely standing.

"Oh my gosh, Liz!" Quinn's heels click-clack on her way over to me. "We didn't even know you were in here." She cuts her eyes over to Lucy so quick, if I'd blinked, I would have missed it. "We could have helped you get ready!"

Lucy steadies me by wrapping an arm around my waist, and Quinn sets the partition upright again. She dusts her hands off like she's accomplished a great feat of manual labor and smiles at me brightly.

"Your makeup isn't even done yet." Lucy *tsk*s and pulls me back toward the mirror they've just abandoned.

"Yeah, it is!" I wave in front of my face. I did a pretty haphazard job of applying some fake blood, but I figure it's good enough for me to hang halfway out of an upside-down Tahoe for an hour.

Now that I can see them in full view, I realize how made up they are. It's not nearly as elaborate as they'll be on prom night, but it's definitely more than just school makeup. They both look thoroughly battered and bruised, but beneath that lies two otherwise picture-perfect prom queen contenders.

Lucy, who spends most of her days donning her pom squad uniform, is wearing a sleek silver gown that would probably drag on the floor if she weren't wearing heels. And Quinn has a pale pink corset top that blooms into a wide silk skirt adorned with watercolor flowers at the bottom.

"No." Lucy shakes her head and drags me in the direction of the vanity mirrors. "No, it's really not."

"Liz, Demo Day is a big deal! We have to make sure you look like a cohesive member of our Dead Girl Posse," Quinn says. We're in the same car for the demo, while Rachel is in Jordan's. Quinn pulls a makeup sponge out of her sparkly pink Caboodle. "But we'll have you performance ready in, like, two seconds. Don't worry."

"Why are you guys helping me?" I ask, looking between their reflections in the mirror. "Rachel would be seething if she saw you two with the competition."

I think briefly about my own best friend, about what she'd say about this moment. She'd probably be pleased that I was aligning myself with the PomBots. Might say something like, "Only hitch your star to one that's rising, my congenial but credulous best friend. Fraternizing with the enemy is okay as long as you end up on top."

But Lucy just clicks her tongue. "Has anyone ever plucked your eyebrows before?"

"Let's do it, Luce!" Quinn claps her hands together. She looks at me. "You have a beautiful brow line, Liz. It just needs some definition."

I shake my head and take a step back. "No way. I'm not letting you two anywhere near my eyebrows. That sounds like the quintessential surefire sabotage plot."

"Liz, if the two of us were going to sabotage you, it would've happened already." Lucy rolls her eyes and pulls me back to her. "Besides, we don't have a problem with you. That's Rachel's thing."

"Yeah, we like you!" Quinn chirps, dabbing a makeup sponge with fake blood down my neck. "You're so nice. Remember that time in elementary school you and Gabi made Ben Burdorf cry because he was being such a jerk to all the girls in our grade?"

Lucy nods. "I remember that! He was such a little snot. He said my mom got Botox! Which is completely untrue. Nobody ever believes her because, I mean, those cheekbones on a woman in her late thirties? Yeah, right. But I swear to God she was just born with, like, naturally tight features. But whatever." She smudges some charcoal-like eye shadow across my cheek to make it look like I've really been in an accident. "The point is, you stood up to him for all of us."

I don't remember it that way. I'm not sure how elementary school lore functions, how a story can evolve into something totally different over time, but I don't correct them.

"You're very Mia Thermopolis," Quinn says almost dreamily.

I knit my eyebrows together in confusion.

"Mia Thermopolis? From *The Princess Diaries*?" Lucy asks, and I keep staring blankly. "Are you seriously telling me you've never seen the classic Anne Hathaway and Julie Andrews film *The Princess Diaries*?" Quinn gasps. Lucy shakes her head and continues, "I was worried you might be a lost cause, and if that isn't proof, I don't know what is."

"I mean, have you guys seen *Drumline*?" And like, yes, *Drumline* and *The Princess Diaries* are in two totally different worlds, but still. They both shake their heads and I smirk. "Okay, then, let's consider it a cultural learning curve." I try not to twitch away as Quinn curls my eyelashes. "Anyways, if you guys like me, why haven't you ever spoken to me outside of prom stuff?"

Lucy pops her gum loudly. "Uh, duh, because you never talk to us. We thought you hated us by association or something, because Rachel is so mean." I must look shocked because she continues. "Look, I think we can all admit that Rachel has some major rage issues that could be worked out in therapy."

"Very major." Quinn giggles. "But she's our friend."

And yeah, I guess I understand that. Loyalty between lifelong friends is complicated and runs deep. More deeply, even, than I think you realize, until just how different you and your friends have become is practically unavoidable.

"And you're surprisingly cool. I never would have guessed from the way you're, like, married to your flute or whatever," Lucy says.

"Ta-da!" Quinn steps back to make sure I can see myself in the mirror. "What do you think?"

I think that I look like I was professionally done up by *The Walking Dead* makeup artists, honestly. Lucy and Quinn have managed to make me look like I am every bit as gruesome as I would if this were real. It's pretty impressive.

"Wow," I say, leaning forward to examine the fake cuts they've put above my needs-shaping eyebrows. "You two are good."

They look at each other and high-five as they respond in unison, "We know."

Outside, the demo is exactly what I've seen every year since I was a freshman, but it's different being a part of it somehow. When the three of us approach the carefully arranged, dented, on-loan-from-the-junkyard Chevy Tahoe, Jaxon is leaning against the frame talking to Jordan. Meanwhile, Rachel is by their car doing what looks like vocal warm-ups. The two guys whistle when we approach, and Jordan admires Lucy and Quinn's handiwork.

"Looks even better than I thought, Lighty!" He examines my neck. He smiles at Lucy and Quinn. "Very believable, ladies."

Jordan leaves to go position himself half in and half out of the windshield of his assigned vehicle. Lucy and Quinn are making jokes about Jaxon's sucky driving skills, and he's laughing and tickling Quinn. And Madame Simoné is directing us on how to position ourselves in our car and reminding those of us with speaking parts not to forget our lines, but Jaxon is poking me in my side and whispering, "And, Lighty, don't you forget to aim out the window when you puke this time, okay? I don't want to have to get my fake-totaled car detailed."

Ugh. He must have heard about my embarrassing moment at Jordan's party. And, okay, not like I blame him for bringing it up, but still.

I smile a little and reply, "Spell 'detailed,' Price."

"You got some fire in you, Lighty. I like it."

It's like some imaginary switch has been flipped, and I don't know when or how it happened, but it feels like I'm on the inside of something I never considered I could be inside of. It's the same feeling from the good part of Jordan's party.

By the time the student body streams out into the parking lot to take in the faux carnage, we're already in our places. There's a moment when my body thrums with anticipation and nerves about how many people are going to be watching us, but I figure that if I have to do this show, I'd rather do it dead than alive.

The whole demo goes by in a flash. There's smoke effects all over the parking lot to mimic small fires, and the firefighters they've dispatched for the demo rush around like they're really attempting to save our heathen lives.

Rachel lets out a bloodcurdling Drew Barrymore scream, Claire rattles off her lines about Chad Davis driving under the influence as she pretends to cry over Jordan's fake-dead body, and Ryan Fuqua groans and attempts to claw his way out of his overturned Prius.

It's not bad, as far as performances go. I even hear a couple of cries of "I love you, Liz!" that don't sound like they belong to just Britt and Stone.

When we walk back inside, Jaxon claps me on my shoulder. "Bonfire at my place this weekend, Lighty. You coming?"

I've never been to one of their bonfires before, even though I've heard about them. People like me don't go to the PomBots' and the Jacket Jocks' bonfires, but I nod before I think better of it. Jaxon whoops. "Perfect. And don't forget, I gotta challenge you in wind sprints! Yo, Jennings, wait up!"

It's so weird, so corny, that I don't want to smile. But I can't help myself. Things almost feel normal, like they're supposed to. And for the first time in maybe ever, I feel like I deserve it.

WEEK FIVE

Hell hath no fury like a PomBot scorned.

thirty

I'm behind the register at Melody listening to the same middle-aged man plunk out the same notes on the grand piano he does every time he comes in, and I can see Amanda weaving through the cars in the parking lot on her board, heading away from the skate shop in the strip out to the parking lot. I don't know how I missed it when she pulled in, but I suddenly know what I have to do. I shout to Kurt in the back to let him know I have to take my break early and run outside.

"Amanda!"

She doesn't look as shocked as I think she should when she turns around. Her hair is pulled up into a topknot, and she's wearing glasses instead of contacts. She doesn't look surprised at all; she just looks tired.

Her hand is on her door handle when I reach her, and, honestly, all I want to do is reach out and touch her. I want to throw my arms around her neck and tell her about this past week, about having a real, honest-to-God conversation with Quinn and Lucy that didn't make me feel like some creature from outer space. I want to tell her how much I hate not talking to Gabi but I don't think I have it in me to forgive her. I want to tell her how sorry I am for lying, for not telling her the truth about why I'm running and what I stand to lose if things don't work out.

But I don't. I decide to keep it short.

"I, um. I saw you from inside." I push my hair out of my face. I've been wearing it out since the party, but it's still an adjustment. "I wanted to say hi."

"Hey." She pushes her glasses up the bridge of her nose. "I've seen your new campaign—your slogan and post and everything. Congrats."

She crosses her arms and leans against her Jeep. She's more than a foot away from me, but the way she says "Congrats" feels like a slap in the face. I step back instinctively.

"Look, I messed up."

"Liz, we don't have to—"

"No, let me just say this. Things are not, um . . . easy for me here." She doesn't say anything, so I just keep going. "But that isn't an excuse to have lied to you. It wasn't fair."

"You let me think you were still not out because it wasn't safe for you here. Do you know how scared that made me for you? And then for it to've been about prom all along . . ."

She bites at her thumbnail, and the gesture is so familiar I kind of want to cry.

"I just didn't know how to tell you the truth." I stuff my hands into the pockets of my jeans before I do something stupid like grab her hand and coax her thumb away from her mouth. "I need that scholarship money to go to college. I can't afford to go unless I win. And I knew I couldn't win if we were, you know, a *thing*."

I wait a beat before looking at her again.

"I'm sorry. I'm sorry for not telling you the truth. And I'm sorry I don't know a better way to do this."

I glance away and swallow a lump in my throat, because I hate this. I hate that it's still true. That despite everything, I still can't tell people. Past the prom thing, past the Amanda thing, I'm just not ready yet.

"Hey. Liz." The toe of her orange Vans nudges at my Chucks until I meet her eyes. "It's cool. And I'm sorry. I guess I just got so caught up in where I was that I didn't see how hard this has been for you. I just . . . I wish you would have told me."

Amanda opens the door of her Jeep and throws her board into her back seat. When she turns back to me, her eyes are shining in a way they weren't before. She doesn't look happy, but she at least looks closer to the Amanda who I kissed that day in the Jeep and the Amanda who I held hands with and danced with and shouted to the ceiling with like nothing could ever stop us.

"I guess I'll see you around?" she asks.

"Yeah." I smile. "I'll see you around."

It isn't the same, but it's close. And close is enough for right now.

thirty-one

Things aren't perfect, but I'm sort of floating by Thursday morning. Everything feels like it might be falling into place.

It's our last week before we find out who made court, so I'm bouncing between absolute gut-churning anxiety and unexpected excitement every day. With no more Gabi to interpret the results of Stone's algorithm, we have no way of telling where I am in terms of stats, but I feel hopeful. I feel like I stand a chance in this thing.

Me and Amanda aren't back together, but we're texting again. Before and after school, I spend more time looking at my phone than I ever have before. I feel like one of those people who can't tear themselves away from Campbell Confidential. I'm afraid that if I'm not looking at my phone, I might miss something—a funny meme, a link to a new Spotify playlist, a cute selfie.

It's not like it was before the concert that led to the kisses that led to the lies that led to the fallout. It's like we've gone back to square one: friendship.

I'm locking my bike to the rack, bobbing my head along to this great Margot & the Nuclear So and So's song that Amanda sent me last night, when Britt and Robbie rush outside. Ro leaves before me most days to meet up with his friends, so I'm not surprised to see him. But I am surprised to see their expressions.

"You two look like someone peed in your Cheerios this morning." I smile and pull my headphones out of my ears. They're on both sides of me as I make my way up the stairs into school. "Whatever it is has got to wait though, okay? Because I have a quiz in—"

"Lizzo, you probably want to stop for a second before—"

But I don't stop. I don't stop because I'm lovestruck and feeling invincible. But that feeling doesn't last long.

Robbie grabs my arm, but it's already too late.

"Oh my God."

Everyone has stopped to gawk at the new display in the Commons. The bodies around me seem to halt on command, everyone going stock still as they see the massive rainbow flag hanging from the glass. In the center of it is a sloppily painted crown that looks dangerously similar to the ones on my posters and buttons. And written on top of it and beneath it in bold block letters the color of blood:

LIZ LIGHTY IS ONLY
QUEEN OF THE QUEERS

The Commons, where last week I'd launched a new type of campaign, one that tried to reclaim all the things this school has tried to take from me, is the site of all my worst nightmares coming true. My throat feels tight, and I'm seeing spots. I can't believe this. It can't possibly be happening.

Suddenly, all the phones in the room ping with a notification at the same time. The people who didn't already have their phones out to take pictures of the flag are unlocking them, and next to me Robbie curses.

"Dammit." He grabs my hand to pull me in the direction of the parking lot before anyone realizes I'm there, but I'm clumsy. My feet are too heavy for my body as I stumble after him, and everyone is turning to look at me. I can hear it before I can see it, different pieces of the same awful conversation broken up and distributed for all my classmates to watch and watch again.

"So Kam from Park Meade, huh? She seems nice. Is she your type?"

"This isn't a fight. We're not fighting."

"You like girls, so do I."

"I understand that you are not *who I thought you were."*

It's like the world's worst reality show, and I'm the sloppy cast member who goes viral every week with a new set of catchphrases immortalized in GIFs.

It's the furthest thing from a fairy tale I could have asked for.

· ♔ ·

Being back in Principal Wilson's office somehow feels even worse now than it did the first time. It's clear from the way he's looking between me and Amanda that we're not here because he wants to help us. We're here because he wants to punish us.

"Well, Miss Lighty, I did tell you to watch your step, did I not?" He leans back in his chair, lips pressed into a thin line. I've never hated a person more than I do in this moment.

Amanda grips the arms of her seat so tight her knuckles go white. I've never seen her look like this before, so angry, so on edge. I feel her energy radiating across the space, and I want to grab her hand. To tell her that this is horrible, of course, but it's also not that surprising. That I've spent every day of the past four years fearing for this moment, and yet even that fear couldn't prepare me for this.

"C'est terrible. C'est terrible!" Madame Simoné paces near the door. She stops briefly to look between me and Amanda. "Something must be done."

"Is no one going to ask how Liz is doing? Your student was just the victim of a hate crime, for goodness' sake." Amanda shakes her head and bounces her leg.

"We don't know that," he responds quickly. "We shouldn't use those words until we know all the facts."

The facts. He's got to be kidding me.

"The fact is that Rachel Collins is behind this!" Amanda says, her face completely red with exhaustion and anger.

"You better quit pointing fingers until you have some evidence to back that up, young lady."

"So what's the point of this meeting?" I ask quickly, impatient. If we're going to do this, I'd rather we just get it over with. After everything we went through to get here, if I'm going to get kicked out of the race, I'd prefer to do it with my chin up. "Because I have a quiz in stats today that I really can't miss."

"Well, yes," he starts. "I imagine you do have some other *things* you two would like to get to."

I don't like his tone, or the way he narrows his eyes slightly, looking between Amanda and me. But I settle into my seat and place both my hands firmly on the armrests.

I try to channel the confidence of a mediocre white man in a boardroom: untouchable.

"We've already been contacted by the president of the PTA. They want you removed from the race immediately," Principal Wilson sighs. "They haven't been too pleased with your little stunts at any point, but they think it's better we cut our losses now than continue with this charade until prom."

"You think this is a *charade*?" I shout. I lean forward, and Principal Wilson recoils slightly. I can tell someone told him that Liz Lighty was a good girl, a quiet girl. Someone who would take this in stride. But I'm not her anymore, not entirely anyway. "You think I wanted someone to do this to me? For what?"

I know the answer, but I can't help but say it anyway. I'm so tired of the way this place treats people who are different, tired of feeling like I exist in the margins of my own life. I deserve better than that.

"Edward," Madame Simoné cuts in, her voice devoid of any French accent, "you and I both know that these girls have done nothing wrong. Goodness gracious, Calliope Vincent and Tatum McGee practically copulated on the floor of the culinary-arts classroom during the Bake-Off last year and didn't receive so much as a slap on the wrist!"

"And you and I both know that what is or is not stated in the rules has nothing to do with it, Roberta," he responds, clearly short on patience. He places both hands on his desk and speaks slowly. "They're already circulating a petition calling for Elizabeth's removal. This is out of my hands."

I can feel the tears threatening to spill over, and I just want to leave. I want to go home, be alone with my music, and forget any of this happened. It's not fair. None of this has ever been fair.

Amanda looks at me, her eyes tender and more than a little sad. She grabs my hand and rubs her thumb in soothing circles over mine.

"Excuse me. Principal Wilson?"

We all turn to the voice that accompanied the knock at the door.

I just want to hug Gabi when I see her. We may not be on good terms right now, but it's hard to unlearn all those years of leaning on someone else when you need it the most. Prom or no prom, you can't change the history that we have together. How she looked out for me after my mom died—I'll never forget the ways she saved me.

"Gabrielle, you really have no reason to be in here right—"

She cuts him off and pushes her way into the room. "Yeah, well, there's something you need to see." She looks over and offers me a sad sort of nod before stoically dropping her phone down on Mr. Wilson's desk.

"Miss Marino, this is very inappropriate. I'm dealing with students right now."

"Two students whom I might remind you have done nothing wrong." Gabi places her hands on her hips. "I know you're one hundred years old, but even you must be able to recognize a viral sensation when you see one."

Amanda snorts, and Mr. Wilson shoots her a dirty look.

"Miss Marino, what's the meaning of this?"

Gabi picks up the phone and turns it around to face him.

"The *meaning* of this, Mr. Wilson, is that since you called these two in here thirty minutes ago, the #JusticeForMighty"—to Amanda and me—"that's your 'ship name, by the way. I didn't come up with it, but I sort of think it works"—and back to Mr. Wilson—"that hashtag has gained almost a thousand posts on Campbell Confidential, and the numbers are still climbing. All your students are talking about the obstruction of justice, the blatant homophobia, that is occurring at your institution. This could turn into a case for the American Civil Liberties Union faster than you can blink."

I joked about Gabi becoming a lawyer, but I hadn't seriously considered it until now. Looking at the way Mr. Wilson shrinks in his seat as he looks at her phone makes it more obvious to me than ever how voracious this girl can be when she gets an idea in her head. It's incredible what she can do when she uses her powers for good and not evil.

Madame Simoné speaks up first. "Edward, be realistic. Does Campbell really need this kind of press? Over prom, of all things?"

"You know how seriously these parents take prom, especially prom court." He sighs and rubs a hand over his face. He looks up at G. "You're right, Miss Marino. This is bad, but not as bad as it could be."

"So what does that mean for us?" Amanda asks, her hand finding mine in my lap and squeezing. "For Liz?"

"It sounds to me," Madame Simoné starts, pushing her glasses up the bridge of her nose. She smiles at us softly. "As though you two girls are free to go. Right, Edward?"

"Well, not exactly. There are still policies to discuss—"

"There's nothing to discuss!" I've only ever seen Madame Simoné raise her voice one other time, and that was out of pure shock during the bake sale debacle. We all snap our eyes in her direction, and even Gabi looks impressed. "I've had enough. I believe in the sanctity of the institution of prom and how it can make us our best selves. And year after year I have watched as good, deserving young people don't enter the race because of how they'll be received. And I won't let it happen again."

I've never heard anyone in the administration say anything like this. The very abuse that the Jennings men have avoided by being athletes, by providing some type of entertainment to the people of Campbell, people like me or even Amanda experience full force. It's the weight, the impact, of being different in a town that hasn't learned how to hold us close and refuses to treat every part of us with as much care as we deserve.

"Elizabeth, we are going to get to the bottom of this. *Je promets.*"

"Roberta, please."

"No 'please.' Either these girls are free to go, and free to continue to express their affection how they see fit, or I swear to you I will start spilling everything I've ever seen and never complained about. And you'll have to worry about a lot more than the damn ACLU."

Principal Wilson looks terrified, but Madame Simoné stands

258

strong. I have no idea what secrets she holds, what she's kept to herself over the years, but Wilson's face tells me everything I need to know. He visibly deflates.

"You two still can't go as dates to prom." He turns to us and his face is hard again. "Rules still matter at my school."

And it sounds like he's saying it more for himself than for us, but it's enough for me. I let out a breath that I didn't realize I was even holding, and Amanda does the same. Gabi smiles smugly and turns on her heel, exiting as easily as she entered. Before I think to do otherwise, I dart out into the hallway after her.

"So, what?" I grab her arm and turn her around to face me. She doesn't look surprised, almost like she knew I would come after her, and that pisses me off a little. I'm not the same predictable Liz whose moves she's successfully predicted for the last twelve years. "You just breeze in and save the day and then take off without speaking to me?"

"You've made it clear you don't want to speak to me, Liz!" she shouts, but doesn't pull her arm away. "You have a new best friend in Jordan and a new girlfriend in Amanda—you don't need me anymore."

And the way she says it, resigned, without bite, is what makes me soften. I drop my hand from her bicep. "G, that's not true. You know that's not true."

When a tear slips down her cheek, I almost reach out to wipe it away for her, like she would for me. But I know her well enough to know that she'd prefer I pretend not to even notice.

"Whatever." She wipes at her eyes quickly. "Everything is messed up anyway. You're right to have dumped me." She looks up and tries to blink away the tears. I open my mouth to speak, but she waves her hand to stop me.

"Good luck, okay?" She turns and rushes in the opposite direction and doesn't leave me so much as a chance to say thank you. Or I love you. Or I miss you.

So I say nothing. Nothing at all.

thirty-two

I roll over at the sound of my alarm, and I am convinced that I'm living inside a nightmare that never ends. I can't imagine going back to school and facing the wolves again.

The rest of the day yesterday was the worst I'd ever had. I couldn't go anywhere without feeling eyes on me. I kept my head down in the hallways, turned my phone off so I wouldn't have to face any of the calls or texts from Jordan and Amanda and Britt and Stone. I just couldn't handle their sympathy, their attempts to make me feel better.

I won't feel better until all this is over.

When I finally climb out of bed and get dressed, I walk into the kitchen, where Robbie is watching *Cosmos* on his phone at the table while scooping handfuls of Grandad's Shredded Wheat straight out of the box and into his mouth. He crunches so loudly, I have to shush him.

"You're going to wake Granny up with all that noise." I take a bowl out of the cabinet, grab the milk from the fridge, and put them on the table in front of him. "And use a bowl, Ro. Act like you got some kind of sense."

He grunts but looks up and addresses me with his mouth full. He smiles, little bits of Shredded Wheat escaping his mouth in the process.

"Big day today, sis. You excited?"

Friday, the day we find out who made court. The day we find out whether or not this whole roller coaster ride has been worth it. I wouldn't even be going to school if it weren't for the prom court candidates' mandatory appearance at the pep rally this afternoon.

My eyes are puffy and my head is pounding, but I have to show up. It's the Lighty Way.

"Tell me I don't have to do this," I groan. "I'm begging you to put me out of my misery."

All the prom court candidates are expected to do a choreographed dance to "Whoomp! (There It Is)" that one of the show choir kids is going to teach us during homeroom. A few days ago after school, we even recorded a little video of us mouthing along to the words around the school that'll play in the background as we dance onstage.

I'm not sure how any of that is going to help the boys' basketball team win 3A state finals tomorrow, but whatever.

Robbie rocks back on the hind legs of his chair with a laugh.

"We were robbed of rhythm and athleticism at birth," he says. "We should sue."

I sigh and lean against the counter. I take a bite of the browning banana that Granny left out for me for breakfast, but I barely even taste it. Robbie stands up, sort of unfolds his long limbs as he walks over to me, and throws an arm around my neck. I lean into him, grateful.

"You remember when I was six and we were playing Beetlejuice at Bryant House?" Beetlejuice was this stupid game where we'd make our voices extra creepy and chase one another around, like a Halloween-themed tag you could play year-round. I'm not even sure who came up with it. "The time I fell and bumped my head on the wood surrounding the sandbox?"

Of course I remember. Ro was such a clumsy kid back then. I learned to look out for him, always, before I even understood his diagnosis. I knew to protect him before I knew what I was really protecting him from.

I nod into his shoulder. He keeps telling the story anyway.

"You leapt into action so quick—sent Abriona McEntire to get Dr. Lamont, told Junior to get the first aid kit, and scooped me up like I weighed nothing, all in one breath." He leans his head against mine. I can hear his smile, even if I can't see it. "And you used to do that for everybody. Got Carlisse Fenton to stop bullying Rodrick for his lisp, practically gave Jamel stitches that one time he fell out of the swing . . . You always took care of everybody."

I suddenly feel like crying. I swallow down the lump that's formed in my throat and shake my head. I look at Ro and realize for the first time that he's still in his pajamas.

"Wait," I start. "What's going on? Are you not going to school today?"

"I'm sorry, sis. I have to tune into the livestream." He shrugs but forces a smile.

I put both my hands on his shoulders and examine him, even though I know what's going on is completely internal. Sickle cell, more often than not, isn't something that you can see by looking at someone. "Robbie, why didn't you tell me you weren't feeling well? Why aren't you in bed? How long has this been going on?"

I don't know how I didn't recognize the glassy tint to his eyes. I can tell the moment he notices me noticing, but he stops me before I can comment on it.

"Chill, chill." He holds his hands out in front of me in the universal "take it easy" position. "I'm fine. On a scale of one to ten, I'm barely even a six. I just don't want it to get any worse, all right? So I'm— What is that thing Stone says? I'm *trusting my body*."

"Trusting your body or not, you should have told me." I cross my arms and look him up and down. "Have you taken your medicine today? Are you drinking as much water as you're supposed to? Make sure Gran has Dr. Fredrickson on standby just in case, because even though you don't think it's bad, it could always get worse. And— Never mind. You know what? I'll just stay home today, how about that? We can watch *The Price Is Right* reruns and—"

"Liz. This is exactly what I was saying. You need to focus on you today." Robbie closes his eyes and takes a quick breath. "You've got a lot to worry about right now, and I shouldn't be one of those things. I'm just a little under the weather."

Under the weather. An inherited blood disease like sickle cell is always more than just being "under the weather." It's not like

Robbie is dealing with a common cold because he forgot to wear a scarf. His body is turning against him. And the difference between those two things is always as serious as life and death to me.

"Robert James." I put my hands on my hips.

"Elizabeth Audre." He stares me down, eyebrows raised in challenge.

I break first. "Okay, fine. But please get back in bed. And call me if there's a problem."

"Did you know stress can give you heart disease? Do you want to have heart disease before your eighteenth birthday?" He puts his hands on his hips, mirroring me, and urges me toward the front door.

Robbie's right. I have to do this.

I pull open the door and look back at him one last time. He has that exasperated expression he used to get when he was a kid and I was babying him, but underneath it I can see there's also an unending tenderness. I know because I recognize that same sensation within myself every time I look at him.

"I love you, Nugget." I throw my arms around his neck quickly before backing out the door.

He smiles, a little wobbly.

"I love you too, big sis. Knock 'em dead today."

I show up outside the gym at the last possible second, wearing the requisite Campbell red and white. The rest of the group has already gathered, but I don't even take the time to look around. I don't want to see anyone. I don't want to say anything to anybody. I just want to get all this over with.

"Lighty!" Jordan rushes up to me when he sees me. I glance over his shoulder and see a worried-looking Quinn flashing a sympathetic look in my direction. I feel like a wounded animal. "I was worried about you, man. You haven't been picking up your phone."

"Yeah, I—"

"Everyone, everyone! *Prenez vos places!*" Madame Simoné claps her hands together to quiet the group. We're supposed to go after the girls' show choir, which is currently performing a rousing jazz square–laden performance of some pop song that I don't know the words to.

"We can talk about it later." Jordan puts his arm around my shoulders quickly in a half hug. "Or not. Whatever you want."

I'm grateful for him giving me the option of distance, because right now the second-to-last thing I want to do is talk about being outed in front of the whole school. Second only to going out in front of a gym full of people who don't know whether to hate me or feel sorry for me and dancing to some song no one has listened to since the Middle Ages. I honestly just wish I was back home with Robbie.

"*Il est temps, les étudiants!* Break a leg!"

She looks so proud as we jog through the doors and get in formation, but that does nothing to quell my fear of performing in front of a large audience of my peers. It's not like band, where I can blend, my one instrument becoming a part of something bigger and beautiful. This is a different beast. I'm in the front row, next to Jordan Jennings, wearing my school colors, and I feel like every eye in the huge space is trained directly on me.

I can see Britt and her bright yellow hair, sitting off to the side with the other rugby girls, pumping her fist in the air as soon as she sees me.

"We love you, Liz!" she shouts. She elbows the girl standing next to her, who is a freshman by the looks of her junior varsity uniform. The girl looks peeved but joins in immediately with a smile of her own. It's probably fake, all things considered, but I appreciate Britt and her strong-arm techniques nonetheless.

As we get into our positions, Jordan looks completely at home, totally comfortable, as he winks back at me and mouths, *Showtime.*

Suddenly the song starts, and muscle memory carries me. We hop up, in tandem, and lean to our left and then back to our right before doing that shoot dance with one arm and one leg that I can't seem to grasp but everyone else is absolutely owning. The crowd is really into it, up on their feet, dancing and singing along with us. During the freestyle dance part, I start feeling extra self-conscious because, honestly, I'm a really bad dancer. Like, embarrassingly bad. And it's made even worse by the belief that all black people have rhythm. It's one of the great shames of my life: being born without the dancing gene.

I start to do the robot, my default move, but Jordan saves me. He comes over and lifts up his foot in a gesture that I recognize immediately. It's our *House Party* dance routine.

He raises his eyebrows like, *Lighty, don't fail me now.* So I step forward and bring my foot up to meet his, then step back and do it again, before we clasp one of our hands in the middle and spin around. I'm laughing, genuinely having a good time, singing the words back and forth with Jordan, when I realize that I'm not scared anymore. I might even be living for it a little.

When we let go of each other and move back into our positions, the crowd is really going wild. I swear I can even hear a repeat chorus of the other night: "Lighty! Lighty! Lighty!" starts up from somewhere in the bleachers. It could be Britt's doing, but it feels bigger than the rugby girls now, like maybe the whole audience is in on it. And okay, it might be my imagination, my newfound comfort onstage, but the room stops feeling like the walls are closing in on me. It feels something like when I perform with the band. Something like right.

When the song ends, I'm smiling, despite everything. I'm waiting for the applause—

And then the lights go out.

I'm convinced that there's going to be the sound of five hundred phones going off next. That there's another secret of mine being broadcast to the entire school. My heart stops in my chest, and I start plotting my escape route. Maybe if I can get out before the lights come on—

But there's no time. It barely takes fifteen seconds, but the light comes back, and my hand shoots up to my mouth.

"Oh my God."

There's no explaining it, no way I could have seen it coming. As I look around the gym, the stands are filled with people who have covered up their Campbell spirit wear with plain black T-shirts featuring a simple gold crown in the middle on the front.

I look to my left, and even Jordan has one on. More than half the gym is wearing the design that has become synonymous with me,

Campbell's infamous, subversive, dangerous, queer-as-hell prom queen wannabe. People are on their feet, and finally the room erupts in applause. But there's no mistaking it this time. This isn't because of our performance.

This is all for me.

thirty-three

I can't believe it. When we're back in the hallway, my hand still hasn't left my mouth. Jordan comes up behind me and wraps his arms around my waist before lifting me up in the air and spinning me around. I don't even care about who else is around, who else might be jealous that we're so close. I'm just happy.

"Jordan, are you behind this?" I turn to face him, and he's grinning and shaking his head.

"I wish I could take credit for this. But it was all those two girls. You know? The one who talks superfast and the one who smiles a lot?" Melly and Katherine. Of course. "They rallied the troops via Campbell Confidential last night. Got a bunch of people in on the plan, and Britt's parents did the T-shirts. It was sort of genius."

I have so many questions, but the pep rally is dismissing and people are flooding out into the hallways. A lot of people are nodding at me as they pass, offering me a fist to bump, apologizing. When my phone starts to vibrate in my pocket, I almost miss it. But I fumble to answer it at the last possible second.

It's my granny. I'm feeling so giddy on hope that I decide right then to tell her about prom. About everything.

"Granny, you won't believe—"

"Lizzie, baby," my granny's voice sounds shaky over the line, and it feels like whatever air was left in the room is suddenly gone. She wouldn't sound like this unless—"You need to come to the hospital right now, you hear? It's Robbie. It's bad, baby."

I hang up without responding. I can't. There's nothing left for me to say.

Jordan's face crumples with concern as he sees me. "Liz?"

I don't have to explain, not really anyway. Jordan pulls his keys out of his pocket and grabs my hand to pull me to the door. It's like I'm no longer in my body, like I'm floating somewhere above myself, wondering how the shell of me is managing to keep moving.

But I mumble the name of the hospital once we reach the car, and Jordan floors it. His usual manner of driving, the one that I've grown all too familiar with over the past few weeks—casual, relaxed—is shot as he peels through the streets of Campbell and onto the interstate that takes us to downtown Indy.

I don't speak as we drive. Neither of us reaches for the aux cord, no one bothers to fill the air with jazz or the newest Kendrick or any of the sound that normally fills the space of his Range Rover. Jordan simply reaches over and drops a hand on mine where it rests in my lap.

It stays there, warm and strong, until we pull into the parking lot.

"I have to get back to school," he starts as I open the door, "but I'll be back later, okay?"

I nod. I still don't have words to thank him, but I hope by now he knows what this all means to me. "You've already done so much. I just— Don't feel pressured to come back. I understand that you have other stuff to do."

"Of course I'm coming back, Lighty." He shakes his head once and offers me a kind smile. For a moment, he looks just like the Jordan who I used to sit next to in middle school band. It makes my heart hurt. "A first is nothing without their second, remember?"

· ♔ ·

It isn't the first time I've been inside a St. Regis hospital—I spent more nights sitting at my mom's bedside than I did at home when things got really bad—but being inside the Jesse Washington Children's Hospital is always . . . different.

It's part of St. Regis, but it's also not. But then again, I guess it should be like that. When you're trying to convince children that they're okay, that they're not here because their own bodies are destroying them, you have to put up paintings of cartoon characters, apparently.

But I know this place just as well as the adult hospital, because it's scarier. Because it could always mean the worst for the person I love the most. Cartoon characters or not.

When I round the corner, Beatriz, my favorite nurse, with her short bob and cartoon-less scrubs, points me in the direction of

Robbie's room without me having to ask. She's barely five feet tall and doesn't smile much, but I've always liked her no-nonsense approach. And if the softness that enters her face when she sees me is any indication, I think she likes me back.

Dr. Fredrickson, Robbie's usual hematologist, is exiting the room right as I reach the door. She places her hand on my shoulder and sort of urges me in the direction she's walking. I glance back at the door but decide not to argue.

"Elizabeth. I wish I were seeing you under better circumstances, but I'm glad you're here. Come sit with me for a second," she says, her rich, honey-like voice soothing as always. "Your grandmother thought it might be best if I was the one to come talk to you. She's still a little shaken up."

Dr. Fredrickson is one of the few black female hematologists in the state, which always makes me so grateful that Robbie gets to have her. She was Dr. L's protégé once upon a time, and I'd always sort of hoped that one day I might be hers. She's about my height, with long, slim fingers, in her late forties but already completely silver-haired.

After all these years of watching her fix my brother in various states of disrepair, she's become a sort of hero to me. She even wrote one of my letters of recommendation for Pennington.

We sit down in some of the chairs in the waiting room, away from any of the children and their parents currently waiting to be seen. There's a LEGO tower in front of us, teetering precariously.

"How are you?" she asks, even though I'm sure she already knows the answer. I normally resent that trait in people, asking questions they already know the answers to, but when it's

Dr. Fredrickson, I let it slide. She doesn't say anything unless she has a reason.

"I've been better," I answer as honestly as I can.

She crosses her legs and places her delicate hands over her knees. Her massive diamond wedding ring sparkles in the nasty hospital fluorescent lights.

"Yes, I imagine you have." She nods. Her lips are in a tight line. "Elizabeth, you know how fond I am of you. I think you are truly one of the most capable and dedicated young women I've ever met. More than once I've told my husband that if we'd decided to have children, I would have wanted a daughter like you."

"I'm not that capable, doc. If I were, we wouldn't be here right now." I swipe at my nose, which has started to run. Dr. Fredrickson hands me a tissue that I didn't even see her holding. "And I think we both know that."

Her eyes soften.

"He hasn't been taking his meds, has he?" I ask. She doesn't respond right away, but I already know the answer. The miracle of Hydroxyurea is that it reduces hospital visits in young patients an almost unbelievable amount. But like any medication, when you don't take it, it's useless.

"I haven't been watching." I shake my head and put my face in my hands. I'm so ashamed, so disappointed. "This is all my fault."

"Don't say that." Dr. Fredrickson's voice is sharp, sharper than I've ever heard it. I snap my head up and look at her, and her normally composed face is colored with something heavier. "You are a good girl, smart and driven. But you are not your brother's keeper, young lady. He's almost sixteen now. And just as I told your grandmother, he's old enough to take his health into his own hands."

"But—"

"But nothing." She places her hand on mine and pats twice. "Your job is to be his sister, not his doctor or his caretaker. You let me do that."

I want to squeeze her hand, to anchor myself with someone solid, someone I can count on. But she's standing, and so I do the same.

"Your brother has acute chest syndrome and was in a great deal of pain when he arrived here. Worse than I've seen in quite some time." She doesn't stop to explain ACS to me, since we both know I've done all the reading there is to do about it. I know how severe it can be, but if Dr. Fredrickson was able to spot it in time, it's treatable. "We're going to keep him here for a little while, track his progress, especially after this afternoon's exchange transfusion."

And it clicks, the reason Dr. Fredrickson didn't want me to walk straight into his room when I arrived. Robbie is currently hooked up to a machine that removes his damaged red blood cells and replaces them with the healthy blood of a donor. Without warning, the sight alone might have been just what it would take to push me over the edge.

She looks down at her watch. "If you're ready, you can have some time with him before I'll need to see him again. Your grandparents are in his room as well."

I straighten as I walk in the direction of his room. I'm still me. And Liz Lighty learned a long time ago how to put on a good face for her little brother.

thirty-four

When I see Robbie lying down, eyes shut against the light and oxygen tubes in his nostrils, and hooked up to the machines that might be saving his life, I am reminded that some people might just not get luck.

"Bea," Robbie whispers, eyes still shut. "Beatriz, will you please ask my sister on a scale of one to ten how pissed she is at me?"

Granny turns to the door where I'm standing, noticing me for the first time. Me and Ro can do this sometimes, just sort of know when the other is in the room without looking. We're not twins, but we have developed an undeniably twin-like connection over time.

"Lizzie, baby." Granny stands and wraps her arms around me. I bury my face into her neck, which smells like it always does, sort of like White Diamonds perfume but mostly like home.

I'm so glad to see her, to be enveloped in her arms like I am every time I walk through the doors of our house, everything feels a little closer to normal. When I pull back, I see Grandad nodding off in the corner. I swear, nothing fazes that man except losing to Robbie at a game of *Jeopardy!*

Beatriz, the nurse, offers me her usual pinched smile as she adjusts the clear dressing over the L-shaped needle sticking out of Robbie's port. I wince at the sight of it. Even though I'm going to be a doctor one day, this has never gotten any easier to stomach.

"Liz, your brother wants to know how pissed you are," she deadpans.

"When Granny and Grandad are gone, I'll make sure to let him know."

Granny tucks me to her side and guides me over to the couch in the corner, like I didn't just threaten to cuss my brother out the minute she leaves the room. I can't blame her. Hospital visits knock everyone off their axes a little bit. And it's been a while since we've had one like this.

Robbie smiles but groans quietly. "Granny, could me and Liz have a second? I want her to"—he intakes a sharp breath with a wince—"rip me a new one while I'm drugged rather than while I'm sober."

Granny laughs and swipes at her eyes quickly. She slaps my grandad on the back of the head, and he wakes with a start.

"What in the Devil!"

"Come on, Byron." Granny grabs his hand and pulls him after her. "Let's see what they're serving up in the cafeteria."

"I don't want that crusty cafeteria food! Last time we were here,

I about cracked a tooth on my biscuit. It's a shame what they're serving the sick and shut in," Grandad mumbles, but he follows her out the door.

Beatriz goes soon after, leaving Robbie and I alone. I almost don't know what to say to him, about any of this. He opens his eyes then, and his face holds no trace of his usual humor, his constant attempts to lighten my mood. "I'm sorry, Liz. I'm really sorry."

I sigh. I'm exhausted. Like, bone-deep, viscerally worn down. I cross the room to sit on the edge of Ro's bed and link our fingers together.

But instead of laying into him like I know he expects, I tell him the truth.

"I should disown you for this, you know. You are literally the cherry on top of a curdled-milk sundae of an emotional roller coaster."

Because the thing is, I'm sorry too. I'm sorry he's sick, that I can't do anything about it—that our lives have been a revolving door of hospital visits and experimental drugs and near-death scares.

"Curdled-milk sundae *and* a roller coaster? You're mixing your metaphors." He snorts. His features snap to attention quickly, the realization dawning on him. "Liz, please tell me you made court. *Please*, I'm begging you, for everything good and holy in this world, please tell me that my sister is going to have her nerdy but some-how secretly amazing self on the prom court docket next week."

"I don't know. I don't even think I want to know right now."

"Well, have you"—he stops and shuts his eyes briefly—"checked Campbell Confidential?"

"I've been a little busy, Ro. I haven't had time to *check Campbell Confidential.*" I roll my eyes. Even sick, this boy can't resist logging in and being nosy. "And whatever. Maybe I should just drop out anyway."

He opens his eyes and looks almost frantic. "Liz, that's the only stupid thing I've ever heard you say."

"Excuse me?"

"You're not serious. You can't be. After all this? No way. Give me my phone." He points at his sweatpants folded on a table next to the window. I grab his phone and place it in his upturned hand, wiggling fingers and all. He scrolls quickly, like the man on a mission he is.

"I am serious." I shake my head. "What's the point? Look what I've already lost in being part of this. I spent so much time doing prom stuff that I could have spent with you. It's not worth it."

"What you've lost? Look what you've gained!" He says quickly, almost breathlessly. "I have never seen you like this before, Liz. You're having fun. And I know that's a foreign concept to a workaholic like you, but fun is a *good* thing." He smirks and nudges me gently with his knee. "You never would have gone viral for becoming Campbell's own FloJo, never would have become friends with Jordan again."

And, okay, so maybe the kid makes some points. But still.

"It just feels like every time I get closer to winning being possible, something else goes wrong."

He looks a little sad, and not just because he's hooked up to this machine.

"You can't keep living your life for me and Granny and

Grandad." He reaches for me slowly, and I take his hand. "We're gonna be fine. We always are—it's the Lighty Way. But look at this! What you've done in this campaign is dope. I can't believe my sister has become the most-talked-about person in Campbell County."

I'm wiping at a tear I don't remember crying, but suddenly my throat feels tight and all I wanna do is wrap my arms around my not-so-little-anymore brother.

"And think about it this way." He looks down at his phone as he speaks, clicking around. "If you hadn't run, you never would have fallen in love."

He shoves his phone at me triumphantly, after finding what he was looking for, the brightest smile I've seen from him all day finally making its way across his face. The prom court list has been posted and reposted all over Campbell Confidential. It's there. My name is there.

My mouth opens and closes without any sound managing to escape.

"Congratulations, big sis." He raises his eyebrows. "Still thinking about dropping out?"

Okay, so I'm full of it.

I am so, so deeply full of it that sometimes I actually believe myself. Because for a second, in the moment that I told Robbie I wanted to quit, I seriously thought I wanted to quit. But now, as I see my name on the girls' list, I'm reminded of how badly I want to win. Want that scholarship. Want to go to Pennington.

Claire Adams
Quinn Bukowski
Lucille Ivanov
Elizabeth Lighty

I'm pretty sure it's dark outside now, even though there are no windows where I'm sitting. I stepped out to let Robbie rest once Granny and Grandad returned from dinner a few hours ago, and decided to hole up in a corner in the waiting room. Granny and Grandad are still camped out in Robbie's room, covered in some thin hospital-issue blankets, drifting in and out of sleep, but I thought it'd be better if I stayed out here. I think that after the past few weeks, maybe some time alone is good for me.

My phone is still turned off, tucked into my back pocket. Which probably explains why I don't expect it when Jordan Jennings comes around the corner—grinning from ear to ear despite where we are—shaking the two greasy white paper bags he has in his hands.

"You come here often?" he says as he approaches. He sits down in the seat next to me and places the bag in my lap. "I brought you dinner. I thought you might be hungry."

I peek inside and smile. "You brought me our first meal."

"I'll never forget Post-Puke Liz Lighty." He laughs quietly. "This double steakburger is officially our thing now."

I plop the bag down on top of an old issue of *Highlights for Children*.

"How you doing, fam?" Jordan throws an arm around my

shoulder, and I lean into it easily. "It's been a wild ride these past few days."

"Yeah." I nod. But Robbie is still here, still safe. So my own drama aside, I can deal. "But it could be worse."

"Just because it could be worse doesn't mean you don't get to acknowledge how much it sucks, you know." I sigh but don't respond. "You've missed a lot since you went off the grid after Rachel pulled that stunt."

I lean back to look up at him, eyes wide.

"Did you forget it's Campbell County, Lighty? Things can always get worse." He rolls his eyes. "Need I remind you about the #ReplacementEmme fiasco?"

I laugh, once, short. "No, you really don't."

Jordan grabs my bag of food as he starts his story, pulls out my burger and shoves it into my hand. He does the same with his and takes a massive bite.

I don't realize how hungry I am until I taste it.

"Yup, eat up. You'll need your strength for when I tell you that Madame Simoné kicked Rachel out of the race."

I nearly choke. "That's why she's not on the list?"

He nods. "Yup. Quinn told Madame Simoné everything: how Rachel had been plotting on you since the start, once it looked like you had a chance of winning. Word on the street is yesterday's stunt was a long time in the making."

"How do you know that?"

"Since you skipped out on lunch yesterday, you missed Quinn screaming at Rachel in the hallway. It was pretty ugly." He shakes his head and laughs. "I didn't even know the girl had it in her. I don't think I've ever even seen Quinn without a smile on her face."

"This is such a mess."

"Okay, but." He chews sloppily, and a little bit of tomato juice ends up on his chin. I reach over with a napkin and wipe it off like it's second nature. Weird how that happens, how you can feel so close to somebody in such a short period of time. He smiles, mouth still sort of full. "You haven't even heard the best part."

"Slow down before you choke."

"Fine. Look." He swallows, his Adam's apple bobbing. He crumples the wrapper and drops it in the bag. He sticks his tongue out, and I swear sometimes this boy reminds me so much of my little brother, it's eerie. "Clean plate club. Now listen! So about yesterday—"

"I don't really want to talk about yesterday," I interrupt softly.

"Have I ever steered you wrong?" Jordan raises his eyebrows at me like he already knows the answer. He begins pulling out his phone when I shake my head with an added eye roll for good measure. "Exactly." He hands his phone to me. "Now watch this."

Every post on Jordan's screen has the same thumbnail image, and to my surprise, it's not of the flag or my reaction. It's the crown from my posters.

"Jordan . . ."

He nods at the screen. "Go ahead. The whole feed is full of #EffYourFairyTale. At least three—no four—times as many as after the mural."

And he's right. The difference between then and now though, is the fact that none of the posts are in opposition to what I'm saying or asking questions about what it means. Almost all the captions look the same:

284

LOVE IS LOVE

Homophobia is for idiots

Get someone who looks at you like Mack looks at Liz! #RelationshipGoals #JusticeForMighty

Even Jaxon Price posted something. There's a picture with his middle finger dominating the frame, but the caption is simple, with no punctuation: *screw haters liz is the realest*

Even Jordan has posted something. A picture of a picture, one of me and him smiling broadly with our arms around each other after a band concert in eighth grade, with the caption: *The first to my second. The best there is.*

My jaw is practically on the ground when I turn back to Jordan. He stands up suddenly and extends his hand to me.

"Jordan . . ." I start, words failing me, my eyes prickling with tears for, like, the thousandth time today.

"Wait! Before you say something ridiculous like 'I don't deserve this!'" He pitches his voice higher to imitate me as he pulls me to my feet. "I have something for you."

"You already bought me dinner, you seriously didn't need to do anything else—"

"One of these days, Lighty"—he smiles that smile where he crinkles his nose a little and pulls me toward the door—"you're going to learn to trust me."

But that's just the thing. I already do trust Jordan—entirely, wholeheartedly. And maybe I've trusted him since the first day he sat next to me in middle school band, since he smiled at me and called me the second to his first, to the moment he brought me dinner while my brother was in the hospital without me having to ask him.

It's why I loved him so much all those years ago, because he's sometimes vulnerable and always honest, and the warmth I feel for him in this moment is proof of every good thought I've ever had about him. Flaws and fears and mistakes all, he is every bit the friend I need him to be right now.

· ♛ ·

I see Gabi silhouetted in the window of the passenger seat of Jordan's Range Rover as soon as I step into the parking lot.

"Talk to your friend, Lighty." He nudges me forward but remains near the door. He jerks his head toward the lobby. "I gotta go talk to one very special, very snappy short nurse about scoring some free pudding."

When I knock on the driver's-side window, Gabi practically jumps out of her skin. She closes her eyes briefly, gathering herself, before unlocking the doors. When I hop in, a wave of relief crashes over me. Despite everything, I'm glad she's here.

"Hi," I say quietly.

"Hi," she replies, turning her body in the seat to face me fully. She's wearing a black wool sweater with sleeves long enough to pull down over her hands. "I heard about Robbie. Is he okay? Are *you* okay?"

"He's going to bounce back," I say. I fold and unfold my hands in my lap. I pluck at a stray thread on my jeans. Seeing Robbie in the hospital, realizing how close I am at any time to losing him, puts things in perspective. "I hate fighting with you, you know."

"I do too." She looks out the windshield briefly, like she can't stand to look at me as she admits it. "I know it's not an excuse, but my dad officially moved out a few weeks ago. Mom has been a mess." She looks back at me with her lips downturned. "I think they're finally getting a divorce."

I don't say anything, even though I want to. G's parents, the former high school sweethearts, have been struggling for years. And Gabi, who works so hard to be *on* all the time, to make things picture-perfect, has always been stuck in the middle. But this seems like the thing that may have broken her.

"But I keep putting my own drama above yours. I did it when we were younger with the whole Jordan thing, and I've been doing it during this race. I tried to control your world because I couldn't control mine, and I'm so sorry. I never should have made you feel like you had to hide parts of yourself. No friend should do that."

"G, you could have told me about your parents," I say. "I would have been there for you. You have to know that."

She nods with a sniffle.

"And you owe Amanda an apology."

"I know," she answers. "She's up next on the Gabi Marino Says Sorry Tour. Stone hasn't let me go a day without reminding me how badly my negative aura is affecting her lately."

I snort, and G smiles.

"I'm really sorry, Lizzie. About everything." And that's all there is to say, really.

Gabi's tiny hand reaches across the space in the car to grab mine. It's like we're kids again, her sleeping on my floor in the weeks after my mom's funeral. We're clinging to each other like lifelines, because in so many ways, we are. And we always have been. We're going to make mistakes. But we're also going to find our way back to each other.

Liz Lighty
View Profile

WEEK SIX

All the world's a game; all the wannabe
kings and queens merely players.

Friends

Messages (315)

LOG OUT?

thirty-five

By Sunday evening, it looks like Robbie is in the clear. Dr. Fredrickson says he should be fine to go home by tomorrow, and honestly, it sounds like music to my ears. My granny's too. She breathes out slowly and allows herself her first smile in days as the doctor talks to us about the updated treatment plan out in the hallway.

When she's done, Granny tells me to come with her for a walk. She doesn't really ask me for anything, never has. Sentences that should have question marks at the end are delivered with periods. I've always loved that about her. She knows exactly what she wants from the people around her, and she's never afraid to let you know. It's a trait I wish I'd been gifted in the genetic lottery.

I glance back in the room before heading down the hall with her. Grandad is snoozing in his usual chair by the window as

Robbie absently clicks through the channels on the hospital TV. His eyes are heavy in that way that tells me he's about five minutes from being completely knocked out.

We round a corner, away from the waiting room, and she sits down unceremoniously.

"I owe you an apology, young lady." She smiles up at me from her seat, and it breaks my heart. I forget sometimes how much my mom favored her. "Sit down."

"Granny, no. *I'm* sorry. I'm so, so sorry that I haven't been home much lately." I sit down and tuck my ankle under the opposite thigh and shift to face her. "I know how important it is to you for us to be together."

And I mean it. I mean it with everything in me. My granny has never asked anything of me other than to get good grades and be on time for dinner every evening. And my grades are still fine. But I've dropped the ball on the thing that matters most to her: family.

"It's not just important to me, Lizzie. It's important to you too. And it was important to your mama." She shakes her head and looks over at the hallway leading to Ro's room, where he's probably asleep by now. "Her only demand when she got real sick—when we had to start thinking about what might happen when she passed—was that you two would stick together. 'They only got each other, Mama,' she said."

I didn't know that. Granny never mentioned it to me before, but it suddenly makes more sense why she was so strict about me missing dinner. It was part of her only daughter's last wish.

And suddenly I'm crying. I'm crying like I haven't allowed myself to cry since my mom's funeral, because I miss her and because I don't have any answers and because the only thing she wanted me to do was to look after my brother and I'm not always going to be able to do that. I was so concerned with my own drama that I didn't watch for the signs that something was wrong. Granny lets me just cry into her soft cotton shirt for a moment without speaking.

"You remind me so much of her sometimes it breaks my heart," she says, her voice hushed. I wrap my arms around her waist, just holding her there, as she rubs big, soothing circles into my back. "The way you take care of your brother, the way you run yourself into the ground to take some of the pressure off me and your Grandaddy paying for your college . . . Looking at you is like looking at LuLu when she was seventeen. You're every bit as feisty as your mama."

Granny rarely uses my mom's childhood nickname, and just the sound of it makes me want to cry more.

"Really?"

She looks down at me and smiles. She wipes at my eyes, and that gesture, like everything she does, is a form of instruction. We cry, but we don't cry long. We feel, but we always fight. It's the Lighty Way.

"Yes ma'am." She nods. "She wanted to be prom queen too, you know."

"What?" I sit up quickly and look her directly in her eyes.

"I know you didn't tell me about running for prom queen because you didn't want me to worry," she says simply. I don't know how she knows or just how much, but I shake my head. "Your brother is the most careless teenage boy I've ever seen. You think he'd at least lock his phone when he forgets it in the bathroom if he's going to keep using that Campbell Confidential mess against my wishes."

"Granny, I—"

"Shhhhhh, don't worry. I'm not mad. Your mama thought about running her senior year. Had a big plan and campaign slogans and everything. But she decided against it at the last minute." Granny rubs the back of her neck, and it's in that motion I realize how tired she is. She looks like she hasn't slept properly in weeks, and I silently kick myself for not noticing this either. "I'll admit, me and your grandaddy weren't the most supportive of the idea."

I pull at one of the frayed threads of the hole in my jeans.

"It was a different time then. Campbell was a different place, but not that different. Now y'all can date who you want and wear what you want, and people will leave you be. They may think what they wanna think, but they won't do the kind of stuff they used to do back then."

I nod. Granny isn't a naturally verbose woman, and something about hearing a story spill from her lips makes me both incredibly happy and incredibly sad all at once.

"I know I haven't said anything about all this prom hoopla you got going on, Lizzie. And I'm sorry about that." Her voice cracks a little. "And I'm sorry I never told you to slow down when I saw how hard you were pushing yourself. I guess I just didn't want to make the same mistakes I made with your mama." She reaches over and wipes the tear that escapes with her thumb. "My Lizzie, my little star. I never want to tell you not to burn as fast and as bright as you can."

Granny is human, and so was my mother, and so am I. We are not above mistakes, not stronger than death, but we sure know how to love. Even if it isn't always perfect, especially when it's a little messy, we know how to love one another fiercely. With everything we have.

"I figured that you're worried about the money. And we don't have much, that's to be sure. But me and your grandaddy have a little bit saved. Enough to help you out a little. It won't cover everything, but it'll help." All those overnight shifts. All those weekends when she couldn't sleep. Granny was worried too. She never left me to fend for myself.

Granny pulls me to her again and speaks impossibly gently into my hair.

"I just want you to know that you can rest, Lizzie, baby." She kisses the top of my head softly. "I got you when you're ready to rest."

thirty-six

The last week before prom is surprisingly calm. The hallways carry the type of buzz that only an event of this magnitude could possibly generate, but things feel less tense somehow. Less scary.

I'm still terrified about not getting the money, of course. But now that the dust has settled and Rachel has been kicked out of the running for prom court, I don't have to look over my shoulder every ten minutes. The votes were cast this morning during homeroom, so now all that's left is for us to wait.

"I'm just saying, I think we should throw out the idea of a limo altogether," Britt says through a mouthful of dessert. Gabi's mom sent her to lunch with a Tupperware container full of vegan cherry-and-almond brownies that we're well on our way to completely devouring. It's the fifth dessert this week. "Let's just take my Prius to prom! Think about it. We're down for making statements now that Liz has paved the way. We should be talking about the environment!"

"I feel like we might need more drama than that." I tap my chin like I'm deep in thought. "Why not ride in on a tank to protest the military-industrial complex?"

"Now you're onto something!" Britt slaps the table.

We're all riding together, like we'd always planned, but something feels off. After everything, I'd sort of thought that me and Amanda would make it work and go as a couple. It was a far-fetched idea, I know, considering the rules. But I couldn't stop myself from hoping.

It will be fine. I'm going to go to prom with my best friends and keep working on this cool new platonic relationship I have going with Amanda. It's cool. I'm cool with being friends with her. The whole thing is very chill.

Okay, I'm lying. I'm not chill at all.

I can't stop myself from cutting eyes over to her desk in AP World History, hoping that I can catch her attention so we can share a laugh about our teacher's habit of wearing pants that ride too low in the back and show off his butt crack. I still spend an obnoxious amount of time waiting for her to text me back or wondering if I should text her first or wanting to ask what she thinks about the newest Kittredge single. I am so freaking gone over this girl I don't know what to do.

"Whatever we do, I might have to do it in my birthday suit, since somebody"—I toss a grape in Gabi's direction and laugh as she dodges it—"finished everyone else's dresses but mine."

In the whirlwind of everything: me and Gabi fighting and not speaking, me being outed, and Robbie getting sick—Gabi ran out of time to finish the dress she was making for me. Although it was less formal than I would've liked, I was okay with wearing the dress she made me for homecoming last year instead. I never got to wear it because I backed out of going to the dance at the last minute. The night of, my anxiety about being seen all dressed up like that just got to be too much. That feels like a lifetime ago now.

The freshmen at the table next to us are whipping out their phones, so I turn my head toward the cafeteria entrance. And when I do, I swear I can feel every hair on my arm stand up. Because Teela Freaking Conrad is playing an acoustic guitar, singing my favorite song, and walking toward me.

Teela's voice quiets the cafeteria almost instantly, but it still doesn't feel like enough. It feels like she could strum the acoustic guitar in her hand while sitting in my lap and I would still want to be closer to her voice, to the song. She's singing "My Life, My Story," the song she wrote after the rumors that she was bi started swirling.

I look around at my friends, and all of them have broad smiles on their faces. They don't look surprised; they just look happy.

> *Someone once told me*
> *You spent your life running.*
> *Well, I wish you'd stand still,*
> *'Cause in this light you're stunning.*
>
> *It's my life, my story,*
> *And I want to share it with you.*

It's my life, my story,
But part of it was always yours too.

I can't even—this is not real life.

Everyone in the cafeteria is recording, and one of the freshmen has fainted into her spasagna. It's officially a faint-worthy event.

When Teela strums the final note, that's when I see her. Amanda rolls into the cafeteria on a skateboard, but not her usual one. As she rolls to a stop in front of our table, she kicks it up into one of her hands and flips it over so the bottom of the deck is facing me. The message is bold, in Amanda's loopy handwriting, but her smile completely shy.

Liz Lighty, will you go to prom with me?

thirty-seven

The morning of prom doesn't feel like waking up on Christmas Day like I thought it might. It's not like that moment of opening your eyes and knowing you're either about to get everything you asked for—everything you ate your vegetables and didn't backtalk your grandparents for—or not. It's like something else entirely.

Something like New Year's Eve maybe. The pressure of it being a big, memorable night that bleeds into a new era and, ultimately, into the rest of your life. I'm sort of terrified.

So I do what I always do when I'm afraid. I connect my phone to the Bluetooth speaker Robbie got me for my birthday last year, find my favorite playlist, and turn it up.

The notes are so familiar, they fly through the room like they live in the air. It's soothing. They feel the way they did the night I applied to Pennington or after the first time Amanda and I kissed. Fear and hope fight for the same space inside my chest. The only difference is now, regardless of the unknown, I'm positive I'll be all right.

No matter what happens tonight, I know I'll be fine.

"Lizzie, baby!" Granny knocks twice but doesn't wait for me to answer before poking her head in the door. Robbie's floating head appears right above hers barely a second later. "Get on up. We got a lot to do today."

Robbie is nodding his head with the biggest smile I've seen on his face in weeks.

"Yeah, Liz, we gotta get you ready for prom!"

I throw my legs over the side of the bed and roll my eyes.

"Don't roll your eyes at your brother, little miss." Granny holds my door open wider with one hand so that I can walk through and nudges me forward gently with the other. Robbie throws an arm around my shoulders and gloats.

"Yeah, *little miss*," Robbie smirks and plants a wet kiss on my forehead before plopping down on the couch next to Grandad. "Be nice to your sickly, can't-attend-prom-and-is-living-vicariously-through-you little brother."

And when I look around the living room, the whole place looks like the Macy's prom section and DSW and the beauty shop Granny gets her hair permed at all got together and had the most massively obnoxious baby known to man. There's a dress form in the center of the room with my mom's prom dress on it, my granny's sewing kit on the coffee table, a box of shoes that must be brand-new are sitting on the couch. Granny's even pulled out her home hair dryer, like the kind they have at the shop, only you can set it on a table and fold it up when you're finished. Grandad is in the center of it all, snoring loudly.

I'm more than a little bit blown away.

I turn to face Granny, and she has her hands on her waist and a tape measure draped around her neck. She's still wearing her scrubs from her night shift, and I know she hasn't been to bed yet. But she smiles at me like she knows what I'm thinking, and I realize that maybe she does.

"You're usually a very sharp girl, Lizzie," Granny says, winding the tape measure around my waist. Her voice is muffled by the pins between her lips. "You should've asked me to alter this dress earlier."

Robbie laughs. "Last-Minute Lizzie has a ring to it, Granny."

"Now you hush, Robert." Granny snaps the tape measure in his direction, and it connects with his bare knee with a light *snap!* Now it's my turn to laugh. "You better learn to mind business that's yours and leave everybody else's alone, little boy."

Granny makes quick work of measuring my waist and bust before jotting down some quick notes.

"What?" she asks, when I open and close my mouth in surprise. "You thought I was going to let you go to prom in a homecoming dress? Not on my watch."

I cut my eyes at Robbie, but he shrugs innocently. The little informant.

"You would have come to me earlier if you knew how difficult it is to alter velvet." Granny's already pinning up the gown. "I made this for your mama nearly twenty-one years ago now. She was going through a Winona Ryder phase."

When she rolls her eyes, it's affectionate, tender.

I look at my mom's dress where it rests on the form. It looks every bit as good now as it did when she went to prom, if the picture of her in it that sits on top of the TV stand is anything to go by. She was so gorgeous. Slightly taller than me, confident, secure in the fact that she deserved to take up space in Campbell. Deserved to take up space anywhere.

The dress reminds me of her: elegant, beautiful, classic. It's a floor-length violet velvet slip dress, with a low back and spaghetti straps.

Robbie asks, "Who's Winona Ryder?" at the same time I say, "What was she like?"

"Like, on the day of prom," I add, ignoring Robbie completely because honestly how has he not seen *Stranger Things* by now? "Do you remember what she was like on prom night? Was she nervous?"

I sit down on the arm of the couch, and Granny looks over at me. She lets out a breath and puts her hands on her hips again with a smile. Her default pose.

"She was excited. Your mama was a real social butterfly, you know. Went with a couple of her girlfriends. She really wanted the full high school experience, even though she spent so much time . . . Even though she wasn't always able to go to school."

Robbie rests his head on my thigh then, and I rub his shoulder.

"She would have found a way to be in the back of the room tonight when you got up on that stage, I know that much," Granny says, turning back to the dress and speaking again through a pin between her teeth. "So let's give 'em a show, huh? For your mama."

By the time Granny is done with me, I see what she means by the resemblance between me and my mom. Granny and I did my makeup together, with the help of some YouTube beauty gurus. It's a simple beat, natural and dewy—compliments of Jackie Aina. My hair is down, but thanks to the deep condition I did this afternoon and the roller set afterward, my hair falls in not-quite-straight but not-entirely-curly waves over my shoulder on one side, and it's pinned up by a beautiful faux-diamond clip on the other. I look like a movie star in her dress—even this updated and altered version—and with the smile on my face as I look in the mirror, I do look like her.

The next half hour happens like a series of snapshots. Like a poorly edited family video from the '90s—all jump cuts, no B-roll.

Robbie does a Campbell Confidential live of Granny and Grandad taking pictures of me on their ancient flip phones—Grandad complaining that "All this technology don't make no type of sense!" before walking to the kitchen and coming back with a disposable camera from who knows where. I'm reluctantly posing in the middle of the room, and suddenly the doorbell is ringing and we all go silent, because this is the moment. This is the big reveal.

And Granny says, "Well, are you gon' let the poor girl inside or are you gon' stand there like a mule looking at a grass sack?"

And Robbie is laughing, and I'm reaching for his phone to end the video and then Amanda is there. Right in front of me, standing in the doorway.

Amanda's dress has a floor-length black skirt with a high waist that cinches in right under her bra line. But the top half is the part that reminds me who I'm going to prom with, the girl whose style can't help but push Campbell past its comfort zone and out of its antiquated ways. The white top is sleeveless with ruffles down the front, the neckline a high Victorian, adorned with a black bow tied in the center, the ribbon left long and draping.

She looks equal parts *Downton Abbey* and Janelle Monáe, and I love every bit of it.

"I didn't think you could look any more beautiful than you did the night of our first date," she says quietly. So quietly, in fact, that I know Robbie can't even hear, despite how hard he's eavesdropping but pretending not to from the couch. "But then you showed up to the party in that black dress, and now . . . now this." She grabs my hand and smiles that smile that she only ever smiles for me. "You are constantly reminding me how ridiculous it is that I got lucky enough to be your date."

And I'm smiling so hard my cheeks hurt, and my granny calls out to us. "Well, come on in here, girl! I'd like to know who has my granddaughter smiling all the time and forgetting to tell me about altering her prom dress."

Amanda is blushing as she steps into my house for the first time. Her face is red as she extends a hand to my grandparents.

"Mr. and Mrs. Lighty, it's nice to meet you."

Grandad is the first to speak, but he lets out a loud cackle first. "Elizabeth, you got this poor girl so scared, even I can see her shaking in her shoes!"

Granny softens considerably. I never thought she'd be one of those have-her-home-by-curfew types, but then again, I never imagined this moment at all. Two months ago, this all seemed impossible.

"Take a breath, baby. I'm not going to hurt you," Granny says. Amanda shakes her hand and offers a tentative smile. "But I might think about it if y'all don't exchange them little corsages and get on out of here."

And so we do. They're identical, little bundles of white orchids with sprigs of lavender interspersed throughout. Even if we couldn't buy tickets as a couple, even though we technically can't hold hands or kiss or dance too close once we get there, there's no mistaking that we're together. And that small act of resistance feels good to me.

We stand together to pose, with Robbie taking over as official prom photographer now that Grandad is all tuckered out and the disposable camera is out of film. And at one point, right before we walk out the door, I swear the kid wipes away a tear.

I don't say anything about that though. I kiss him once on the cheek and do the same for both my grandparents before walking outside. Amanda links our fingers together and just looks at me once we reach the car. Neither of us reaches for the door handle. We just kind of watch each other.

We're supposed to be headed to meet Britt, Stone, and Gabi for our dinner reservation at Rick's Café Boatyard, but I can't bring myself to rush.

"Hey," I say, tucking one of her strands of hair behind her ear with my free hand. "Whatever happens tonight, there's no one else I would rather be doing this with." I'm so happy I could burst.

"You're not the only lucky one."

thirty-eight

I've always thought downtown Indianapolis was sort of magical, which, I know, is a ridiculously Midwestern thing of me to say. But it's true. It's only a few miles away, but it's worlds different from Campbell. And that's always made it feel like something special to me.

But the Arts Garden is magical tonight by anyone's standards.

The sun has just barely set by the time we walk inside, and you can see every bit of the pinkish-purple light of the early evening sky once you step through the doors. The Arts Garden is one of the coolest things the city has to offer, and I'm not surprised Campbell makes it a point to host prom here every year. The entire space is made of glass, steel beams crossing back and forth above our heads and keeping us firmly seven stories above the rest of the city. It's like we're on display for everyone to see but somehow tucked away in a world of our own making up here.

Like I said, it's very Campbell.

We're still reeling from the yearbook-paparazzi camera flashes on the Cougar-red carpet just moments before when Amanda stops suddenly. "Whoa, this is . . ."

"Yeah." I nod. "Just wait until they start the fireworks later."

The theme is Midnight in Paris, and even I have to admit that the prom committee went above and beyond with this one. The entire room is glowing in blues and golds, and they've even managed a massive, very impressive Eiffel Tower replica that people keep stopping to gawk at. There's a six-foot-tall ice sculpture of the Louvre Pyramid, with sparkling cider spouting from a fountain at its peak, near the stage. In the back of the room is an elaborate photography setup, with full lights, a huge backdrop, and Anabella San Junipero—the photographer who shot the *Vanity Fair* young Hollywood cover a few years back—carefully positioning a couple of juniors in front of her lens.

I suddenly get what all the hype is about. This is enough to turn any cynic into a believer.

It's weird, being raised in a small town. There's not much to do there except drive into the city, and not much to look forward to but getting out one day. But prom is the thing that binds the whole place together. It's the one event of the year where everyone participates, parents forget who said what at that one PTA meeting, and we get to become the stars of the fairy tales we've been reading since we were kids. Maybe it has to do with the performance of it all, how elaborate and ornate it can be—about feeling like royalty in the midst of a place surrounded by cornfields.

Prom is a lot of things to a lot of people, and I'm not sure I'll ever understand some of them. But that part I sort of get: Feeling special in a town that doesn't feel special at all is worth all sorts of madness.

Mr. K is the chaperone on duty for check-in when we arrive, and I'm so happy to see him.

"Look at you!" He beams when we approach the table to check in— Gabi, Stone, and Britt in front of me and Amanda beside me. We're not holding hands, but her knuckles keep brushing against mine, and it's a very near thing. "You guys look like a million bucks! Let me just find your names here."

Our tickets had to be bought separately, but Mr. K checks off my name and then Amanda's. When he hands us our goodie bags— each of them filled with a pair of AirPods, some gift cards to local restaurants, and a commemorative mug—he holds on to mine for a second longer than everyone else's, and I tell the rest of the group to go on without me.

"I have good news," he says, his smile wide.

The last time I saw him look this hopeful was before my audition. I smile back on instinct.

"Is this about—" I start, but he jumps in before I can finish.

"I sent your newest arrangement to my old advisor at Pennington! He loved it, and they agreed to give you another audition in a few weeks, if you want to give them another chance."

I scream. I can't help it. I put my hands on my knees and happy-screech at the floor. When I look back up, Mr. K is laughing so hard his eyes are watering.

He wipes at them quickly, and I start to thank him for this audition, for everything.

"Mr. K, I don't even know what to say. Thank you so much—"

He waves his hands in front of his face and beams.

"Don't even think about it. You deserve this. We'll talk more about it on Monday. But for now"—he points over to where Amanda is standing with my best friends. She's talking to Britt, waving her hands around as she tries to prove a point—"it looks like you have a date to get back to."

"What was that about?" Amanda pushes close to me when I catch up to her by the table she's claimed as ours. There are a couple of folks from concert band sitting down already who wave as I approach.

"I—" I stop myself and shake my head with a grin. It can wait until Monday morning. Right now, all I want to focus on is this. "I'll tell you about it later. You want to dance?"

And of course she wants to dance. My date is nothing if not unafraid of letting go, of being unabashedly excited about something. And when she pulls me to the dance floor, I feel that same energy. I start off with a simple sway, but as Amanda throws her hands into the air and spins and smiles at the Beyoncé and Jay-Z song they're currently playing, I can't help but join in.

I'm out of breath when Jordan taps me on the shoulder.

"Mind if I cut in?" he asks Amanda with that little crinkle-nose smile of his. I throw my arms around his middle, so happy to see him I can barely contain myself. "Whoa, Lighty! If I had known you were already this in tune with your emotions I wouldn't have used up all my best relationship advice on you."

He hugs me back just as tightly as I angle my face up to look at him.

"You look different," I say, stepping back to examine his face. He looks great, of course. His tuxedo is perfectly tailored, and his gray bow tie is serving me definite Met Gala vibes. "What's different about you?"

He doesn't say anything, just sort of smiles shyly, and then Emme Chandler peeks out from behind him and extends a hand to me, and I get it.

"I think I might be to blame." Her voice is soft like I remember.

I bypass her hand altogether and hug her too. Because I guess prom has just turned me into the type of person who hugs people all willy-nilly.

Emme looks amazing. Her white-blond hair is half up, half down and falling in loose waves down her back. Her silver dress is simple and sophisticated, like a young Grace Kelly.

"Emme"—I look from her to Jordan and back—"you're here! I can't believe you're here."

I'm genuinely excited to see her. Not because I've ever known Emme all that well, but because I know what she means to Jordan. I know what it must mean to him to have her here on this night.

"Can I talk to you for a second?" Emme leans in and whisper-shouts in my ear.

I glance back at my friends, who are all in their own world. Gabi is shaking her hips like there's no tomorrow, Stone has her eyes closed and is swaying to no real rhythm in particular, while Britt just sort of aggressively fist pumps.

Amanda is still dancing but smiles at me, like, *Go ahead, I'll be waiting for you when you get back!* And I realize that she always looks like that, like she'll always be there when I come back.

I follow Emme off to the side of the room, and we stand at the edge of the snack table. They wouldn't dare leave a bowl of punch out like they do in all those movies, because—let's be honest with ourselves here—who trusts a room full of teenagers with too much privilege and not enough supervision *not* to do something reckless? But there is a water dispenser, and some finger foods catered by Guy Fieri in a seriously decadent spread.

Two senior PromBotsPomBots, the worst kind, whisper near the water and keep looking in our direction. I sigh. I can't wait to be past all this.

"Sorry about that," I say with a sigh. I know it must be hard enough to come back after being away, and the whispers can't be helping.

"No apologies needed from you." She smiles at me gently and places a hand on my arm. She lowers her voice like she's telling a secret. "Did you hear I got arrested for being part of an illicit capuchin monkey smuggling ring in Arizona?"

I laugh thinking of all the ridiculous rumors that spread about where Emme went after she first left. They've slowed down a bit, become less extreme over the past few weeks, but they're still pretty pervasive.

"What?" I feign surprise. "I heard it was tropical birds in Nebraska!"

"Campbell is good at blowing things out of proportion," she adds with a laugh of her own.

"Jordan's missed you," I offer. It feels appropriate in this moment. "This whole place just about shut down after you left."

"It was hard to be away from him." She lowers her voice. "He's probably told you some of what's been going on with me. And I just wanted to say thank you for being there for him when I needed to take some time away to get my head on straight. It's hard to . . . grow here sometimes."

I don't ask her where she's been, or if she's back for good, because it's none of my business. I just nod, because I do understand the most important part of what she's saying. This town has never been good at allowing people to be their full, imperfect-but-still-worthy selves.

"You know, Jordan hasn't said anything about where you've been—not even to me." I look over to the dance floor, where he's currently having a twerk-off with Jaxon, and roll my eyes. "You are the one thing he never takes lightly."

"Well, well, well. Look who's graced us with her presence!" Rachel cuts in, quick and stumbling, and points between the two of us.

I think briefly that she might have pregamed a little too hard before getting here, but I realize she's not stumbling because she's drunk, she's stumbling because she broke away from a flustered-looking Claire, who was very clearly trying to keep her from doing exactly what she's doing now.

"Hello, Rachel," Emme says, cool as ice. "Lovely dress. Red has always been your color."

"Like Satan himself. Very appropriate," I mumble, because I've never been as nice as Emme.

"I heard that, Liz," Rachel seethes. "And give it a rest, Emme. You don't get to disappear to *rehab* and come back playing the princess."

Claire walks over, embarrassment dotting her features. I wonder where Quinn and Lucy are and if they're watching their old friend completely unravel at the snack table, of all places.

"Emme, Liz, hey." Claire attempts a smile for the two of us before turning her attention to Rachel. "Rach, seriously, let's go outside for some air. I hear some freshman is crying by the Cinnabon because her senior boyfriend just broke up with her."

Claire tries to tug Rachel toward the door, but she's immovable. Hate can really make a mountain out of a person.

"I'm not going anywhere, *Claire*. I want to know why these two are so chummy all of a sudden." She narrows her eyes at Emme. "You go away and come back playing for the other team, huh, Em?"

Rachel is talking too loud, and now people are paying attention. The girls who were whispering before are back, arms crossed, and ready to CC Live a showdown between the former queen and the reigning dictator who took her place. I'm not sure what my role is in that metaphor, but something tells me it's nothing good.

Quinn walks up with Lucy, Jaxon in tow holding her purse. I see now what Jordan meant about not knowing Quinn had the capacity to look so angry.

"What is your problem, Rachel? Gawd!"

"Yeah, this is beneath even you, Rach." Lucy purses her lips and rolls her eyes, half bored with the whole thing, as usual.

Rachel looks around, clearly unsure what to do with not being the one whose side everyone is automatically on.

Her fists curl at her sides and she rounds on me, reaching for my hair. My reflexes are normally trash, but tonight they're quick enough to grab her wrist before it connects. It's not even hard—

I'm barely touching her—but she immediately bursts into tears.

"You stole this from me! You ruined everything!" Her mascara is running, and I let go of her, jumping back like she burned me. "You're not even—you're not even supposed to *be here*!"

I open my mouth, but no sound comes out. I don't know what I would have said even if it did.

"I think you're the one who shouldn't be here, Miss Collins," Principal Wilson's voice booms from behind her. I'm not sure when he got here or how much he saw, but something tells me that Mr. K and his satisfied smile by the door have something to do with it.

And as Principal Wilson escorts her out the door, I don't know who starts it, but there's scattered applause around us, loud enough to hear over the still-pulsing music. I don't know the song, but I know the sound. And it's every bit the soundtrack I've been waiting for.

thirty-nine

The next two hours are surprisingly uneventful, given how things started. Uneventful but perfect. They're playing more music that I only vaguely recognize because of Jordan and Robbie, and the beat is sort of giving the whole room a pulse.

I mean, there's a lot of white people in here, so the movements lack a certain type of finesse, but it's still good. Jordan, Emme, Amanda, and I have formed a dance circle, and eventually Britt, Stone, and Gabi find their way over and jump around with us for a while. And I'm happy to be here. I'm genuinely, unabashedly happy to be in this place with these people on this night.

Britt, G, and Stone insist on getting pictures together, so we snap some selfies and then do a group photo with the professional photographer, making sure that they're *extra* corny. We line up in height order and do that thing where we put our hands on one another's waists, and we laugh so hard we can barely get a picture where the four of us are even looking at the camera.

"I'm gonna miss you weirdos." Britt throws her arm over my shoulders as we walk back to the dance floor.

"I'll send you to Pennington with sage, Lizzie. For you to cleanse the space," Stone offers. She leans her head against my shoulder and wraps her two arms around the one of mine. "And to remember me by."

"This isn't the end, guys! We have more than a month until graduation!" I shout over the music, in part because it's true and also because if I think about it too hard, I might get more emotional than I want to get while standing next to a couple of juniors who have their tongues so far down each others' throats it looks like it might be a legitimate health hazard.

"Okay, ladies, let's move. They're announcing queen in five!" Gabi shoos us back to the dance floor.

We rush back to dancing, and Amanda is right where I left her. She smiles at me and links our hands together between us. I'm not sure if anyone notices, but I find that I don't care. We deserve our small moments too.

"You ready?" She whispers into my ear.

With you, always, I think.

"As I'll ever be," I say.

They turn down the music as Madame Simoné clears her throat into the mic. She looks good tonight, in all black and a cute little beret. I have a feeling she had everything to do with this theme choice.

Behind her sits a table with a huge, Miss America–esque tiara for the queen and a much more modest gold crown for the king.

"Bonsoir, les étudiants!" Her expression is coy, like she knows she has everyone in the room's attention and she's not going to let it go. "Crowning the king and queen of Campbell County prom is my honor every year.

"I believe the king and queen should represent the very best of what Campbell has to offer, and I do truly believe that this year, we *have* had some of the very best candidates we've ever seen."

Everyone claps again, on cue, as Madame Simoné begins to unfold the envelope in her hand.

"And your 2020 Campbell County prom king is . . . Jordan Jennings!"

I look to my left, and Jordan is weaving his way up to the stage, smiling brightly. Emme is clapping furiously and crying happy tears. Everyone in the room could have seen this one coming—even Jaxon is hollering his praises as Jordan gets crowned—but it still feels good to watch. It isn't often people get the things they deserve, but Jordan deserves this. If king and queen are really what Madame Simoné says—that they represent the best of what Campbell has to offer—then this was always his to win.

He's the best Campbell has to offer.

Jordan hasn't taken his eyes off Emme since he got onstage, but as Madame Simoné gears up to make the announcement for queen, he looks at me and winks. And, like, I'm eighty-five percent sure this overwhelming, obnoxious, definitely-too-soon feeling in my chest is love for the girl to my right whose hand I'm holding and who happens to be the only person I want to kiss at the end of the night—but I'd be lying if I said the other fifteen percent isn't sheer terror about what's coming next.

"Now for the *pièce de résistance*, your 2020 Campbell County High School prom queen is . . ."

She unfolds the envelope, and my heart stops.

Amanda squeezes my hand once.

The room goes quiet, and I swear I can hear the shouts of an indignant Rachel Collins from the street below.

And it's as if I've been here before. I know this feeling like I know the way my hands feel wrapped around my instrument, spine straight and ready to perform.

It's the moment before the first movement of an orchestra. It's the split second before a conductor drops their arms to signal the beginning of a song. When you wait with bated breath and you feel the energy in the room and you don't have to wonder anymore because you just *know*. You just know it's all out of your hands from there. Call it fate or magic or miracle or whatever, but you've done what it takes for a flawless performance—practiced and rehearsed until your calluses had calluses—and yet, everything hangs in the balance. Anything could go wrong. Or—on the best nights—go very, very right.

"Elizabeth Lighty!"

I know people are clapping because I can see them, but I can't hear anything except a dull roar in my ears. She couldn't have said— There's no way it's—

"Liz, you won!" Amanda shouts. She's holding my face in both of her hands, and she's smiling a smile I've never seen before—a little wild, more than a little proud. "It's you! You won, Liz!"

And I don't know how I get onstage, because I can't even think to move my feet, but suddenly I'm standing next to Jordan and crouching down so that Madame Simoné can place the tiara on my head, and I'm crying a little, and I'd probably be embarrassed if I didn't look down into the audience and see Gabi, Stone, and even Britt all crying too.

Madame Simoné places a bouquet of flowers in my hands and whispers in my ear.

"*Tu es la meilleure*. The best queen I've ever crowned, Elizabeth." She kisses both my cheeks before pulling back and gesturing for me to step up and stand by Jordan. "The very finest."

I sort of stumble forward, and the room comes into sharp focus in that moment. I can see and hear everything, and it's almost sensory overload. The shouts from my friends I can distinguish easily, mingling with the clapping and the cheering of people I don't know. Everyone in the room, it seems, is locked into this moment with me. With Jordan.

Jordan grabs my hand with his and gives it a squeeze.

"What did I say, Lighty? A first is nothing without a good second." He waves at the audience with his free hand but smiles down at me. "But this is all you—you've always been first."

"Now, now!" Madame Simoné is back on the mic, calling for everyone to quiet down. "If everyone would settle down. It's time for our king and queen's official first dance."

Jordan lets go of my hand and smiles at me one more time, and I've never loved him more than I do in this moment.

"It's time for you to get that grand finale."

Jordan hops offstage like it's nothing, and the crowd parts for him like Moses and the Red Sea. But he stops, removes his crown, and places it directly on Amanda's head. He whispers something in her ear that makes her blush, turns to Emme, grabs her hand, and pulls her away for a dance of their own.

When I step down, Amanda is bouncing between looking at me and looking up at her too-big borrowed crown and trying to keep it from falling off her head. There are a couple of "Awwwws" around us and a couple of annoyed groans too. I may have won, but this is still Campbell. Things still aren't perfect, not by a mile.

"I think I owe you a dance, Queen Liz." She smiles and places her hands on my waist. Her—or Jordan's—crown tilts slightly to the left. "I know you're sort of against them, but I have to say, this feels like a fairy tale to me."

I drop my flowers on the ground between us and wrap my arms around her neck to pull her close. Because let's face it, I've never been much of a dancer.

So I kiss her instead. There in the middle of all our classmates, with the spotlight on us and those gaudy, coveted crowns on our heads, I kiss her with everything I have. Like I'll never kiss her again. Because this is real, we finally made it to this place, and it's better than any fairy tale. Because I'm done letting people stop me.

Because here, *always*, we deserve this good thing.

Acknowledgments

Acknowledgments might be the toughest part of this whole bookmaking thing because I owe so much of who I am and what this book has become to so many. But the first thank-you for this book, this life, always, is due to God, who has shown me an almost-unbelievable amount of grace and mercy over the past twenty-five years. I know that's kind of your bag and everything, but I'd be lying if I said it didn't still amaze me every day.

Thank you to my incredible agent, Sarah Landis, who read an essay of mine two years ago and decided that I was a writer worth taking a chance on. That is a gift that no amount of gratitude can repay. This book (and everything I write, honestly) wouldn't be what it is without your early guidance and endless tenacity.

Thank you to Maya Marlette, my genius editor. You have been a supreme blessing in my life since the moment you told me we were going to make a book together. You have made and continue to make me not only a better writer but a better thinker. Thank you for helping me usher our complicated, incredible girl, Liz, into the world, and for allowing me to write the book we both needed when we were fifteen. I'm grateful every day to have shared this journey with you. Ugh, your *mind*.

Thank you to my incredible team at Scholastic, without whose love and care and attention *Crown* would not exist. *pulls out megaphone* Taylan Salvati, David Levithan, Mallory Kass, Nikki Mutch, Melissa Schirmer, Stephanie Yang, and Josh Berlowitz: You all are the squad of my dreams. Even now, as I hold this book in my hands, I struggle to believe the fact that I got to do this with you. Thank you for making this dream of mine a reality. I have no choice but to stan.

Thank you to Heather Peacock, who has always answered all my questions and indulged all my comments. Thank you for pushing me to be unendingly curious and bold to a fault. This story began in your classroom fifteen years ago, even if I didn't know it at the time. And to the folks at the Sarah Lawrence College MFA in Writing program, thank you for giving me the space to find my voice and for the brilliant community of writers who I now get to create alongside forever.

Thank you to the friends who might as well be my blood—CRR, NG, SS, JS, RTW, QM, DE—touches of you all are scattered throughout this book. No matter how far apart we are, I carry pieces of each of you with me every day. Thank you all for being the family that I get to choose every day.

Thank you to my earliest reader on this manuscript and platonic life partner, Khadija. You're a madwoman and a national treasure. Thank you for being there to remind me—especially on days when I forget—that stories matter, that meet-cutes are always worth believing in, and that pop culture died in 2009. Now go check your DMs; I just sent you a Hozier meme.

Thank you to my critique partner and the other half of the Duffy Collective, Arriel. What can I say except thank you for seeing me, for matching my energy, and for understanding what it means to be "down bad" in a way that only we can. You saw me and this book through all its many highs and lows, and I look forward to the day I get to do the same for you.

Thank you to my very best friend and the light of my life, Ally. You are my greatest gift and the brightest mind I've ever known. This life is better because I've gotten to spend twenty-two years of it with you by my side. Thank you for loving me, for always being willing to share stories with me, and for speaking exclusively in obscure pop culture references with me at all hours of the day. Everything I write is made possible because of the dreams we shared in that bright yellow bedroom.

Thank you to my family, wholly, entirely for your love and support. To Jon, for those years we performed monologues in the living room every Monday and talked about what it will take to get ourselves free. To Sissy, for your constant encouragement and faith in me. To Granny, for teaching me to have a heart for stories, even before the world was ready to hear them. And to Mom and Pack: There isn't a better pair of parental units. Thank you for being my twin beacons of light, for never asking me to be anything other than exactly who I am, and for showing me what it means to love unendingly. I'll love you forever, and I'll like you for always.

And finally, thank you to black girls everywhere—in all our flawed, free, fantastic glory. I see you, I am honored to share this sisterhood with you, and I'm so grateful for the chance to write our stories. There is no world in which we're not both miracle and magic, in which we're not worthy of every happy ending. Thank you for teaching me how to wear my crown.

About the Author

Leah Johnson is a writer, editor, and eternal Midwesterner currently moonlighting as a New Yorker. She is a graduate of Indiana University and Sarah Lawrence College, where she received her MFA in fiction writing, and currently teaches in their undergraduate writing program. When she's not writing, you can usually find her on Twitter, ranting about pop culture and politics, at @byleahjohnson. *You Should See Me in a Crown* is her first novel.